THE SORROW OF WAR

Bao Ninh was born in Hanoi in 1952. During the Vietnam war he served with the Glorious 27th Youth Brigade. Of the five hundred who went to war with the brigade in 1969, he is one of ten who survived. A huge bestseller in Vietnam, *The Sorrow of War* is his first novel.

Bao Ninh

THE SORROW
OF WAR

A Novel

ENGLISH VERSION BY
Frank Palmos

FROM THE ORIGINAL TRANSLATION BY
Phan Thanh Hao

V

VINTAGE

Published by Vintage 2005

1 3 5 7 9 10 8 6 4 2

Originally published as *Thân Phân Cua Tinh Yêu* by
Nhà Xuät Ban Hoi Nha Van (Writers' Association
Publishing House, Hanoi, 1991)

First published in Great Britain by
Martin Secker & Warburg Limited in 1994

First published by Vintage in 1998

Vintage
Random House, 20 Vauxhall Bridge Road,
London SW1V 2SA

Random House Australia (Pty) Limited
20 Alfred Street, Milsons Point, Sydney
New South Wales 2061, Australia

Random House New Zealand Limited
18 Poland Road, Glenfield,
Auckland 10, New Zealand

Random House (Pty) Limited
Endulini, 5a Jubilee Road, Parktown 2193, South Africa

The Random House Group Limited Reg. No. 954009
www.randomhouse.co.uk/vintage

A CIP catalogue record for this book
is available from the British Library

ISBN 0 099 48353 X

Papers used by Random House are natural, recyclable
products made from wood grown in sustainable forests. The
manufacturing processes conform to the environmental
regulations of the country of origin.

Printed and bound in Great Britain by
Cox & Wyman Ltd, Reading, Berkshire

O N THE BANKS of the Ya Crong Poco River, on the northern flank of the B3 battlefield in the Central Highlands, the Missing In Action body-collecting team awaits the dry season of 1976.

The mountains and jungles are water-soaked and dull. Wet trees. Quiet jungles. All day and all night the water steams. A sea of greenish vapour over the jungle's carpet of rotting leaves.

September and October drag by, then November passes, but still the weather is unpredictable and the night rains are relentless. Sunny days but rainy nights.

Even into early December, weeks after the end of the normal rainy season, the jungles this year are still as muddy as all hell. They are forgotten by peace, damaged or impassable, all the tracks disappearing, bit by bit, day by day, into the embrace of the coarse undergrowth and wild grasses.

Travelling in such conditions is brutally tough. To get from Crocodile Lake east of the Sa Thay River, across District 67 to the crossroads of Cross Hill on the west bank of the Poco River – a mere fifty kilometres – the powerful Russian truck has to lumber along all day. And still they fall short of their destination.

Not until after dusk does the MIA Zil truck reach the Jungle of Screaming Souls, where they park beside a wide creek clogged with rotting branches.

The driver stays in the cabin and goes straight to sleep. Kien climbs wearily into the rear of the truck to sleep alone in a hammock strung high from cab to tailgate. At midnight the rains start again, this time a smooth drizzle, falling silently.

The old tarpaulin covering the truck is torn, full of holes, letting the water drip, drip, drip through onto the plastic sheets covering the remains of soldiers laid out in rows below Kien's hammock.

The humid atmosphere condenses, its long moist, chilly fingers sliding in and around the hammock where Kien lies shivering, half-awake, half-asleep, as though drifting along on a stream. He is floating, sadly, endlessly, sometimes as if on a lorry driving silently, robot-like, somnambulantly through the lonely jungle tracks. The stream moans, a desperate complaint mixing with distant faint jungle sounds, like an echo from another world. The eerie sounds come from somewhere in a remote past, arriving softly like featherweight leaves falling on the grass of times long, long ago.

Kien knows the area well. It was hére, at the end of the dry season of 1969, that his Battalion 27 was surrounded and almost totally wiped out. Ten men survived from the Unlucky Battalion, after fierce, horrible, barbarous fighting.

That was the dry season when the sun burned harshly, the wind blew fiercely, and the enemy sent napalm spraying through the jungle and a sea of fire enveloped them, spreading like the fires of hell. Troops in the fragmented companies tried to regroup, only to be blown out of their shelters again as they went mad, became disoriented and threw themselves into nets of bullets, dying in the flaming inferno. Above them the helicopters flew at tree-top height and shot them almost one by one, the blood spreading out, spraying from their backs, flowing like red mud.

The diamond-shaped grass clearing was piled high with bodies killed by helicopter gunships. Broken bodies, bodies blown apart, bodies vaporised.

No jungle grew again in this clearing. No grass. No plants.

'Better to die than surrender my brothers! Better to die!' the Battalion Commander yelled insanely; waving his pistol in front of Kien he blew his own brains out through his ear. Kien screamed soundlessly in his throat at the sight, as the Americans attacked with sub-machine-guns, sending bullets buzzing like deadly bees around him. Then Kien lowered his machine-gun, grasped his side and fell, rolling slowly down the bank of a shallow stream, hot blood trailing down the slope after him.

In the days that followed, crows and eagles darkened the sky. After the Americans withdrew, the rainy season came, flooding the jungle floor, turning the battlefield into a marsh whose surface water turned rust-coloured from the blood. Bloated human corpses, floating alongside the bodies of incinerated jungle animals, mixed with branches and trunks cut down by artillery, all drifting in a stinking marsh. When the flood receded everything dried in the heat of the sun into thick mud and stinking rotting meat. And down the bank and along the stream Kien dragged himself, bleeding from the mouth and from his body wound. The blood was cold and sticky, like blood from a corpse. Snakes and centipedes crawled over him, and he felt Death's hand on him. After that battle no one mentioned Battalion 27 any more, though numerous souls of ghosts and devils were born in that deadly defeat. They were still loose, wandering in every corner and bush in the jungle, drifting along the stream, refusing to depart for the Other World.

From then on it was called the Jungle of Screaming Souls. Just hearing the name whispered was enough to send chills down the spine. Perhaps the screaming souls gathered together on special festival days as members of the Lost Battalion, lining up on the little diamond-shaped grass plot, checking their ranks and numbers. The sobbing whispers were heard deep in the jungle at night, the howls carried on the wind. Perhaps they really were the voices of the wandering souls of dead soldiers.

Kien was told that passing this area at night one could hear birds crying like human beings. They never flew, they only cried among the branches. And nowhere else in these Central Highlands could one find bamboo shoots of such a horrible colour, with infected weals like bleeding pieces of meat. As for the fireflies, they were huge. Some said they'd seen firefly lights rise before them as big as a steel helmet – some said bigger than helmets.

Here, when it is dark, trees and plants moan in awful harmony. When the ghostly music begins it unhinges the soul and the entire wood looks the same no matter where you are standing. Not a place for the timid. Living here one could go mad or be frightened to death. Which was why in the rainy season of 1974, when the regiment was sent back to this area, Kien and his scout squad established an altar and prayed before it in secret, honouring and recalling the wandering souls from Battalion 27 still in the Jungle of Screaming Souls.

Sparkling incense sticks glowed night and day at the altar from that day forward.

There were civilian souls loose in the wood, too. Quite near to where the Zil truck parked on this rainy night there was once a tiny trail leading to Leprosy Village. Long ago, when Regiment 3 arrived, the village had been empty. Disease and successive famines had erased all life.

Still, it seemed the naked, warped and torn souls had continued to gather, emitting a stink that penetrated the imagination. The regiment sprayed petrol and set the village alight to cleanse it, but after the fire the soldiers were still terrified and none of them would go near the place again for fear of ghosts and lepers.

One day 'Lofty' Thinh from Squad 1 courageously went into the village and there, in the ashes, shot a big orang-utan. He called in three others to help him drag it back to the squad huts. But, oh God, when it was killed and shaved the animal looked like a fat woman with ulcerous skin, the eyes, half-white, half-grey, still rolling. The entire squad was horrified and ran away screaming, leaving all their kit behind. No one in today's regiment ever believed the story, yet it was true. Kien and his colleagues had buried her, making a little headstone for the grave.

But none escaped her vengeful, omnipresent soul. 'Lofty' Thinh was soon killed. Gradually the entire regiment was wiped out. Only Kien remained.

That had happened during the rainy season. Before marching to the South Wing to attack Buon Me Thuot, Kien's regiment had been based on this very spot for nearly two months. The landscape was much the same and the roads over which they passed had not become overgrown.

At that time the scout platoon had built its huts on the bank of this same stream by which they were now parked, but further along, where the stream hits the foot of the mountain, divides, then continues along as two separate streams. Now, perhaps at that branching of the stream, their old grass huts remained. Thatched roofs, side by side, near the rushes by the water.

The area had been used then to house front-line soldiers called back to the rear for political indoctrination. Politics continuously. Politics in the morning, politics in the afternoon, politics again in the evening. 'We won, the enemy lost. The enemy will surely lose. The north had a good harvest, a bumper harvest. The people will rise up and welcome you. Those who don't just lack awareness. The world is divided into three camps.' More politics. Still, the scouts were treated lightly, not being pressured as much as others to attend the indoctrination sessions.

They had plenty of time to relax and enjoy themselves before returning to the battlefields. They hunted, set traps, caught fish and played cards.

In his entire life Kien had never developed such a passion for cards as he developed here. They played all the time. At dark, straight after dinner, the game started. In the warm air which smelled of sweat and mosquito repellant the gamblers gathered enthusiastically, concentrating on their cards. The kitty was usually stinking 'Compatriot' cigarettes, made from wild leaves. Or, if the stakes were higher, it would be snuff, or pieces of flint, or the roots of *rosa canina* plants, which were smoked like marijuana. Or dried food, or photos; photos of women of all kinds, foreign or Vietnamese, ugly or beautiful, or anyone's sweetheart. Any photo was valid currency. When the kitty was gone they used to get lamp-black and paint moustaches on each other. Some played, others watched, joyfully, noisily, sometimes all through the night. It seemed a period of happiness and calm. An easy, carefree time.

They were really happy days because for most of that rainy season they didn't have to fight. The entire platoon of thirteen was safe. Even 'Lofty' Thinh spent a happy month here before being killed. Can hadn't yet deserted. His mates Vinh, 'Big' Thinh, Cu, Oanh and Tac the Elephant were all still alive. Now, only the torn, dirty set of cards, fingerprinted by the dead ones, remained.

Nine, Ten, Jack.

'Lofty', 'Big' Thinh and Can,

Queen, King, Ace!

Cu, Oanh and Tac!

Sometimes in his dreams these cards still appear. He shouts their names and plays Solitaire. 'Hearts, diamonds, spades . . .' They had bastardised the regimental marching song and made it a humorous card-players' song:

'We'll all be jokers, in the pack,
Just go harder, in attack.
Dealing's fun, so hurry back,
Enjoy the game, avoid the flak.'

But one by one the card players at their fateful table were taken away. The cards were last used when the platoon was down to just four soldiers. Cu, Thanh, Van and Kien.

That was in the early dawn, half an hour before the barrage opened the campaign against Saigon. On the other side of an overgrown field was the Cu Chi defence line. The Saigon defence forces then started returning fire with artillery and machine-guns and they registered some lucky hits. In the trenches and in shelters the infantry were trying to enjoy last moments of sleep. But for Kien's scouts, who were going to lead the attack as the advance guard, it was going a bit too fast. They were spooked by their cards, not at all liking how the hands fell as they played the game called 'Advance'.

'Slow down a bit,' Kien suggested. 'If we leave this game unfinished Heaven will grant favours, keeping us alive to return and finish the game. So, slow down and we'll survive this battle and continue the game later.'

'You're cunning,' said Thanh, grinning. 'But Heaven's not stupid. You can't cheat Him. If you play only half the game the Old Chap up there will send for all four of us and we'll torment each other.'

Tu said, 'Why bother to send all four there? Send me with the cards. That'll do it. I'll play poker, or tell fortunes from cards for the Devils in charge of the oil urns. That would be fun.'

The dew evaporated quickly. Signal flares flew into the air. The infantry noisily came to life and began to move out. Armoured cars motored to the front line, their tracks tearing the earth, the roar of their engines reverberating in the morning breeze.

'Stop, then!' Kien threw the cards down, adding petulantly, 'I just wanted to slow down for good luck, but all of you rushed the game to the end.'

'Hey there,' 'Thin' Van slapped his thigh happily, 'I didn't know until now just how much I enjoyed playing cards. I'll have to learn to play better. If I die, remember to throw a deck of cards on my grave.'

'We have only one deck and Van wants it for himself. Selfish bugger!' Thanh shouted back as he moved out. Before an hour was up Van was burned alive in a T54 tank, his body turned to ash. No grave or tomb for them to throw the cards onto.

Thanh died near the Bong bridge, also burned in his tank together with the tank crew. A big, white-hot steel coffin.

Only Tu had fought, together with Kien, to Gate 5 of Saigon's Tan Son Nhat airport. Then Tu was killed. It was the morning of 30 April, with just three hours to go before the eleven-year war ended.

Late in the night of 29 April and into the 30th when the two of them met for the last time at the airport, Tu had taken the deck of cards from his knapsack and given it to Kien. 'I'll go in this fight. You keep them. If you live on, gamble with life. Deuces, treys and fours all carry the sacred spirit of our whole platoon. We'll bring you permanent luck.'

Kien sinks into reminiscence.

Whose soul is calling whom as he swings gently and silently in his hammock over the rows of dead soldiers?

Howls from somewhere in the deep jungle echo along the cold edges of the Jungle of Screaming Souls. Lonely, wandering noises. Whose soul is calling whom this night?

To one who has just returned the mountains still look the same. The forest looks the same. The stream and the river also look the same. One year is not a long time. No, it is the war that is the difference. Then it was war, now it is peace. Two different ages, two worlds, yet written on the same page of life. That's the difference.

Kien recalled: At the time of our first stay here it was late August. Between the jungle and the forest along this stream, *rosa canina* blossomed in the rain, whitened everywhere, its perfume filling the air, especially at night. The perfume vapour permeated our sleep, fuelling erotic, obsessional dreams and when we awoke the perfume had evaporated but we were left with a feeling of smouldering passion, both painful and ecstatic. It took us months to discover that our nightly passion-frenzied dreams were caused by the *canina* perfume. Those diabolical flowers! Kien had seen them in the jungles along the western ridge of the Ngoc Linh mountains and even deep inside Cambodia around Ta Ret, but nowhere did they grow the way they did here, with such powerful scent.

The *canina* here grows close to creek banks, within reach of the mountain carp, who nibble at their roots, so when caught their taste is exquisite but instantly intoxicating. The local people say *canina* thrives in graveyards or any area carrying the scent of death. A blood-loving flower. It smells so sweetly that this is hard for us to believe.

Later, it was Kien's scout platoon, taking a break in some idle moments, who decided to try drying the *canina*, slicing the flowers and roots, then mixing them with tobacco, as a smoke. After just a few puffs they felt themselves lifted, quietly floating like a wisp of smoke itself floating on the wind. The tasty *canina* had many wondrous attributes. They could decide what they'd like to dream about, or even blend the dreams, like preparing a wonderful cocktail. With *rosa* one smoked to forget the daily hell of the soldier's life, smoked to forget hunger and suffering. Also, to forget death. And totally, but totally, to forget tomorrow.

Smoking *rosa canina* Kien would immerse himself in a world

of mythical and wonderful dreams which in ordinary moments his soul could never penetrate. In these luxurious dreams the imagined air was so clean, the sky so high, the clouds and sunshine so beautiful, approaching the perfection of his childhood dreams. And in those dreams the beautiful sky would project pictures of his own lovely Hanoi. The West Lake on a summer afternoon, the scarlet flame trees around the lake. Once in his dream-picture he had felt the waves lapping the side of his tiny sampan and looking up he had seen Phuong, youthful, innocently beautiful, her hair flying in the Hanoi breeze.

The soldiers each had their own way of smoking *canina* and ridding themselves of their shared harsh realities. For Cu, cassava alcohol or *rosa canina* conjured up images of returning home. Cu could relate the scenes vividly, making them sound so joyful that tears fell from everyone's eyes as he unfolded the scene in soft words. Vinh dreamed only of women, describing his imagined and planned love affairs with youthful enthusiasm. As the affairs dragged on the women became more voluptuous and the affairs more complicated, the descriptions more erotic and explicit. As for 'Elephant' Tac, he dreamed mainly of food. He spoke of long tables laden with wonderful and exotic dishes and of sitting down to savour the moments, morsel by morsel, dish by dish.

The lethargy brought on by *rosa canina* spread from Kien's scout platoon huts through the entire regiment. It wasn't long before the Political Commissar ordered the units to stop using *rosa canina*, declaring it a banned substance.

The Commissar then ordered troops to track down all the plants and cut all the blooms then uproot all the trees throughout the Screaming Souls area to ensure they'd grow no more.

Along with the gambling and smoking of *canina* went all sorts of rumours and prophecies. Perhaps because the soldiers in their hallucinations had seen too many hairy monsters with wings and mammals with reptilian tails, or imagined they had smelled the stench of their own blood. They imagined the monstrous animals plunging about bleeding in the dark caves and hollows under the base of Ascension Pass on the other side of the valley from the jungle.

Many said they saw groups of headless black American soldiers carrying lanterns aloft, walking through in Indian file. Others paled in terror as horrible, primitive wild calls echoed inside their skulls in the rainy, dewy mornings, thinking they were the howls of pain from the last group of orang-utans said to have lived in the Central Highlands in former times.

The rumours and the predictions were all seen as warnings of an approaching calamity, horrible and bloody, and those who leaned toward mysticism or believed in horoscopes secretly confided these fears to their friends. Soon there sprang up tiny altars in each squad hut and tent, altars to the comrades-in-arms already fallen. And in the tear-making smoke of the incense soldiers bowed and prayed, whispering in prayer:

> '. . . suffering in life, pain in death,
> the common fate of us soldiers.
> We pray the sacred souls will bless us,
> that we may overcome enemy fire,
> and avenge our lost comrades . . .'

The rain had kept pounding, day after day. The fighting seemed blanketed by the immense dull sea of rain; if one stared hard and long into the dark, grey, wet-season sky, or listened to the rain falling on the canvas canopies, one thought only of war and fighting, fighting and war.

The rain brought sadness, monotony, and starvation. In the whole Central Highlands, the immense, endless landscape was covered with a deadly silence or isolated, sporadic gunfire. The life of the B3 Infantrymen after the Paris Agreement was a series of long, suffering days, followed by months of retreating and months of counter-attacking, withdrawal, then counter-attack. Victory after victory, withdrawal after withdrawal. The path of war seemed endless, desperate, and leading nowhere.

At the end of the wet season the echoes of cannon fire could be heard a hundred kilometres away, a harbinger of a poor dry season over Con Roc, Mang Den and Mang But.

That September the NVA forces attacked Kontum township's defence lines. The firing was so loud that it shook the earth as if every square metre would rise in a groundswell and burst. In the 3rd Regiment, hiding in the Screaming Souls Jungle, the soldiers waited in fear, hoping they would not be ordered in as support forces, to hurl themselves into the arena to almost certain death.

Some of those waiting found they were hearing a musical air in their heads, the sound of guitars rising and falling with the sounds of the Kontum carnage. Soldiers of that year 1974 sang:

> 'Oh, this is war without end,
> war without end.
> Tomorrow or today,
> today or tomorrow.
> Tell me my fate,
> when will I die . . .'

Late in the afternoon of Can's escape, that wet, boring autumn afternoon, Kien was sitting by the stream, fishing. The drizzle was relentless, the day lifeless and gloomy. The stream was swollen, its waters turbulent and loud, as if it wished to wash the banks away. But where Kien sat fishing there was a silent eddy around bare tree roots, exposed where flood waters had bitten deep.

Kien nestled in his jute raincoat, hugging his knees, staring blankly into the rolling stream, thinking of nothing, wanting nothing. Now that the *rosa canina* had all gone there was nothing for his soul to grab hold of. So it wandered, meandering freely. Every day Kien would sit for hours by the stream, motionless, letting its sorrowful whispering carry him along.

That autumn was sad, prolonged by rain. Orders came for food rations to be sharply reduced. Hungry, suffering successive bouts of malaria, the troops became anaemic, and their bodies broke out in ulcers, showing through worn and torn clothing. They looked like lepers, not heroic forward scouts. Their faces looked moss-grown, hatched and sorrowful, without hope. It was a stinking life.

To buoy himself up, Kien sometimes tried to concentrate on uplifting memories. But no matter how hard he tried to revive the scenes they wouldn't stay. It was hopeless. His whole life from the very beginning, from childhood to the army, seemed detached and apart from him, floating in a void.

Since being recruited he'd been nicknamed 'Sorrowful Spirit' and this now suited his image and personality, just as the rain and gloom fitted the character of the Jungle of Screaming Souls.

Kien waited for death, calmly recognising that it would be ugly and inelegant. The thought of his expected end brought a sense of irony.

Just the week before, in a battle with Saigon commandos on the other side of the mountain, Kien had truly made fun of death. When the Southern ARVN had faced his own Northern NVA troops both sides had quickly scattered, rushing to take cover behind tree trunks and then firing blindly. But Kien had calmly walked forward. The enemy had fired continuously from behind a tree ahead of him but Kien hadn't even bothered to duck. He walked on lazily, seemingly oblivious to the fire. One southern soldier behind a tree fired hastily and the full magazine of thirty rounds from his AK exploded loudly around Kien, but he had walked on unscratched. Kien had not returned fire even when just a few steps from his prey, as though he wanted to give his enemy a chance to survive, to give him more time to change magazines, or time to take sure aim and kill him.

But in the face of Kien's audacity and cool the man had lost courage; trembling, he dropped his machine-gun.

'Shit!' Kien spat out in disgust, then pulled the trigger from close range, snapping the ARVN soldier away from the tree, then shredding him.

'Ma . . . aaaaaa!' the dying man screamed. 'Aaaa . . .'

Kien shuddered and jumped closer as bullets poured from all sides towards him. He hadn't cared, standing firm and firing down into the man's hot, agonised body in its death throes. Blood gushed out onto Kien's trousers. Walking on, leaving blood-red footprints in the grass, he slowly approached two other commandos hiding and shooting at him, his machine-gun tucked carelessly under his arm, his shirt open. He was unconcerned and coldly indifferent, showing no fear, no anger. Just lethargy and depression.

The enemy backed away and dispersed in retreat.

Despite that imprudent, risky action Kien was invited on return to the military personnel section and told he was on the list of officers selected to attend a long-term training course at the Infantry Institute near Hanoi. The order would soon come down from the Divisional Commander and Kien was to travel back up north.

'The fighting is endless. No one knows when it will stop,' the hoarse, gloomy personnel officer told Kien. 'We must keep our best seeds, otherwise all will be destroyed. After a lost harvest, even when starving, the best seeds must be kept for the next crop. When you finish your course and return to us your present officers will all be gone, and the regiment with them. The war will go on without you.'

Kien remained silent. A few years earlier he would have been proud and happy, but not now. He did not want to go north to do the course, and felt certain he would never join them, or become a seed for successive war harvests. He just wanted to be safe, to die quietly, sharing the fate of an insect or an ant in the war. He would be happy to die with the regular troops, those very soldiers whose special characteristics had created an almost invincible fighting force because of their peasant nature, by volunteering to sacrifice their lives. They had simple, gentle, ethical outlooks on life. It was clearly those same friendly, simple peasant fighters who were the ones ready to bear the catastrophic consequences of this war, yet they never had a say in deciding the course of the war.

Someone was coming up to him from behind, but Kien didn't turn. The person came closer then silently sat down behind Kien as he fished on the edge of the stream. At that late hour the bamboo forest on the other bank seemed to make the dusk thicken. The brief, rainy day faded away quickly.

'Fishing?' the person asked.

'Obviously,' Kien replied coldly. It was Can, chief of Two Squad. A small thin boy, nicknamed 'Rattling' Can.

'What's your bait?'

'Worms.' Kien added: 'I thought you had a fever. What're you doing here in the wet?'

'Caught anything?'

'No. Just killing time.'

Kien mumbled. He hated any confidences, any sharing of personal problems. Hell, if everyone in the regiment came to him with personal problems after those horrendous firefights he'd feel like throwing himself over the waterfall. He knew Can was going to unload some personal problems on him.

'It's raining heavily in the north,' Can droned on in his gloomy, dispirited voice. 'The radio says it's never rained as hard. My home district must be flooded by now.'

Kien just cleared his throat. More rain was falling. The air was getting colder and now it was quite dark.

'You're about to go north, I hear.'

'What if I am?'

'Just asking. Congratulations.'

'Congratulations? Congratulations?'

'Please. I'm not jealous, Kien. I'm sincere. I know you don't like me but can't you understand a little of what I mean. Accept what heaven gives you. You've survived down here and now you'll go north and continue to survive. You've suffered a lot. You were from an intellectual family, so it's not right for you to die anyway. Just go, and let events unfold here. We feel pleasant envy for you. You deserve it.'

'I'm not going anywhere to make others happy. I know you're scared of being killed, but you have to overcome your fear by yourself. You can't place that responsibility on others' shoulders.'

Can seemed to ignore the taunt.

'As for me, I've always longed for the opportunity to get into an officers' training course. Truly, that was my dream. I'm younger than you. I was top of the class at school. I've tried to discipline myself, to fulfil all my duties. No disobedience, no gambling, no alcohol, no dope, no women, no swearing. And for what? All for nothing! I'm not jealous, just depressed.'

Kien felt uneasy about what was coming. He feared it, yet he expected it.

Can continued, 'I haven't lived yet and I want very much to live.'

Kien remained silent.

'For just one week in the north I'm prepared to lose everything. Everything.'

'So I'll tell Personnel to put your name down, instead of mine,' said Kien sarcastically. 'Don't moan! Please, go back to your hut and lie down.'

'Don't patronise me! I'm telling the truth, not trying to change things. I can look after myself. I'm not afraid of dying, but this killing and shooting just goes on, forever. I'm dying inside, bit by bit. Every night I have the same dream, of me being dead. I swim out of my corpse and turn into a vampire going off to suck human blood. Remember the Playcan fighting in 1972? Remember the pile of corpses in the men's quarters? We were up to our ankles in blood, splashing through blood. I used to do anything to avoid stabbing with bayonets or bashing skulls in with my rifle butt, but now I've got used to it. And to think that as a child I wanted to take orders and go into a seminary.'

Kien turned and looked curiously at Can. You occasionally found such traumatised misfits in the army. Their chaotic minds, their troubled speech, revealed how cruelly they were twisted and tortured by war. They collapsed both spiritually and physically. But it was curious that after fighting alongside Can for so long Kien had never heard him go on like this. He had seen Can only as a trusty farmer who'd gradually adjusted to the hell of the battlefield.

'You're an experienced front-line soldier, but you're starting to whinge and moan. That will make you even more miserable, Can. You'd better transfer out of the scout group. We're the first to go into the fight.'

Can continued his gloomy confessions as though he had not heard a word. 'I used to ask myself why I'm down here while my old suffering mother is at home, helpless, day and night crying for her distant son. When I joined up my village was flooded and it was hard for mother even to get by. Who was left to help her? My brother was already in the forces. I could have been exempted as the only son left but the village chief wouldn't agree. We have so many of those damned idiots up there in the north enjoying the profits of war, but it's the sons of peasants who have to leave home, leaving a helpless old mother, exposed to hardships. So, Kien . . .'

Suddenly, Can burst into tears, burying his face in his knees, his shoulders heaving and trembling, his thin back wet and shivering.

Kien stood up, picked up his fishing rod and looked down, frowning, at Can. 'You've been reading too many enemy pamphlets. If someone reported you to the upper levels you'd be a goner. Are you going to desert?'

Can remained sitting, his head on his knees. His voice came low, mixing with sounds from the stream and the rain. 'Yes. I'm going. I know you're a real friend. You'll understand. Say goodbye to my mates for me.'

'You're nuts, Can. First, you've no right to escape. Second, you can't. You'll be caught and brought back. Court-martialled. Shot. You'll be worse off than now. Listen to me. Calm down! I won't rat on you.'

'Too late. I've already hidden my bag in the jungle.'

'I'm not letting you desert. Go back to the huts. Try to hang on a bit longer. The war has to end sooner or later.'

'No. I'm off. Win or lose, sooner or later, that means nothing to me. My life is fading fast, and I still have to see my mother once more, and my village. You won't stop me? What for? Why would you?'

'Listen, Can, leaving like this is suicidal. And shameful.'

'Suicidal? Killing myself? I've killed so often it won't mean a thing if I kill myself. As for the shame,' Can stood up slowly, looking into Kien's eyes. 'In all my time as a soldier I've yet to see anything honourable.

'Back home I might be even more humiliated. They won't let me live. Even so, these nights all I dream of is my mother calling me. Perhaps my brother is dead already and she's ill and suffering. I can't wait any longer. It's you, not me, who's been chosen for the officers' course and being sent back. Me, I'll just have to find my own way home. I hope my mates take pity on me.

'I won't get caught, not if the scouts don't chase me. And that's you, Kien, you're in charge, you're the one who can guarantee my safety. Let me go.'

Can continued softly, 'When this is all over, well, you know my village in the Binh Luc district, Ha Nam province. Drop in when you get a chance.'

In the darkness Can grasped Kien's wrist with his cold, thin hand. Kien slowly took the hand away and turned his back without saying a word, leaving Can by the stream.

Nearing his hut Kien seemed to awaken, and change his mind. He dropped his fishing gear and turned back, running to the stream, calling 'Can. Caaaaaan!'

He called again, 'Caaan, wait.'

He rushed back through the heavy rain along the dark path to the edge of the stream. Can was gone. In the tiny clearing Kien felt imprisoned by the rain and the thick bamboo jungle wall on the other side of the stream.

The restricted visibility compressed the space. The only movement was the stream, which gurgled on.

Kien stood there, staring, then burst into tears, the rain washing over his face as the tears gushed out.

Desertion was rife throughout the regiment at that time, as though soldiers were being vomited out, emptying the insides of whole platoons. The authorities seemed unable to prevent the desertions. But the commanding officers issued specific orders for Can to be traced. They feared he would desert to the enemy and betray the secrets and the battle plans of the entire regiment.

After many days splashing around on their search the military police finally found Can the deserter. He'd only made it to a small dead-end track between hills, two hours from the huts. He still had months to travel, so many obstacles between him and home in Binh Luc.

In late September, just before the regiment's departure from the Jungle of Screaming Souls, the men got mail from their families, their only delivery for the wet season. Kien's scout platoon got just one letter. It was for Can, from his mother.

'. . . the whole hamlet shares my joy at having received your letter and I write back immediately with the hope that the kind military post officers will take pity on me and deliver it as quickly as possible to you. I might already have died, but thanks to your letter I now continue to live and hope, my dear son.

'. . . Oh, my son, since receiving word of your brother's death from his unit, then having his commemoration ceremony in the village, and getting the Patriotic Certificate, my dear son, I have worked night and day in the ricefield, ploughing land and transplanting. And I pray always to Heaven, and the ancestors, your late father and brother, to bless you in that distant battlefield, praying you and your comrades will return safely . . .'

Kien read and re-read the letter. His hands trembled, tears blurred his eyes. Can was no more. The military police had found his rotten corpse. Only his skeleton was complete, like that of a frog thrown into a mudpatch. Crows had pecked away Can's face; his mouth was full of mud and rotting leaves.

'That damned turncoat, he really stank,' said the military policeman who had buried Can.

His eye-sockets were hollow, like trenches. In that short time moss and slime had already grown over him. The MP had gagged, spitting at the memory.

No one spoke of Can again. No one bothered to find out why he had died, whether he was killed, or had just exhausted himself in the jungle, or whether he'd committed suicide. No one accused him, either.

The name, age and image of someone who'd been every bit as brave under fire as his comrades, who had set a fine example, suddenly disappeared without trace.

Except within the mind of Kien. Can's image haunted him every night, returning during the night to whisper to him by his hammock, repeating the final, gloomy lines he'd spoken by the stream. The whisper would turn to a suffocating gasp, like the sound of water blocking the throat of a drowning man.

'. . . my soul swims away from my body . . .'

Kien recalled Can's voice. And each time Kien knelt in prayer before the platoon's altar to the war martyrs Kien would whisper a word for Can's soul, the soul of a mate who had died in humiliation, uncared for and misunderstood, even by Kien.

In the past months of the wet season Kien had been posted to the MIA team charged with gathering the remains of the dead from the worst battlefields. He had crossed almost all the northern sector of the Central Highlands, returning to the sites of innumerable battles. The MIA team had uncovered a vast family of forgotten members of their regiment, dead under the mantle of the warm jungle. The fallen soldiers shared one destiny; no longer were there honourable or disgraced soldiers, heroic or cowardly, worthy or worthless. Now they were merely names and remains.

For some of the other dead, not even that. Some had been totally vaporised, or blasted into such small pieces that their remains had long been liquidised into mud.

After some final touches with the shovel their graves would be done, their remains laid out. Then, with their final breath their souls were released, flying upwards, free. The uprush of so many souls penetrated Kien's mind, ate into his consciousness, becoming a dark shadow overhanging his own soul. Over a long period, over many, many graves, the souls of the beloved dead silently and gloomily dragged the sorrow of war into his life.

Tonight, back at the camp, how strange that it is a night which is perhaps the most mystical of the hundreds of dark nights in his life, with Can's soul whispering to him. And now his whole fighting life parades before him, with troops of dead soldiers met on the battlefields returning through a dim arch in an endless dream. The echoes of the past days and months seem like rumbles of distant thunder, paining then numbing his own turbulent soul.

Near dawn Kien suddenly shivers and half awakens to a piercing, horrible, sorrowful howl, flying up from the cliffs like an echo. Kien moves to get up but then stops and flops back into the hammock, closing his eyes, still listening to the howl.

That howl, the howl first heard in this damned Screaming Souls Jungle right by this same stream in the rainy season last year, the last rainy season of the war. The howl from the valley on the other side of the mountain, echoing down to us. Some said it was mountain ghosts, but Kien knew it was Love's lament.

At the time, right here in the sad wet jungle, Kien's B3 scout platoon had lived a moment of love which was strange and fascinating, fuelled by a passion both wanton and unique, born of a magical meeting.

Kien had unfortunately not been included in this ambience of love. He recalled his unit had arrived and chosen to build huts at the foot of this very mountain. After the first two nights had passed everyone sensed something unusual was happening to the platoon. Kien had done more than sense that mysterious atmosphere. He had listened to it, and had seen vague figures flitting by. On the third night, a rainy August night, Kien, fitful after three days of fever, was distressed and could not sleep. Uneasy, just before dawn, he put on his raincoat and with machine-gun at the ready went to check the huts. The forest floor was muddy and slippery and lightning sparked the air, lighting the jungle every few moments.

Kien slipped around, groping his way through the rain, his machine-gun swinging. Approaching Squad One's hut, Kien stopped. Laughter? Yes, peals of laughter. But who would be laughing like that in this sorry platoon? And imitating a girl's voice? It sounded ghostly. Kien approached, looking inside. It was dark, but there was no sound of snoring. Just a heavy silence.

Kien was wary: 'Who laughed in there?'

'Why, Kien?' Thanh's voice. Alert.

'Who? Maybe an angel,' said another.

'Don't piss around. Someone laughed. I'm not that feverish, you baboon.'

'So come in, platoon commander. Check for yourself.'

Kien was confused. Shit! Was there another ghost in this Screaming Souls Jungle? Kien dropped the flap, then left. Still, the laughter had seemed clear, sharp, genuine. A girl's laughter, not a ghost's. He was not imagining things.

Walking slowly back he sensed a movement and stopped, stiffening to stay still and alert. He could hear his own heart come almost to a standstill. In the reflection of the stream he saw a lovely young girl. Her midriff was bare, her skin shone like the light dancing on the water, her hair, long and flowing, hung down on her thighs. She walked slowly out of his vision, leaving her reflection dancing on the reeds along the bank.

Kien stared after her into the jungle, then shook himself free of the vision and shouted out, 'Stop! Who's there?' He stepped forward with his hand on the trigger. 'Code Five!' he called. No answer.

The rain, the thunder and the lightning seemed to halt abruptly.

'Stop! I'll shoot!' Kien shouted angrily.

'It's me, mate, Thinh!'

'What?'

'It's me. My turn on duty,' answered 'Lofty' Thinh clearly. 'What's wrong?'

'Who's been in there with you?'

'No one.'

'Didn't you see anyone?'

'No. What's up?'

Kien swore through his teeth. Just then the lightning and thunder flared up again. Kien stared into the swaying trees, looked again at the swirling stream, then back at Thinh.

Thinh stood before him, looking innocent. He wore shorts, his bare midriff glistening in the rain.

Kien groaned softly, then trudged back slowly to his tent. He threw himself back into his hammock, overcome by a sense of self-pity and impending doom.

What had he seen? Ghost or girl?

The next morning the matter was not mentioned. Neither Thanh nor Thinh said a word, but Kien felt they and the others shared a secret, while pretending nothing unusual was happening. It was the first time he had felt cut off from his mates.

Kien slowly discarded fears that he had imagined things. Something was happening, something strange. No more beautiful ghost-girls slipped by the huts near the stream. But he sensed other mysterious movements.

At midnight, shadows slipped silently from the hammocks. Gently creeping to the hut doors, making signals to the night guards, they disappeared in single file into the dark jungle. The shadows slipped quietly into the stream and headed, in teeming rain, towards the great dark mountain.

Night after night these shadows moved around, until one night

Kien, too, awoke. He lay still, feigning sleep, listening. At first he heard the whispers, then movements from hammocks, then bare feet stepping into mud. Then muted conversation with the guards. Someone slipped over. Muffled laughter.

Some nights they were shadows from own his hut: the next night from another hut: once from the hammocks near him. They were going out every night, returning hours later, just before dawn. He could hear them, out of breath, muddy and shivering from the drizzle and cold air.

After a few nights Kien began caring for them, worrying for the welfare of these shadows. He would lie awake until every one of them had returned. When the last one had returned he would hear a long, mournful call from the base of the mountain, like a call of farewell. At the return of the last shadow Kien would sigh with relief and drop into a slumber.

Not the entire platoon of thirteen were involved. Three regulars, he was certain, made the dangerous journey at night to the dark mountain through a wild, gloomy valley. He now recalled there had been a prosperous farm there by a waterfall, before the war had spread inland.

The farmhouse had been abandoned, then commandeered by the district military officers as their headquarters, then abandoned again many years ago. There had been three very young girls from the original farming family. It dawned on him that the girls, who would now be in their late teens, had returned home despite the farm's vulnerability.

Kien felt he now knew what was happening and that he understood their feelings. Which is why, as a commander, instead of stopping the undisciplined and dangerous liaisons, he did nothing. He recalled the standing orders from the Political Commissar: 'It is necessary to readjust, rectify, and re-establish the rules, the morals and behaviour of your men when there are breaches.' Of course that would have meant pulling the soldiers out, snapping them out of their romantic spells. Kien's heart would never allow him to truly discipline those boys. It begged him to keep silent and sympathise with the young lovers. What else could they do? They were powerless against the frenzied forces of young love which now controlled their bodies.

At the time Kien felt old. Only he and Can were over twenty. All the others were still teenagers, still boys.

It was then that the honeyed dreams began, and in his sleep he saw his beautiful girl from Hanoi appear before him. During those rainy nights she would come to him from the back door of his memory, stepping lightly like a sprite. His body would shiver, then tremble, starved and thirsty for desire, wanting to savour the heightened sensations of smooth body contact. 'We two may die as virgins, our love is so pure. We ache for each other, unable to be together,' Phuong would say, causing their seventeen-year-old hearts nearly to break.

In his dream he knew that he was dreaming and he would writhe, trying to change the images, trying to get away from the pain and desolation he suffered from knowing it was all a dream.

When he awoke he heard his mates' footsteps from far away. Now, he had no need to await their return. He could tell long before. In their hut, along with the gentle perfume of dope, there was now a new fragrance, distinctly soft, tender and ethereal, which lingered vaguely in the wind.

Kien thought back to the source of his own love, when he had been young. That was now hard to imagine, hard to remember a time when his whole personality and character had been intact, a time before the cruelty and the destruction of war had warped his soul. A time when he had been deeply in love, passionate, aching with desire, hilariously frivolous and light-hearted, or quickly depressed by love and suffering. Or blushing in embarrassment. When he, too, was worthy of being a lover and in love, as his troops were now.

But war was a world with no home, no roof, no comforts. A miserable journey, of endless drifting. War was a world without real men, without real women, without feeling.

War was also a world without romance. He couldn't avoid the drain on his soul, the ruin his young men were escaping from as they set about squeezing the last remaining drops of love from their nightly adventures. Tomorrow, they might be dead. We might all be dead.

But the love he knew had been within him seemed now to have drained away. He despaired that he could never again share the frivolities and elations of ordinary love.

Closing his eyes, looking back, Kien remembered the pain of those weeks. Those young girls and the boys of his platoon were all dead now. A constant fear for them had wrenched his heart. True, it was war, and the times were abnormal. The great issues, the important tasks of fighting and their sacred duties, had become the most important matters in life. Whereas the tiny issues, those filigree-fine joys and sorrows of human destiny, like the boys' dalliance with the three farm girls, seemed less important. They were such rare occurrences they were considered by some as a bad omen, as though happiness must necessarily call down its own form of retribution in war.

It was indeed true; those small acts of love were an omen of terrible events to come.

Kien recalled the scene as if it were only yesterday. He was standing there in the pelting rain in the wet grassy yard of the small farmyard in the isolated valley at the base of a huge mountain where every night his young men had secretly met their new lovers.

His face, clothes and hair were all sopping wet. The sub-machine-gun was about to slip from his shoulder. Around the farmhouse the huts and storage areas from the district head-quarters days seemed to send off vapour from the teeming rain as the drops bounced off their roofs. The sky gradually lightened and a few rays broke through, although some light rain persisted.

'Ho Bia-aaaaa!' 'Lofty' Thinh had started calling.

Kien had simply gone along with the search. After Thinh's calls the other scouts scattered around the farm all shouting the girls' names: 'Ho Biaaaaa, May, Ma-aaay, Thom, Th-oom.'

There was no reply. From the high waterfall by the cliff between the farm and the foot of the mountain a huge fountain of white water arose, rumbling and foaming, sounding like perpetual thunder.

But no one replied.

The other sounds were from the rain. Water running off roofs, dripping into pools. Kien went inside. It was a lovely three-roomed house with bamboo roof, covered with perfumed wild lily. The furniture was in good condition, and tidy. A full set of rattan chairs and table, a flower pot, tea and teacups. An opened book. Beds, pillows, blankets. Mirrors and combs.

At the back, clothes were hanging on the line, washing that should have been brought in by then.

The larders were well stocked with paddy, rice and cassava. The smell of dried mushrooms, honey, and stores of other fragrant foods and spices filled the little kitchen. All seemed in perfect order. The kitchen table had been laid neatly, as though a full dinner had been prepared but the family had been called away. Bowls of dried fish, eggplants, rice, had been placed in the centre of the table and covered with insect-proof netting. For each person there were chopsticks, bowls, salt, pepper and small side plates. The main rice pot was still on the stove and below it, the charcoal and ash glowed dimly, still warm.

Kien and his men stepped out back, through peanut plants,

eggplant, thyme and oregano. They walked cautiously, down the yard to banana trees and marrows. Beyond this vegetable garden a simple low wooden gate opened onto a tiny narrow path leading to a stream which ran into the main river a little way down. They stood there looking over the stream and up into the dim shadows of the mountain under which the little farmhouse stood.

Though it rained day and night, the farm girls had used water from the stream, wisely saving their well-water for the dry season. Kien approached the well. It seemed in good order, the lid fitted snugly and around its base a gutter had been dug, to drain away muddy water during heavy rains. The silence was unnerving.

Kien left the others and on a hunch turned towards the stream and noted the girls' tiny toilet built over the stream, almost totally hidden from view behind bamboo. The narrow track from well to toilet was gravelled, weed-free.

Kien approached not by the path, but circuitously, by stepping quietly into the water and wading upstream.

The door of the toilet was open. He kneeled, unslinging his machine-gun. He was certain someone was in there . . .

That had been so long ago, yet now it was still vividly clear in his mind. The door of the toilet hadn't been opened. It had been ripped off its hinges and thrown aside onto the bank. Inside, there had been two buckets part-full, a dipper, a pair of rubber sandals, and soap. A thin, worn housecoat and an embroidered towel hung on a tiny line. A piece of muddied clothing lay by the toilet wall, near a green canvas raincoat.

Something on the smooth rocks caught his eye. It was a torn white bra. In the dim light it looked like a strange, large flower with smooth, soft petals. On one petal there was a trace of blood.

Kien shivered, as though twine had been wrapped tightly

around his heart. Then he pictured several greenish, ghostly enemy forms passing silently under the jungle's canopy, quietly arriving at the jungle's edge to find the farm, then entering . . . finding three young girls. One girl had been in the bedroom, another in the kitchen near the table, the third at the bathroom. There had been no time to react. No cries. No shots. No escape.

'The commandos! The commandos, they did it,' someone howled.

'Oh, Kien,' said Thinh in a whisper, his voice hoarse and trembling.

Beyond them the bamboo branches scratched eerily against the bamboo walls. Kien sighed, tightening his lips.

'Did you hear anything this morning?' he asked.

'No. Nothing,' they replied.

Kien tried to put the picture together. So, what had happened? These young men had been here with the girls last night, enjoying themselves.

This was 1974, not the dark times of 1968 and 1969, the worst years of the war. This was now a day's walk to the front line. Yet this morning the young lovers in the platoon had sensed something wrong. They had persuaded Kien to take a look. Kien now agreed their hunch had been right.

'How do you know they're commandos?' Kien asked, aware that whoever the visitors had been, they were still alive, and not far away.

'We found a Rubi cigarette-end. And footprints,' Thinh said.

'What made you sense something was wrong this morning? You were happy enough when you came back,' Kien said, letting them know he had known all along of their nocturnal visits.

'Nothing specific. We suddenly felt unbearably anxious, that's all.'

'Now you tell me! Did any of you go back looking for them this morning?'

'Yes. But we found no trace.'

'You missed this,' said Kien, pointing to the blood-stained bra. Thinh stepped out front, slowly kneeling down. His AK rifle dropped from his shoulders, clattering on the rocks.

'It's Ho Bia's! This is Ho Bia's bra!' he whispered, raising the bra to his lips. 'Oh, darling, where did they take you? Why? You were so innocent! Why would they hurt you? What can we do?'

Thinh sobbed and moaned, uttering urgent prayers in a despairing voice.

Later, many years later, while watching a pantomime where an artist bent over, writhing his body in agonised desperation, by magical association Kien recalled the moments when Thinh had similarly crouched in sobbing despair, praying for Ho Bia.

The audience around him in the theatre had seen Kien suddenly sit bolt upright, remembering the war scene clearly. His attention on the pantomime faded as the sharp detail of the tragic love story of his men and the three farm girls unfolded in his mind. He drifted off into a reverie as he dreamed of that day, blind to the pantomime before him.

How deeply moved he was, and how he trembled at the joy and the pain the memories brought. He wanted to etch into his heart these memories, and wondered how he could have forgotten this tragedy for so many years.

It was almost dark that same day before they found the commandos' hiding-place. They had not killed the three girls on their own farm, but had chosen to take them down the valley, away from the farm. The rain had erased their tracks and it was by total chance that Kien's platoon had discovered the seven commandos at the foot of a hill.

They had ambushed the commandos, killing three of them in the first attack and capturing the remaining four at gunpoint.

'Lofty' Thinh, one of the lovers, was killed in close fighting, getting a bullet through his heart. No time for tears or for vengeance. He fell, his face to the earth, without seeing Ho Bia again.

Kien stood before the captured men. They were not tied up, but they were exhausted from their lost battle, their clothes torn, filthy with mud and blood, offering no further resistance. They stood still and silent, shuffling their feet but indifferent to questions.

'Where are the three girls?' he asked calmly.

No answer.

'Well, where are they? If they're still alive, you might live.'

The biggest of the four commandos, his left eye torn away by a bullet, looked over at Kien with his good eye. Blood and mud ran down his cheeks. He laughed scornfully, showing white teeth.

'The girls? We sacrificed them to the Water Spirit, sir. We used their bodies as an offering. They cried and carried on like crazy.'

Kien's scouts drew their bayonets. Kien held them back.

'Stop! Don't. Perhaps these guys might also want to cry like crazy as the girls did before they died. They won't want to die immediately, will they?'

'Motherfucker! Kill us if you like!' another of them shouted. 'Look at my hands, look, red from the bitches' blood!'

'Shut up!' Kien said. 'Don't worry, we'll do as you wish. I just want to know something. You came here to track us, the regular army, right? So why attack them? Why kill three young girls so brutally?'

No answer.

Kien cursed himself for wasting his time on them. Worse, he'd even been polite.

He ordered them to dig their own graves.

The four of them dug a common grave, digging quickly, enthusiastically, as though they were on contract.

'It doesn't have to be so deep, it's just for lying down in so that arms and legs won't show,' said Kien. 'And hurry up! It'll soon be dark.'

Each of the four had a shovel, the usual collapsible multi-purpose sharp tools. They were all healthy, muscled men. They dug violently, digging, scooping, throwing. The hole widened, deepened, then began to fill with reddish water.

'That's enough, get out!' Kien ordered. He explained: 'You have to get out before you throw in the bodies of your three friends. You don't want to leave them to stink up the forest, do you?'

They asked permission to wash and have a last cigarette. Kien agreed, but his troops were not satisfied.

One said, 'Why string it out? Give them some bronze candy!' It was the troops' slang for bullets.

'I can't stand these four arseholes either,' said Kien. 'They'll be treated like dogs before they die, but there's something I have to know.'

The four southern commandos went down to the stream and washed their hands slowly, carefully. They also washed the blood from their uniforms, then returned.

'Please have a cigarette, sir!' said the youngest of them, a round-faced, pale-skinned boy who spoke with a sweet northern accent. He politely offered the Rubi cigarette, offering it in cupped hands to Kien.

'Keep it!' Kien waved him away. 'Offer it to your pals when you're under the ground.'

The young commando sighed, then looked imploringly at Kien,

lowering his voice. 'Sir, the one who has been impolite to you is our commander. Yes, he's a lieutenant.'

'Is he? Well, he'll just be an ordinary soldier below ground. Not your commander, so forget it, don't worry.'

'Please don't kill me,' the young man said. 'I didn't rape any of those girls. I didn't stab them even once. I swear I didn't. I'm a Catholic.'

'You don't have to swear to me. Back in your line!' Kien replied.

But the young man, tears running down his cheeks, kneeled down in front of Kien. 'Please take pity on me, sir, I'm still so young, sir. I have an old mother. I'm going to get married. We love each other, I beg you!'

Trembling, he took a leather purse from his pocket and from it produced a small coloured photograph which he placed in Kien's hands. Kien held the photo, looking at it. A young girl wearing a black swimming-costume stood with her back to the sea. She smiled happily, her wavy hair surrounding her face and covering her shoulders. She held an ice-cream in one hand and waved with the other. A tiny, graceful wave from a girl so beautiful that he could look at her forever. Kien wiped the rain-drops from the photo and handed it back to the boy.

'She's beautiful. Nice photo. Put it away or it'll get wet.'

The commando gasped, his mouth dry. His eyes shone with hope. 'You mean you'll let me live? Really? Oh, thank God!'

'Back to your hole!' shouted Kien. 'Son of a bitch! Light your last smoke, or your time is up! You others too, be quick!'

The young man joined the three others who now sat on the edge of the grave dangling their feet over the bodies of their three mates who had been tossed into the hole. Around the scene light blue cigarette-smoke, warm and pleasant, drifted lazily into the drizzle of rain. Darkness was descending from the slopes and the stream gurgled around them.

'Now!' said Kien, pulling the AK from his shoulder. 'Line up!'

The four pale faces looked up, afraid and intense.

'Stand up, in one row,' Kien repeated casually, pressing his thumb into the trigger guard in the sub-machine-gun. 'Move!'

'Sir, let us finish our cigarette!' It was the same young man with the northern accent.

'Stand up!' Kien shouted again.

'Let them finish, Kien,' a scout whispered hoarsely into Kien's ear.

The condemned men stood up, leaning against each other. Imminent death had left them fearless, their faces hardened. They looked with hatred at Kien, who became angry as he looked at them sneering at death.

'So, you don't mind dying? I'll satisfy you, with as much blood as you want. Like you did the girls.' Kien was shouting, then laughing grimly.

He fired. Over their heads.

The young northern Catholic began crying. He rushed forward to Kien and knelt, his face on Kien's feet. Whining, praying, sobbing, he writhed close to the ground, but no words came.

'You're volunteering to go first?' asked Kien, placing the gun-barrel against the boy's forehead.

'No, please, let me live, I beg all of you! Let me live, I pray, sir, I beg you!' Kien shoved the barrel hard on his head and the young commando fell back. The blow seemed to bring him to his senses and he stopped crying. Still kneeling, he raised himself slightly, looking wearily around first at Kien, then the others. His hands wandered over his wound. A cut on his forehead had started blood streaming down his nose.

'I volunteer to fill in the grave,' he said. 'You don't have to tire yourself doing it. I'll also tell you all the information I know. Your Party's policy is to punish those who run away and forgive those who return, so you have no right to kill me. No right! Please, I beg you, beg you!'

Someone behind Kien touched his arm, whispering to him in a trembling voice. 'Kien, why don't we forgive them for now and send them to our superiors to decide?'

Kien turned. It was Cu. Kien burned with anger and he let fly in fury, sticking his gun into Cu's mouth. 'If you want to show your love for them go stand in the line with them. I'll kill you too! You too!'

'Kien, Kien, what the hell makes you cry so loudly?'

The truckdriver's beefy hand pushed through the hammock onto Kien's shoulder, shaking him awake.

'Get up! Get ready! Quick!'

Kien slowly opened his eyes. The dark rings under them revealed his deep exhaustion. The painful memory of the dream throbbed against his temples. After some minutes he got up, then slowly climbed down from the hammock and dropped from the back of the truck to the ground.

Seeing how sluggishly Kien ate, the driver sighed and says, 'It's because you slept back there, with nearly fifty bodies. You'll have had nightmares. Right?'

'Yes. Unbelievably horrible. I've had nightmares since joining this team, but last night's was the worst.'

'No doubt,' the driver said, waving his hand in a wide arc. 'This *is* the Jungle of Screaming Souls. It looks empty and innocent, but in fact it's crowded. There are so many ghosts and devils all over this battleground! I've been driving for this corpse-collecting team since early '73 but I still can't get used to the passengers who come out of their graves to talk to me. Not a night goes by without them waking me to have a chat. It terrifies me. All kinds of ghosts, new soldiers, old soldiers, soldiers from Division 10, Division 2, soldiers from the provincial armed forces, the Mobile Forces 320, Corps 559, sometimes women, and every now and again, some southern souls, from Saigon.' The driver spoke as though it was common knowledge.

'Met any old friends?' asked Kien.

'Sure! Even some from my own village. Blokes from my first unit. Once I met a cousin who died way back in sixty-five.'

'Do you speak to them?'

'Yes, but . . . well, differently. The way you speak in hell. There are no sounds, no words. It's hard to describe. It's like when you're dreaming – you know what I mean.'

'You can't actually do anything to help each other?' asked Kien. 'Do you talk about interesting things?'

'Not very. Just sad and pitiful things, really. Under the ground in the grave human beings aren't the same. You can look at each other, understand each other, but you can't do anything for each other.'

'If we found a way to tell them news of a victory would they be happier?' Kien asked.

'Come on! Even if we could, what would be the point? People in hell don't give a damn about wars. They don't remember killing. Killing is a career for the living, not the dead.'

'Still, wouldn't peacetime be an ideal moment for the resurrection of all the dead?'

'What? Peace? Damn it, peace is a tree that thrives only on the blood and bones of fallen comrades. The ones left behind in the Screaming Souls battlegrounds were the most honourable people. Without them there would be no peace,' the driver replied.

'That's a rotten way to look at it. There are so many good people, so many yet to be born, so many survivors now trying to live decent lives. Otherwise it's not been worth it. I mean, what's peace for? Or what's fighting for?' Kien asked.

'Okay, I'll grant you we have to have hope. But we don't even know if the next generation will get a chance to grow up, or if they do, how they'll grow up. We do know that many good people have been killed. Those of us who survived have all been trying to make something of ourselves, but not succeeding.

'But look at the chaotic post-war situation in the cities, with their black markets. Life is so frustrating, for all of us. And look at the bodies and the graves of our comrades! The ones who brought the peace. Shameful, my friend, shameful.'

'But isn't peace better than war?'

The driver seemed astonished. 'This kind of peace? In this kind of peace it seems people have unmasked themselves and revealed their true, horrible selves. So much blood, so many lives were sacrificed for what?'

'Damn it, what are you trying to say?' Kien asked.

'I'm not trying to say anything. I'm simply a soldier like you who'll now have to live with broken dreams and with pain. But, my friend, our era is finished. After this hard-won victory fighters like you, Kien, will never be normal again. You won't even speak with your normal voice, in the normal way again.'

'You're so damn gloomy. What a doom-laden attitude!'

'I am Tran Son, a soldier. That's why I'm a bit of a philosopher. You never curse your luck? Never feel elated? What did the dead ones tell you in your dreams last night? Call that normal?' he asked.

On the way out the Zil truck moves in slow, jerky movements. The road is bumpy, muddy and potholed. Son stays in first gear, the engine revving loudly as if about to explode. Kien looks out of the window, trying to lighten his mood.

The rain stops, but the air is dull, the sky lead-grey. Slowly they move away from the Screaming Souls Jungle and the whole forest area itself. Behind them the mountains, the streams, all drop away from view.

But strangely, Kien now feels another presence, feels someone is watching him. Is the final scene, the unfinished, bloody dream of this morning, about to intrude itself in his mind. Will the pictures unfold against his wishes as he sits staring at the road?

Kien called to Son over the roar of the engine, asking if he'll be finished with MIA work after this tour of duty.

'Not sure. There's a lot of paperwork to do. What are your plans?'

'First, finish school. That means evening classes. Then try the university entrance exams. Right now my only skills are firing sub-machine-guns and collecting bodies. What about you, will you keep driving?'

The truck reached a drier section of road and Son was able to go up a gear, dropping the loud engine revs.

'When we're demobbed, I'll stop driving. I'll carry my guitar everywhere and be a singer. Sing and tell stories. "Gentlemen, brothers and sisters, please listen to my painful story, then I'll sing you a horror song of our times." '

'Very funny,' said Kien. 'If you ask me we'd do better to tell them to forget about the war altogether.'

'But how can we forget? We'll never forget any of it, never. Admit it. Go on, admit it!'

Sure, thinks Kien, it's hard to forget. When will I calm down? When will my heart be free of the tight grip of war? Whether pleasant or ugly memories they are there to stay for ten, twenty years, perhaps for ever.

From now on life may be always dark, full of suffering, with brief moments of happiness. Living somewhere between a dream world and reality, on the knife-edge between the two.

I've lived all these lost years. No one to blame for that. Not me, not anyone else. All I know now is that I'm still alive after twenty-nine years and from now on I have to fend for myself.

There's a new life ahead of me, and a new era for Vietnam. I have to survive.

But my soul is still in turmoil. The past years out here imprison me. My past seems to enfold me and move with me wherever I go. At night while I sleep I hear my steps from a distant peacetime echoing on the pavement. I just have to shut my eyes to conjure up those past times and completely wipe out the present.

So many tragic memories, so much pain from long ago that I have told myself to forget, yet it is that easy to return to them. My memories of war are always close by, easily provoked at random moments in these days which are little but a succession of boring, predictable, stultifying weeks.

Not long ago, in a dream, I was back, standing in the Screaming Souls Jungle. The stream, the dirt road, the empty grass plots, the edge of the forest of days gone by, were sparkling in sunshine. I was standing in this peaceful, picturesque scene looking south-west towards the four olive-green peaks of Ngoc Bo Ray mountain, when my new dream adventure began.

The whole night long I reviewed the life of my scout platoon. Each day, each memory, each person, appeared on a separate page of the dream. At last there was the scene by the stream where the whole scout platoon gathered around 'Lofty' Thinh's grave, the afternoon before we left for a major battle in the Central Highlands.

'Thinh, you stay here in the forest. We're leaving to fight a battle,' I heard my voice echoing from that afternoon. On behalf of the whole platoon I said farewell to Thinh's soul.

'From the depths of the earth, dear friend, please listen to your mates and give your blessing to us as we now must fight and break through the enemies' lines. Please listen for the sounds of our guns. Your mates will shake sky and earth with the guns to avenge your death,' the prayer concluded.

Oh my lost years and months and days! My lost era! My lost generation!

Another night with bitter tears wetting the pillow.

Another night, also in a dream, I saw pretty Hoa in the Screaming Souls Jungle. She'd been born in Hai Hau in 1949, but killed a long way from home in 1968, when not even twenty. Hoa's story was part of my mental war films, but somehow buried along with many others until now.

We were only able to meet for a moment in my dream, a passing glance at each other. In the thick mist of the dream I could only see Hoa vaguely, far away. But I felt a passionate love and a grieving intimacy I'd not felt for her at the time of our traumatic, violent parting after Second Tet in 1968. During our brief time together I'd only felt a shameful impotence, a feeling of defeat and desperate exhaustion.

For the entire night I floated in the sea of suffering called Mau Than, the tragic year of 1968. When I awoke it was almost dawn yet the dream images were then transferred to my waking hours: Hoa fallen in a grassy plot in the jungle, the American troops rushing towards her, then surrounding her, like bare-chested apes, puffing and panting, grabbing her, breathing heavily over her body. My throat still hurt from screaming during the nightmare, my lips were bleeding, the buttons of my pyjama coat had been ripped off, my chest was deeply scratched and my heart beat painfully, as though I were in danger, not our courageous Hoa.

Since returning to Hanoi I've had to live with this parade of horrific memories, day after day, long night after long night. For how many years now?

For how many more years?

Often in the middle of a busy street, in broad daylight, I've suddenly become lost in a daydream. On smelling the stink of rotten meat I've suddenly imagined I was back crossing Hamburger Hill in 1972, walking over strewn corpses. The stench of death is often so overpowering I have to stop in the middle of the pavement, holding my nose, while startled, suspicious people step around me, avoiding my mad stare.

In my bedroom, on many nights the helicopters attack overhead. The dreaded whump-whump-whump of their rotor blades bringing horror for us in the field. I curl up in defence against the expected vapour-streak and the howling of their rockets.

But the whump-whump-whump continues without the attack, and the helicopter images dissolve, and I see in its place a ceiling fan. Whump-whump-whump.

I am watching a US war movie with scenes of American soldiers yelling as they launch themselves into combat on the TV screen and once again I'm ready to jump in and mix it in the fiery scene of blood, mad killing and brutality that warps soul and personality. The thirst for killing, the cruelty, the animal psychology, the evil desperation. I sit dizzied, shocked by the barbarous excitement of reliving close combat with bayonets and rifle-butts. My heart beats rapidly as I stare at the dark corners of the room where ghost soldiers emerge, shredded with gaping wounds.

My life seems little different from that of a sampan pushed upstream towards the past. The future lied to us, there long ago in the past. There is no new life, no new era, nor is it hope for a beautiful future that now drives me on, but rather the opposite. The hope is contained in the beautiful pre-war past.

The tragedies of the war years have bequeathed to my soul the spiritual strength that allows me to escape the infinite present. The little trust and will to live that remains stems not from my illusions but from the power of my recall.

Still, even in the midst of my reminiscences I can't avoid admitting there seems little left for me to hope for. From my life before soldiering there remains sadly little. That wonderful period has been heartlessly extinguished. The lucky star of fortune I once had seems also to be gone forever. It once shone brightly, but quickly burnt out. The aura of hope in those early post-war days swiftly faded.

Those who survived continue to live. But that will has gone, that burning will which was once Vietnam's salvation. Where is the reward of enlightenment due to us for attaining our sacred war goals? Our history-making efforts for the great generations have been to no avail. What's so different here and now from the vulgar and cruel life we all experienced during the war?

Even me, I'm nearly forty. I was eighteen at the start of the war in 1965, twenty-eight at the fall of Saigon in 1975. So, how many long years have passed? Ten or eleven? Twelve. No. Thirteen? Another year with the MIA team. Or was it longer? And more time wandering as a Veteran. Closer to fourteen years lost because of the war.

And me already forty. An age I once thought distant, strange, somehow unattainable.

From the horizon of the distant past an immense sad wind, like an endless sorrow, gusts and blows through the cities, through the villages, and through my life.

Kien lays his pen down. He turns off the table lamp, pushes his chair away, stands up and silently walks to the window. It is very cold in the room, yet he feels hot and breathless. He is uneasy, as though he feels a violent summer thunderstorm approaching, heralded by gusts of alternately hot and cold air.

So bitter is his frustration that he feels his pen takes him closer at first and then more distant from what he wishes to say.

Every evening, before sitting at his desk and opening his manuscript, he tries to generate the appropriate atmosphere, the right feelings. He tries to separate each problem, the problem of paragraphs and pages, wishing to finish them in a specific way and by a specific time. He plans the sequences in his mind. What his heroes will do and what they will say in particular circumstances. How they'll meet, how they'll part. He lays the design of this out in his mind before taking up his pen.

But the act of writing blurs his neat designs, finally washing them away altogether, or blurs them so the lines become intermixed and sequences lose their order.

Upon rereading the manuscript he is astounded, then terrified, to read that his hero from a previous page has, on this page, disintegrated. Worse, that his heroes are inconsistent and contradictory, and make him uneasy. The more uneasy he feels the quicker the task at hand slides from his mind.

On some nights, he energetically follows a certain line, pursuing it sentence by sentence, page by page, building it into a substantial work. He wrestles with it, becomes consumed by it, then in a flash sees it is all irrelevant. Standing back from it he then sees no value in the frantic work, for the story-line stands beyond that circled arena of his soul, that little secret area which we all know intuitively contains our spiritual reserves.

Kien seems to write only to rid himself of his devils. Neither the torment of regret brought on by wasted writing efforts, nor the loss of his health, can overcome his urgent desire to be a perfectionist. The threat of being pinned to his writing-desk for great lengths of time similarly does not concern him. He continues his quest for perfection, crossing out, erasing, crossing out again, editing, tearing up some pages, then tearing up and destroying all. Then he starts over again, making out each syllable like a learner trying to spell a new word.

Even so, he still believes in his writing and his talent. It is something else that needs to be addressed, something intangible, other than the writing. So, he begins again, writing and waiting, writing and waiting, sometimes nervous, over-excited.

He seems to mature as he works, and grows more confident from this belief, and pushes on with new confidence, despite all the past failures, patiently savouring the end result he anticipates from his artistic endeavour and creativity.

Despite this growing confidence, he frequently relapses and once again feels like a man standing on the edge of an abyss.

Despite his conviction, his dedication, he also sometimes suspects his recall of certain events. Is there a force at work within him that creates this suspicion?

He dares not abandon himself to emotions, yet in each chapter Kien writes of the war in a deeply personal way, as though it had been his very own war. And so on and on, frantically writing, Kien refights all his battles, relives the times where his life was bitter, lonely, surreal, and full of obstacles and horrendous mistakes. There is a force at work in him that he cannot resist, as though it opposes every orthodox attitude taught him and it is now his task to expose the realities of war and to tear aside conventional images.

It is a dangerous spin he is in, flying off at a tangent, away from the traditional descriptive writing styles, where everything is orderly. Kien's heroes are not the usual predictable, stiff figures but real people whose lives take diverse and unexpected directions.

After all his trial essays, short stories and novellas comes this novel, which he suddenly realises is his last adventure as a soldier. Curious, for it is at the same time his most serious challenge in life; in writing this work he has driven himself to the brink of insanity. There is no escape, no saviour to help him. He alone must meet this writing challenge, his last duty as a soldier.

In contemplation an odd idea takes root in his mind – or has it been there for many years? At the bottom of his heart he believes he exists on this earth to perform some unnamed heavenly duty. A task that is sacred and noble, but secret. He begins to believe that it is because of this heavenly duty that he had such a brief childhood and adolescence, then matured in time of war. The duty imposed on him in his first forty years a succession of suffering with very few joys. Those who selected Kien to perform these sacred tasks also ordained that he should survive the war, even in battles where it seemed impossible to escape death. The heavenly glow which streaked, sparkled and vanished like a falling star had bathed him in serene light for just a few moments, then disappeared so suddenly that he had no time to understand its full import.

The first time he had felt this secret force was not on the battlefield, but in peacetime, on his post-war MIA missions gathering the remains of the dead. The sacred force nurtured him, protected him and willed him on, renewing his thirst for living and for love. He had never before acknowledged this sacred heavenly duty, yet he had always known it existed within him as an integral part of him, melded with his soul.

From the time of that realisation he felt that day by day his soul was gradually maturing, preparing for its task of fulfilling the sacred heavenly duty of which the novel would become the earthly manifestation.

It was in summer five years ago that, totally by chance, on a lovely warm day he had stopped by the Nha Nam township. And from there he went on to revisit Doi Mo, a tiny, ancient hamlet where twenty years earlier his newly formed battalion had been based and had trained for three months while awaiting transportation to the front, called the 'Long B'.

The landscape looked to Kien as though it had been forgotten by time. The pine plantations, the myrtles, grassy slopes, and eucalypts in desolate and gloomy lines between fields were exactly as he remembered them as a young recruit. The houses were scattered about as he had remembered them, one on each small hilltop and each as dull and unimaginative as before.

With no particular plan in mind, Kien left the only road through the hamlet and turned down a dirt track almost overgrown by grass.

He knew the track led to Mother Lanh's house. She had been godmother to the many young recruits, especially his own three-man special team.

The house was still there, looking exactly as he had seen it the day he left; earthen wall, thatched roof, kitchen at the rear facing onto an overgrown small garden. Near a flight of steps, almost obscured by wildflowers and shrubs, was the same old well, with its windlass. Godmother Lanh had died. So now it would be Lan, her youngest daughter, who lived here.

When Lan opened the door and stepped outside she recognised Kien immediately. She even remembered his platoon nickname, the Spirit of Sorrow. Kien had forgotten everything about her.

'In those days I was just thirteen years old. I still called you uncle. And we girls of the backwoods have always been shy and unattractive,' she added in self-deprecation. But what Kien saw before him now twenty years later was an intelligent woman, quietly attractive, with mistily sad eyes.

Tears welled up in those sad eyes when Kien told her that the other two in the three-man squad who had stayed with Lan's mother had been killed on the battlefield. 'What a cruel time,' she said, 'and so very long. The war swept away so many people. So many new recruits used to be based in my house. They used to call my mother their mother, and called me younger sister. But of all of them only you have returned. My two brothers, my classmates and my husband, too, were all younger than you, and joined up years later than you. But none of them has returned. From so many, there is only you left, Kien. Just you.'

She went with him to pay tribute to her mother. Kien burned

incense sticks and bent his head in prayer for some time, letting the painful memory of those days throb through his temples while he tried in vain to conjure up the image of the godmother's face. The last rays of the sun were slanting over the long grasses, now tinged pink in the sunset.

She began speaking quietly: 'If people had been patient in those days and let parents know of their son's deaths one at a time, my mother would still be alive today. But in the first weeks of peace the bureaucrats wanted to speed up the delivery of bad news, to get it out of the way quickly. My mother was here one fateful morning when an official arrived bringing a death certificate for my brother, her first son. She took the news badly, although she had feared and expected it. She was buoyed only by the expectation of her second son coming home soon. But a few hours later another courier arrived with a second death certificate telling her my other brother, her second son, had also been killed. Mother collapsed in a faint, then lapsed into a coma. She hung on for three days without uttering another word, then died.'

Kien stared down at Lanh's tombstone, noticing for the first time a second, much smaller grave alongside it. She said quietly: 'My son. He was almost eight pounds when he was born, but he only lived two days. His name was Viet. My husband was one of the Tay tribe, far from his province of Ha Giang. He had been based here for less than one month, so there was not even time to complete the formal wedding ceremony. Six months after he left I got a letter, but not from him. It was from one of his mates, writing to tell me he'd been killed on the way into Laos. I'm sure that's why our baby faded fast and died. It had no will to live.'

They rose and slowly walked down to the house.

'So, that's the short story of my life. First my brothers, then my mother, then my husband, then my son. No wonder I feel a little weaker every year. I live in this shell of loneliness, going from house to hill, hill to house, and around the hamlet, with no one paying any attention to me and me not noticing others.

'By a strange quirk of fate, my husband's was the last unit based here. After his group left no others came to Doi Mo. Now, after many years of peace you are the only one to return here. Just you. None of the others.'

She asked him to stay the night and he silently agreed. The short summer night softly enfolded them and all that was heard was the sound of a nightbird calling from the edge of the forest and the distant rippling of the hamlet's slow stream.

Kien and Lan walked out together early in the morning; she stayed with him beyond the first hill, neither of them saying a word. The sun was warming them and the dew evaporated, rising around them. Lan's face seemed pale and drawn.

'A few years ago I decided to leave here,' she said suddenly. 'I intended to go south and rebuild my life. But I changed my mind. I just couldn't leave my mother and my son lying over there. I just wait and wait, without knowing what I'm waiting for. Or for whom. Perhaps I've been waiting for you.'

Kien remained silent, avoiding her gaze.

'I knew who you were straight away, although you look very different now. Back then I was so small. But I knew. Perhaps you were my first love and it took all this time for me to realise it.'

Kien tried to smile but his heart felt constricted. He gently raised Lan's hand to his lips, bent his head, and kissed it a long time.

'Stay. Live peacefully, my sweet. Try not to be sad, and try not to think poorly of me.'

Lan leaned forward, caressing his shoulders and his greying hair.

'Forget me. Your life is an open road, go out and enjoy it. I'll find a foster-child and we'll live together peacefully. I wish I could have had your child, Kien, but it's impossible. That doesn't depress me. Just for a moment let's imagine that we've both come back from the past, while our loved ones were still alive.

'I ask you to remember one small favour for me. If you come to the end of your wandering and seem to have nowhere left to go and no one to turn to, remember you have a place here with me, always. A home, a woman, a friend. Doi Mo hamlet was where you started this war. You can make it your point of return, if you want to.'

Kien hugged Lan, pressing her to his chest. She said in a muffled voice, 'Please go now. I'll never forget you. Please, don't forget me completely, my unexpected lover.'

He left, bending his head into the summer morning sun which spread across the grassy roadside. When he turned he saw his long shadow reaching back, pointing to Lan in the distance. She had not moved.

She had watched as he slowly walked away, and was still watching as he turned out of sight, over a distant hill.

Some years after that meeting, also on a summer afternoon, Kien and some journalist colleagues, riding a jeep back from the border, again passed through the same valley. The sight of the hills and streams, the smell of the earth brought to him on a pleasant wind, brought back powerful memories. Only he and the driver were still awake. Kien reminisced in silence, with a tinge of regret. It was here, this very place, where Lan had promised him a final refuge. 'There is always one place and one woman here for you,' she had said.

The sad, doomed meeting echoed back to him, reminding him of that final act of kindness.

Some of his loved ones he had not bothered to stay in contact with. Others had vanished. He had left yet others in his wake. He had lived selfishly these last years without looking back. Time and his work had taken over his life. He had sought neither opportunities nor responsibilities. The memory that afternoon reawakened in him the sense of sacred duty. He felt he must press on to fulfil his obligations, his duty as a writer.

It was necessary to write about the war, to touch readers' hearts, to move them with words of love and sorrow, to bring to life the electric moments, to let them, in the reading and the telling, feel they were there, in the past, with the author.

Why choose war? Why must he write of the war? His life and that of so many others was so horrible it could hardly be called a life. How can one find artistic recognition in that kind of life? They gossip about me, the author who wishes to write of the war. They say of me that the war author cannot even bear to enter a cinema where people may be shooting each other on the screen.

Is this the author who avoids reading anything about any war, the Vietnam war or any other great wars? The one who is frightened by war stories? Yet who himself cannot stop writing war stories, stories of rifles firing, bombs dropping, enemies and comrades, wet and dry seasons in battle. In fact, the one who can't write about anything else?

The author who will later have to give all credit for his unique writing style and story-telling fame to those war stories?

When starting this novel, the first in his life, he planned a post-war plot. He started by writing about the MIA Remains-Gathering team, those about-to-be-demobilised soldiers on the verge of returning to ordinary civilian life.

But relentlessly, his pen disobeyed him. Each page revived one story of death after another and gradually the stories swirled back deep into the primitive jungles of war, quietly re-stoking his horrible furnace of war memories.

He could have written about the macabre, or about cruel brutality without writing about the war. He could also have written about his childhood which was both painful and happy.

He could have written: 'I was born and grew up ... My late parents ...' and so on. And why not write of his father's life and his generation? That was a generation both great and tragic, a generation bursting at the seams with ambitious Utopians, people of elegant spiritual and emotional qualities, sadly now long forgotten by Kien's generation.

But when thinking of his childhood or his father, Kien becomes depressed. He feels that as a son he had not sufficiently loved or respected his father. He had not understood his father's life and remembered almost nothing about his family tragedy. He still doesn't know why his parents separated and knows even less about his mother. So it is strange that he remembers his mother's second husband so clearly.

His mother's second husband was a pre-war poet who had gone into hiding to escape the anti-intellectual atmosphere of the state ideologies that came with Communism.

Kien had visited him just once in an old house in the Hanoi suburb of Chem, on the edge of the Red River. There was a small window facing the northern dyke. Kien remembered the scene clearly. His real father had just died, five years after his mother, who had left him and remarried, to the poet, who became his stepfather. Kien decided he should visit his stepfather to say farewell before going away with the army. He was seventeen at the time and the visit left an indelible impression.

The house was old and greyish, surrounded by a sad, unkempt winter garden which itself was ringed by wispy eucalypts that rustled in the light breeze.

The entire scene reflected his stepfather's extreme poverty. On a dusty family altar his mother's photo rested in a frame with broken glass. The bed in the same room was limp and bedraggled.

A writing table was a mess of books, papers and glasses. The atmosphere was depressing. Yet in sharp contrast his stepfather lived in a style which belied his conditions. His thinning white hair was neatly combed back, disguising some scars, his beard was well shaven and tidy, and his clothes were clean and pressed.

He treated Kien warmly and politely and with the correct intimacy for the occasion, making him hot tea and inviting him to smoke and generally feel at home.

Kien noticed that his eyes were blurred and his scraggy and frail old hands trembled.

He looked over to Kien and said gently, 'So, you're off to the war? Not that I can prevent you. I'm old, you are young. I couldn't stop you if I wanted to. I just want you to understand me when I say that a human being's duty on this earth is to live, not to kill,' he said. 'Taste all manner of life. Try everything. Be curious and inquire for yourself. Don't turn your back on life.'

Kien was surprised by the integrity of his stepfather's words and he listened intently.

'I want you to guard against all those who demand that you die just to prove something. It is not that I advise you to respect your life more than anything else, but for you not to die uselessly for the needs of others. You are all we have left, your mother, your father and me. I hope you live through the war and return home to Hanoi, for you still have many years ahead of you. Many years of joy and happiness to experience. Who else but you can experience your life?'

Surprised, and far from agreeing with him, Kien nevertheless trusted his stepfather's words, feeling an affinity with his sentiments. He saw in the old man a wise multi-faceted intelligence with a warm, romantic heart that seemed to belong to another era, a sentimental era with all its sweet dreams and heightened awareness, alien to Kien, but attractive nonetheless.

He understood then why his mother had left his father and come to live with this wise, kind-hearted man.

For the entire afternoon he sat with his stepfather in the room in which his mother had lived her last years, and where she had died. And that winter afternoon became his only memory of his mother, a memory of warmth and a special atmosphere conjured up by his stepfather as he read old love poems he had composed for her when he was young. He took a guitar down from the wall and started singing in a deep voice a song by Van Cao, a song his mother had loved. It was a slow, melancholy song recalling loved ones who were forever gone, decrying life's unhappiness yet with a strain of underlying hope:

> Don't lament, don't bathe in the sorrows,
> look up and live on . . .

After joining the army, Kien had written to his stepfather, but had no reply. After the war, ten years after his visit that afternoon, Kien returned again to find him.

But when he arrived neighbours told him his stepfather had died many years earlier. Even the house had gone. It had been destroyed long ago. No one remembered the circumstances of his death, or even how the house had been destroyed.

Such a man, such a story, Kien pondered. But there were so many romantics like him now; some close to him, others from just outside his immediate circle.

Once, at his desk in the editorial office of his magazine, a strange man who wished to remain anonymous approached him, asking for his story to be run in the magazine. It was a love story. The main characters were this man and his wife. 'If the names are changed we can then really tell the truth of this very beautiful but tragic story,' he told Kien. It was to be an extraordinary present for his sick wife, to commemorate their thirtieth anniversary in marriage. Wasn't that great?

Kien thought the story was a load of rubbish and very boring. Yet the courage and determination of the man, and his strong desire to create this unusual present, impressed him, set him thinking.

He could, for example, write a novel about his neighbours, above, below and on the same floor as his own apartment in the one building. It could be a story of symphonies. Not a war story.

Stories, humorous, heart-rending, arose every day. Anywhere people were jammed up close together and forced to share their lives. On summer evenings when there were power blackouts and it was too hot inside, everyone came out to sit out in front, near the only water tap servicing the whole three-storey building.

The tap trickled, as drop by drop every story was told. Nothing remained secret. People said that Mrs Thuy, the teacher widowed since her twenties, who was about to retire and become a grandmother, had suddenly fallen in love with Mr Tu, the bookseller living on the corner of the same street. The two old people had tried to hide their love but had failed. It was true love, something that can't be easily hidden.

Or Mr Cuong, on the third floor, who when drunk once set about his wife with a big stick but by mistake whacked his own mother. The latest gossip was about Mr Thanh, the retired sea captain, whose family was always having problems. The family was so poor they would even squabble over a bowl of rice. Poor Thanh wanted no more of it so decided to commit suicide. He tried once with a rope, then with insecticide, but both times he was discovered and rescued.

Thanh was still better off than old Mrs Sen, blind and lonely, the mother of two sons killed in action. Mrs Sen's nephew and his wife cheated the poor old lady out of her room by having her sent to a mental hospital to die. The nephew was not only well educated, but well heeled. He had graduated from the University of Finance and Economics, he travelled abroad frequently, spoke two foreign languages, and lived an easy life. On returning each afternoon he would eat a huge meal, then go out onto the balcony to rest, belching repeatedly and yawning. His wife, a boring, tight-lipped serious woman, worked in the courts. Not once had she ever been seen to smile at her neighbours.

There was Mr Bao, also on the third floor, living with his parents, Dr Binh and his wife. He had been released from prison in the recent New Year Amnesty and quickly won the sympathy of all the people in the building. He had originally been sentenced to death, then had that reduced to a life sentence, then to twenty years. Bao didn't look like a criminal. His many years as a prisoner had turned him into a devout, religious man. Only a short time after being released this formerly dangerous convict surprised his fellow apartment dwellers with many acts of kindness, and kind helpful words. The only reservation was his obvious sadness, betrayed by his deep, sad eyes. When he looked sad everyone felt sorry for him.

Even such a tiny stream of life, running through this apartment building, contained so many waterfalls, so many cliffs, so many eddies and whirlpools. Children were born to life, sprouted like mushrooms after a shower of rain, grew up, became adults. The adults grew old, some of them falling away every year. Generation after generation, like the waves of the sea.

Last summer, old Du – the great barber of Hanoi – had died in his ninety-seventh year. He was the last survivor of the pre-war generation known to Kien.

'No one, neither Genie of Jade nor King of Hell, will allow me to live the last three years of my own century,' his loud voice had declared. He had tried to make a joke of it when Kien came visiting him. 'Please write a play for me, entitled *The Barber of Hanoi*. I'll come up from hell to see the first performance.'

He had been a barber from the time when Hanoi gentlemen followed the ancient Chinese custom and wore their hair braided into queues. 'These days they call them pigtails, but that would have been an insult. Queues denoted authority and culture,' he had said. 'Under my hands three hundred thousand heads and faces have been beautified, turned from messy and rough to tidy and perfumed. Under my sculptor's hands, rough stone is turned into beautiful statues.'

Before the war his children, his grandchildren and all his great-grandchildren were gathered around him in one big family and although not one of them followed in his footsteps as a barber everyone enjoyed his influence and his style as a raconteur. He worked hard, creating a large, kind family, all pleasant and fun-loving. In his childhood memories Kien sees old Du's scissors and hears the snip, snip, snip, as Du tells his funny stories, interspersed with bars from the *Marseillaise*, sung out of tune.

For Kien, the most attractive, persistent echo of the past is the whisper of ordinary life, not the thunder of war, even though the sounds of ordinary life were washed away totally during the long storms of war. The pre-war peace and the post-war peace were in such contrast.

It is the whispers of friends and ordinary people now attempting ordinary peacetime pursuits which are the most horrifying. Like the case of Father Du, who presided over a very large and happily noisy family. Today he is the only living male. And Huynh, the train-driver, whose three sons all died on the battle-field. Like Sinh, wounded in the spine, more dead than alive until he finally died where he had lain for so long.

The spirits of all those killed in the war will remain with Kien beyond all political consequences of the war.

So many friends of the same age have long departed, never to return. Their houses are still here in Hanoi, their images part of them. Their images also endure in the faces of the new generation.

Kien remembers Hanh, a single girl who lived in the pre-war days in the small room close to the stairs, a room which now belongs to Mr Su. Hardly anyone now remembers why Hanh left, or when.

Hanh was older than Kien. When he was very young he would see men quiver with lust when Hanna walked by. They would fight each other to get close to her door. The ones on Hanh's side of the street tried to fight those from the even-numbered houses across the street to stop them encroaching on their territory, meaning the doorways on the odd-numbered side, where Hanh would walk by at least twice a day. Every time Hanh passed, walking nonchalantly, her long tresses swaying, she would exude a youthful charm that aroused the men. They would stiffen, stop what they were doing, and stare after her with feverish, blatant desire.

The girls around there hated her, calling her a bitch, a whore, or a witch, because of her innocent influence, of which she remained either unconcerned or completely ignorant. Kien felt their passionate hatreds were based on envy and lies. Hanh was a normal, neighbourly girl, he felt. 'Good morning, sister,' he would say politely when she emerged. 'Good morning, younger brother, you're really a nice boy,' she would say, tousling his hair. At the Lunar New Year celebrations she gave Kien a gift of money, just as she did the other children in the building. Brand-new crisp banknotes, and wishes for a happy school year. 'Be a good pupil. Why, you already look almost grown up. Just take care not to be big in body but tiny in brain, my younger brother!' she laughed.

But it was not very long before she began to change her style of address to Kien. He had turned into a handsome and strong seventeen-year-old and was about to graduate. But he and Phuong, his classmate and sweetheart from childhood, were both so intensely occupied with each other that neither seemed to notice what Hanh had observed, that Kien had matured into an impressively attractive young man.

War was looming. Hanoi was considered a non-combat area yet the authorities ordered the population to practice evacuation, to dig shelters, to heed air-raid sirens and to wear dark clothing. During a lunch break at home from school one day Kien was startled when Hanh slipped quietly into his room. 'Hey, younger brother, how about helping me later. I want to dig an air-raid shelter under my bed so I don't have to tear down the street every time that siren goes off.'

'Okay, sister, I'll help you.'

That evening was his first time in a room alone with a girl. It was small, but sensitively decorated. Kien wanted to ask her not to destroy the harmony of the room but she had already started on the digging work. He started to dig in the corner, by her small bed, about ten tiles in from the wall. He used a crowbar to break into the foundation, then a hoe and a shovel. Bit by bit, through bricks and the rubble of the foundations, they dug deeper.

Hanh had prepared a nice dinner, and bought beer for Kien. After dinner Kien began to feel a little uneasy, but said nothing, starting on the digging again. In the middle of the work there was a blackout and they had no electric light. Hanh brought out a small kerosene lantern and they continued, with Kien digging and Hanh carrying away the soil in buckets. Both worked silently, patiently for a long time.

'This is probably deep enough,' said Kien, panting, 'it's above my chest which means the level of your chin. Don't make it too deep.'

'Yes. Let's stop there. But let me try it. We might need some steps for me to get down into it easily,' she said, holding her arms out to slip into the shelter.

Hanh didn't look much shorter than Kien, but once inside the shelter in the dimly lit room, she only came up to his chin. Her body pressed into his tall, muscular body as he lifted her down.

She sensed the intimacy and seemed to change her mind, wishing to get back out, but the shelter was too narrow and deep. Her urgent mood transferred itself to Kien whose body began heaving uncontrollably with a burning male sensation that he'd never felt before. He breathed heavily, trying to cope, but the sensations produced by her closeness, her perfume, her hair, her shoulders, her breasts pressing under her thin shirt hard against him, slowly overpowered him.

Confused and trembling out of control, Kien hugged her tightly, bending to kiss her neck, then her shoulders, as she twisted her body to get clear of him. Clumsily he pressed her against the earthen wall, triggering tensions in his muscles, which snapped a shirt button, springing it wide open and bringing him suddenly to his senses.

He threw his head back, stepped away and released Hanh, then lifted himself quickly out of the little shelter onto the floor, poised to run out of the room. But in his rush he knocked over the kerosene lamp, which went out.

'Kien,' Hanh called in a low voice. 'Don't go, don't run off. Please help me. I can't see a thing.'

Trembling, Kien bent down and grasped her under her arms and lifted her out, ripping his shirt open even wider as he lifted. Hanh raised her arms and placed them around his neck, whispering to him: 'Go upstairs for a moment, but don't stay long. Come down soon. There's something I want to tell you,' she said.

Kien went quietly back to his room, took a bath and slowly put on fresh clothes. But he couldn't summon the courage to return downstairs. He started, but stopped. He sat down. He lay down, but he couldn't sleep. His emotions were running riot, willing him to return. But his conservative training in restraint anchored him to the spot. The hours dragged by, until he saw the first glint of dawn. He sat up suddenly, walked barefoot to the landing and tip-toed downstairs to Hanh's room, where his courage ran out again. He pressed his face to the door, his heart beating loudly. He didn't dare knock, even when he heard a slight scratch of footsteps on the other side of the door and a latch being lifted ever so gently. Breathlessly Kien sensed Hanh's body pressing on the inside of the door, a centimetre of timber between their bodies. He lowered his hand to the ceramic door-handle, trembling, but it froze on the handle for some seconds, then minutes, and he found no strength to turn it. He finally released the handle, turned round noisily and ran back upstairs, throwing himself on the bed in defeat.

From that day on, Kien avoided her. If their paths accidentally crossed, Kien would bend his head and weakly mumble, '. . . Sister.' Hanh would look quietly and sympathetically at him and say, 'Good day, younger brother.' She seemed willing to say more, to tell him something she had long wanted to say, but Kien's continued avoidance of her acted as a deterrent. The words she longed to say would never be voiced. Perhaps in their dreams, for soon she was gone.

When Kien joined up Hanh had already become involved with the Volunteer Youth Brigade which had gone off to the Fourth Military Zone. When Kien returned to Hanoi before heading south he found a new occupant in Hanh's old room. The deep shelter had been filled in and tiled over and there was no indication that the floor had ever been disturbed.

'There's something I want to tell you,' she had said. The words lingered with him for years.

When later he recalled his actions, her words, his timidity, he would grieve, and regret his loss.

The passing of beautiful youth had been so rapid that even its normal periods of anxiety and torment, of deep intensive blind love, had been taken from him as the war clouds loomed. A moment so close, yet so far, then totally lost to him, to remain only as a memory forever.

Kien sighed and pressed his face to the cold glass window, looking out into the dark night. He could see the top of the tree in front of his house, the leaves brushing wetly against his window.

In the streets below, scattered lights shone, the light mixing with the rain. Illumination stopped at the end of the street, marking the start of the vast lake. Swinging his vision to the right he saw the dark cloud canopies low over the familiar tiled roofs of Hanoi, although hardly any of the houses emitted light. There were no cars on the street, and not a single pedestrian.

At this moment the city was so calm that one could practically hear the clouds blow over the rooftops. He thought of them as part of his life being blown away in wispy sections, leaving vast, open areas of complete emptiness, as in his own life.

The spirit of Hanoi is strongest by night, even stronger in the rain. Like now, when the whole town seems deserted, wet, lonely, cold, and deeply sad.

When they slept in the jungle the rain fell on forest canopies, and Kien would dream of Hanoi in the rain. Hanoi with leaves falling. Now, as he watched the leaves falling, he remembered the jungle rains and the dreams of Hanoi. The dreams focused and refocused until past scenes and the present became a raging reality within him, images of the present and the past merging to double the impact and the smell and atmosphere of the jungle there in the room with him. Wave after wave of agonising memories washed over his mental shores.

*

One year in the seventies a false spring had appeared in Hanoi. The sun shone during the day and the air was as light and clean as any April or early May. The trees whose branches had turned bare during winter suddenly sprouted beautiful green buds. In the parks the flowers began blooming and migratory birds began returning to nest under the eaves of city buildings. For those few moments in a season Hanoi lost its lonely, desolate look.

One day after that week of sunny midwinter days the sky darkened, an icy cold wind began gusting along the newly greened streets, and a sorrowful, drizzling rain began. The newly-emerged buds retreated, the blooms wilted, the birds remained hidden, and the colours and the new hope that had arrived like a golden promise evaporated into the reality of harsh grey winter.

Phuong, his childhood sweetheart, his classmate, his female lead in one of the strangest opening nights of the war theatre, and his self-created ikon for salvation in peacetime, had left him again. She had gone from him when the false spring faded and real winter returned.

Phuong had left no note and since departing had not written to him. She had probably decided never to return. The doors and the windows in her apartment were shuttered and locked and had the look of permanency about them. That had been their first parting since he had returned from the war. Her sudden, cruel departure had cut Kien deeply.

Kien sat forlornly in his apartment, emotionally exhausted. A glint caught his eye and he turned to face a small mirror. What he saw astounded him; his hair, his beard, his wrinkles, the circles under his eyes. He tested his voice; even that had changed; it was now deep and sad. His looks, his voice, seemed to upset others these days. Was it the empty, blank stare he now saw in the mirror? Was that what they turned from, avoiding his glances?

He became bored with his university studies. One morning he simply decided he wouldn't attend. From that point on he ended his easy student life, quietly, and for no apparent reason. He stopped reading newspapers, then books, then let everything go. He lost contact with his friends, then with the outside world in general. Except drink. And cigarettes. He couldn't care less that he was penniless, that he drank and smoked almost non-stop. He wandered around outside, pacing the lonely streets. When he did sleep, it was a heavy, drunken slumber.

In his dreams he saw Phuong now and then, but more often he dreamed of crazy, twisted things, distorted apparitions of loneliness and sorrow. Horrible, poisonous nightmares brought back images that had haunted him constantly throughout the war. During the twilights of those cold nights the familiar, lonely spirits reappeared from the Screaming Souls Jungle, sighing and moaning to him, whispering as they floated around, like pale vapours, shredded with bullet-holes. They moved into his sleep as though they were mirrors surrounding him.

He would often awake to find himself writhing on the floor, tears streaming down his face, shivering with fear and cold. His numbed heart was seized up and his emotions overcame him. When the icy winds outside blew fiercely and rain pelted heavily against his dark windows, he would just sit there, still, not wishing to move. Sad, foolish self-pity washed over him.

He had tried desperately to forget Phuong, but she was unforgettable. He longed for her still. Nothing lasted forever in this world, he knew that. Even love and sorrow inside an aging man would finally dissipate under the realisation that his suffering, his tortured thoughts, were small and meaningless in the overall scheme of things. Like wispy smoke spiralling into the sky, glimpsed for a moment, then gone.

*

That cold spring, Kien was frequently out on the streets late at night. On one memorable night, near the Thuyen Quang park by the lake, he saw two figures struggling on the ground under a kapok tree. One of them, a man, rose quickly and drew a knife from his belt. Kien jumped into the fray, kicked the man, then knocked him into a gutter, before chasing him off. He turned and saw that the second figure was an attractive young girl. Kien called a pedicab going past, bundled her into it and headed for home. Once inside, he saw she was made up in the familiar, tartish way made famous by the 'Green Coffee Girls' of the area. These were the most notable Hanoi prostitutes, so called because they waited for their men in a certain group of coffee houses.

'You know whose life it is you've just saved, and brought into your home. Well, do you?' she asked. 'I'm a Green Coffee Girl.'

She stood, feet slightly apart, looking directly at him. Not yet nineteen, but sure of herself. A little paler, a little less healthy than he had first thought. And on closer scrutiny her bright clothes, attractive from a distance, had seen better days.

'That punch was worth a lot to me. That was real trouble for me. I owe you,' she said, taking charge. 'You were just wonderful,' she added, stepping out of her skirt slowly. She continued to undress for him, ending by pulling her blouse lightly over her head. It was a smooth performance, but something was wrong. She began to shiver, smiling hesitantly, shyly. Kien noticed her smooth skin was blue with cold, that her ribs formed sharp lines under her breasts. She was starving.

'Let's share that cigarette,' she said, in a final effort to retain her composure. But after only one puff she slid into his bed, sighed like a sleepy child, and was soon in a deep sleep.

When she woke up she saw Kien sitting over by the table and realised with astonishment that she knew him. In the morning light she could see him clearly and recognised him as the friend of her big brother, in the same platoon, from years ago. Kien came over, lighting a new cigarette, then sat down on the bed beside her. In the light of the new day, he had recognised her, too, despite the make-up.

As she slept he had wondered how she came to be in town. Why had she left her village? How had she joined the most famous of all the street girl groups, the Green Coffee Girls?

She was embarrassed by the recognition. The shared memory of her brother Vinh, with him in the same platoon, at M'Drac battlefield with him, was with them both. And of their only other sad meeting.

After the war Kien had taken his mate's last possessions to Vinh's family, in a hamlet on the outer edges of Hanoi. The landscape was half marsh, half rubbish dump. The scrawny children wore rags. Dirty dogs ran here and there and the flies, mosquitoes and rats were numerous and evident. The hamlet's inhabitants were semi-beggars, gathering garbage for their meagre living, and there were small dumps of obviously stolen goods lining the paths where thieves had set up tiny stalls.

Someone pointed out Vinh's family house to Kien. It was like all the others, a shanty of tin and old timber, surrounded by garbage. Vinh's little sister was barely fifteen then. Her eyes had swollen and sent tears down her cheeks as she recognised her brother's knapsack and his personal belongings. There was no need to ask why Kien had come to visit them. The sad news was there for them to touch. Vinh's blind mother sat with the girl, feeling the items as she handed them over. A cloth hat. A folded knife. An iron bowl. A broken flute. A notebook. When Kien rose to leave the old lady had reached up and touched his cheek. 'At least you came back,' she said quietly.

He stared at the little sister, now naked in his bed, a blanket wrapped around her shoulders. He had forgotten her name and was now too embarrassed to ask. She began to speak, quietly:

'My mother died that same year. I stopped collecting garbage. In fact the dump doesn't even exist now. I came to town, alone.'

They each spilled their stories, talking throughout the morning. She in bed, he beside it. Kien found some rice then fried it over his kerosene stove, and they shared a small meal. She rested again.

Later, she opened her eyes, looking over to him with a small smile. She reached out and began tugging his arm, inviting him to slide in beside her. Kien held back.

'Come on, please. You saved me,' she said.

When Kien declined again, she seemed thankful and didn't persist. 'You're funny,' she said. 'Strange, I mean.'

Kien moved around the room picking up anything of value he could find. Paper money, lottery tickets, anything. After she'd dressed and was preparing to leave he handed her the money and the tickets. She started laughing gaily, but took them. He saw her out into the street and back up to the Thuyen Quang lake, where he had helped her the long night before. 'You'd better make yourself scarce,' she told him. 'People will jump to wrong conclusions if they see you with me. I'll never forget you, though. You're really nice, and strange.'

The girl withdrew her hand and walked away. He felt so dry, so vulgar, so impotent and spent. The result of those months and years at war.

He was at a stage when he had no idea how he would spend the rest of his life. Study? Career? Business? All those things he had once considered important, and attainable, suddenly seemed meaningless and beyond his reach. He was still alive – just. He had no idea of how he would earn his daily living. It was a time of utter isolation, of spiritual emptiness, of surrender.

Yet the city was now coming alive again, this time in a synthetically generated frenzy of patriotism. Another war was about to break out! Pol Pot had been chased out of Cambodia by Vietnamese troops and because of that Pol Pot's allies, the Chinese, were threatening Vietnam's northern border. This would be another turning-point in their lives. Kien's friends emerged to advise him to rejoin the army. Long live his career! Long live the army of Vietnam! A good soldier would always be invaluable, they said. That went on for weeks.

In the streets, on the trains, in offices, in shops, in teahouses and beer gardens, the talk once more was of fighting and weapons. Passionate discussions on the situation on the northern border, with China threatening to invade because of their humiliation in losing Pol Pot, removed from power in Cambodia by the glorious Vietnamese Army.

And night after night express trains packed with soldiers rumbled through Hanoi on the way to the northern front. Tanks and guns were jammed into goods wagons, compartments were filled with young soldiers, and the smell of soldiers' sweat wafted out from train doors and windows. Kien caught the familiar smell of excited fear, of young men soon to be burdened with hardships, bullets and blasting, hunger and cold. This time on the northern border.

'Just like old times, eh?' said someone in the crowd close by. 'Like in 1965 in the early days against the Americans,' the rich city people commented.

'At least we're much stronger compared to those days,' others commented, confident of another victory.

Kien listened, thinking they might be right. But he knew it wasn't true that young Vietnamese loved war. Not true at all. If war came they would fight, and fight courageously. But that didn't mean they loved fighting.

No. The ones who loved war were not the young men, but the others like the politicians, middle-aged men with fat bellies and short legs. Not the ordinary people. The recent years of war had brought enough suffering and pain to last them a thousand years.

Kien wasn't involved in this new war. For him there had been just the one war, the one which had involved the Americans. That had been the final war as far as he was concerned. It was the one which now determined all events in his life; the happiness, the unhappiness, the joys, the sorrows, the loves, the hatreds.

It was that spring which had begun so sadly, so inauspiciously, with his country once more on the brink of war, when something moved within Kien's heart, taking him from turmoil to peace. Something inside him, powerful and urgent, pumped life back into his collapsed spirit and snapped life back into him. It felt like love. Perhaps it was recognition of some wonderful truth deep inside him.

That same chilly dark spring night Kien started to write his first novel.

Kien returned home to find Tran Sinh, a former classmate of his and Phuong's, lying in agony. Sinh had been in hospital for months but had now been sent home to await death. The time to die had come.

Sinh had been home in his first-floor room for two days now, awaiting death. He had joined the army after Kien but was wounded, then demobilised, before Kien. At first, when Sinh returned home, he had not looked like an invalid. He even planned to marry.

But, day after day, paralysis crept over his body, first travelling down his left leg, then his right, then along his trunk. By the time Kien was demobilised Sinh was walking with the help of a walking-stick, but within a short time his health had deteriorated further and he was confined to his bed. The doctors wondered how he had survived his terrible spinal wound, surprised he had not been killed outright. Instead, Sinh had lived and his suffering had been prolonged. 'Incurable,' the doctors had said. The more they tried to help him the worse matters became for him and the relatives caring for him, and this unhappy situation continued for four years.

Sinh's parents had died. His brother had married and left. Sinh was left in the room at the end of the corridor on the first floor, a room dark and wet, with its only window facing the toilet. Kien pushed the door open and stepped in. Through the dim light he saw two children and a thin woman, Sinh's sister-in-law, sitting on the floor assembling cartons for the local biscuit factory, earning a little extra money. None of them looked up.

'How is he?' asked Kien, whispering.

'The same,' the sister-in-law replied in a tired, bored voice. 'Everyone who visits admires him for hanging on so long.' She sighed.

The dying man lay on a bamboo bed in the far corner of the room. Kien approached and caught a whiff of an unbearably foul smell. The stench came from the filthy bedclothes.

Sinh's hair had all fallen out, revealing a darkening scalp, dry as old timber. His nose had flattened, and his cheeks had collapsed, revealing his teeth and eye-sockets. Kien couldn't guess if Sinh had his eyes open or closed. He leaned over and asked: 'Do you recognise me, Sinh?'

'He still recognises you,' interrupted the sister-in-law, 'but he can't speak because his lungs have collapsed.'

'Can he eat?'

'Yes. But it just flows out the other end.'

Kien sat down on the stool by the bed, not knowing what to say. Sinh could move a little, but his desire to live was clearly gone. Fifteen minutes passed, then twenty. If he watched carefully Kien could discern a slight rising and falling of the blankets. The room was still. Now and then the sister-in-law mumbled something about how harshly fate had treated her. Sinh's brother, sleeping in a loft above Sinh, suddenly began to snore.

Poor Sinh, the poet of Class 10A. What a great pity!

The summer before Kien had visited Sinh in hospital. He could still move then, but his will to live was dwindling. He would sit in his wheelchair and speak with a clear mind, ignoring the certainty of his fate, that he would soon die. He didn't complain or bemoan his destiny. Above all he had never made his visitors feel uncomfortable.

Often, he would work up enthusiasm and act delighted, smiling all the time at his visitors. He would chat away in his weak voice, speaking of schooldays and classmates, the pretty girls and the teachers and other matters removed from his present state. He would act as though everything Kien told him was fascinating: 'Right, excellent, how could I have forgotten!' And: 'Now I remember! How could I have forgotten that!'

Kien had pushed Sinh's wheelchair out into the hospital's pretty garden, past some mimosa shrubs in beautiful bloom. The afternoon had been so calm, the air so clean. The sunshine had slanted over the green lawn.

They stopped under the canopy of a spreading *boddhi* tree. 'The sun divides the afternoon into halves,' he had said, 'and the mimosa petals close ... see, that's a poem,' Sinh smiled. 'I didn't dare think of myself as a real poet when I joined the army,' he said. 'I hoped to be someone like Le Anh Xuan, our southern hero whose works will endure from this war into the next century. Well, that was my dream. And while I think of it, I must confess I wrote many romantic poems for Phuong and for ages I was frightened you'd find out and beat me up.'

There was nothing to say. The two childhood friends were now in completely different situations in post-war life. After so many years of fighting they were able to speak to each other wordlessly, using the language of their hearts.

Kien saw Sinh back to his ward and said goodbye. He hugged him and kissed his cold thin cheeks.

'Come and see me, some time,' Sinh called after Kien as he left.

'Please,' he had said, beginning to sob in a rare bout of self-pity. 'Sometimes I wish I could kill myself and end everything quickly. War has robbed me of the liberty I deserve. Now, I'm a slave . . .'

And now, as he sat near the dying Sinh in his bedroom, Kien was choked with emotion. He buried his face in his hands, unable to bear it. He then got up and ran from the half-bedroom, half-mortuary, without even saying goodbye to the sister-in-law.

Back in his room, his muddy jacket and shoes still on, he lay on his bed and stared at the cracked and yellowing ceiling, his hands behind his head. Hot and painful tears silently ran down his cheeks.

What was to be done? What could be done? He coughed, wanting to moan out loud to ease the pain.

In truth he had been deliriously happy to return home to Hanoi when the war ended. He had spent more than three days travelling on the trans-Vietnam 'Unification' troop train after the fall of Saigon. It was a happy feeling and some soldiers now regarded it as the best days of their army life. Still, there had been some pain, even then.

The train was packed with wounded, demobilised soldiers. Knapsacks were jammed together on the luggage racks and in every corner. Hammocks were strung vertically and horizontally all over the compartments, making them look a little like resting stations in the jungle.

At the start, there had been a common emotion of bitterness. There had been no trumpets for the victorious soldiers, no drums, no music. That might have been tolerated, but not the disrespect shown them. The general population just didn't care about them. Nor did their own authorities.

The railway station scenes were just like afternoon markets, chaotic and noisy.

The authorities checked the soldiers time after time, searching them for loot. Every pocket of their knapsacks had been searched as though the mountain of property that had been looted and hidden after the takeover of the South had been taken only by soldiers.

At every station the loudspeakers blared, blasting the ears of the wounded, the sick, the blind, the mutilated, the white-eyed, grey-lipped malarial troops. Into their ears poured an endless stream of the most ironic of teachings, urging them to ignore the spirit of reconciliation, to beware of the 'bullets' coated with sugar, to ignore the warmth and passions among the remnants of this fallen, luxurious society of the South. And especially to guard against the idea of the South having fought valiantly or been meritorious in any way.

But we 'meritorious' and victorious soldiers knew how to defend ourselves against this barrage of nonsense. We made fun of the loudspeakers' admonishments, turning their speeches into jokes, ridiculing them.

By the time we reached the northern Red River Delta areas, where the roads were running alongside us showing the way home to Hanoi, we were all deliriously happy. All the dreams and wishes that had so long been pent up inside suddenly burst from us.

Even the most conservative among us expressed wildly passionate ideas of how they would launch into their new civilian, peacetime lives.

Kien had befriended Hien, a girl soldier from Zone 9 battlefield in the south. She had travelled south in 1966 and been badly wounded in battle. Although her native home was Nam Dinh she had a Ha Tien provincial accent. At night, Kien had carried her to his hammock and they had spent the night together. The rocking of the train set the hammock swinging and despite the cheerful teasing from the soldiers around them they had hugged each other and slept together, awakened together, dreamed together and hugged some more. They had kissed hurriedly, sharing the last moments of their uniformed lives, the last kilometres of their battlefield of youth, in passionate embrace.

When the train stopped at her station, Kien helped Hien down from the train. He told her he wanted to leave the train there and take her home, but she had laughed and refused.

'That's enough. Let our stories become ashes now,' she had said. 'You need to get home, too. Go home as quickly as possible and take care of your house. See if there's anyone or anything left for you to live for. Maybe someone's expecting you.'

'Won't we see each other again?' he had asked.

'Who knows? In peacetime anything can happen. Now there's no war and we're not soldiers we needn't make promises to each other. Maybe we'll meet again, by chance.'

Alone, Hien had turned away from him, dragging herself along on crutches, her badly wounded leg swinging uselessly. Her slim body swung from one side to the other gracefully as she moved along, her shoulders raised by the crutches. Just before she went through the crowded platform gate she turned to look at Kien for a last time. Her eyes were sad, but misting over. She staggered a little, nearly losing her balance, then swung determinedly around and went through the gate and out of view.

From there to Hanoi the train's siren seemed to sound continuously, saying 'good times, good times, good times,' and the wagon wheels clipping over the rail joints replied, 'happy days, happy days, happy days.' As they neared beautiful old Hanoi Kien was intoxicated by the excitement, as though he'd been lifted to a higher level on a fragrant cloud. Swept up in the fever of anticipation of returning home, his eyes blurred over with tears for a homeward journey he had never dreamed possible.

It was already dark when he arrived at his old home after walking through quiet dark streets from the Hang Co railway station. He stopped and looked at the old building which itself was also strangely dark; perhaps the families were all asleep. He entered the front yard cautiously, then approached the front door. Perhaps someone had waited up for him, he thought, for the door was unlatched. Surely no one would wait for me. How would they know? But as he began to climb the stairs he felt a dark sense of urgency and his heart tightened in foreboding.

A pale light shone from a yellowish lamp on the first landing, throwing a dim glow down the corridor. The door to the rooms where he and his father lived was still the same, with the bronze plaque bearing his father's name. His hands began to shake, then his body, and tears of joy welled up inside him. He stood, swaying gently, fixed to the spot before the door.

Suddenly, another door down the corridor opened and a tall, slim woman wearing a nightgown appeared in the hallway. She stared directly at him, a mute cry in her eyes. Phuong!

He was transfixed, confused.

'Kien!'

She stepped gently forward, leaning into his arms.

Kien responded, gradually coming to his senses, and bent a little as her smooth arms tightened around his neck.

'Phuong, my darling,' he murmured, as he began kissing her, kisses for ten long years. An unforgettable embrace for each of them, from one heart to the other, an embrace they would remember forever, for nothing so wondrous had touched their lives in those lost years apart.

She gently rubbed her cheek on his lips, then his collar, then his rough army shirt. They whispered urgently to each other. 'It's been ten years. Ten years. I was sure I'd never see you again.'

'We've each been ghosts in the other's mind,' he said.

She continued to murmur, 'But from this moment on we'll never be apart, will we darling?'

Kien tensed a little. A feeling of deep embarrassment began to creep over him, a shadow of concern intruding into his happiness, a feeling of uneasiness that seemed to stem from the supple body he held in his arms.

He tensed. He could hear padded footsteps. Someone was watching them in their embrace.

Phuong, oblivious, began undoing the top button of her blouse, from which she took a shiny key, slung like a necklace. His eyes blurring, Kien unlocked his door and went in. The air, stagnant for several years, flowed out, emerging like a dying gasp.

Kien turned and grasped Phuong's arm and began pulling her into his room. He had seen a shadow inside the door of her room and had suddenly become brusque. She had not been alone.

Phuong turned pale, her gaze defensive. Kien reached down in front of her and picked up his knapsack, then, letting her go, stepped into his room alone and closed the door in her face.

So this was what the peace and happiness would be! The glorious, bright rays of victory, his grand, long-awaited return. So much for his naive faith in the future. He swore: 'Wretched man that I am!'

And every time after that when he recalled the first night home of his new post-war life, his heart was wrenched in anguish and bitterness and he would involuntarily moan.

Having stepped into the room and unslung his knapsack he began pacing the room to make sense of the second presence with Phuong. So, the divine war had paid him for all his suffering and losses with more suffering and loss at home. Throughout his years at the front he had dreamed – when he had dreamed of home at all – of little else but the magic moments of return and

Phuong, seeing them both in a Utopian dream. He sat down. A succession of images passed through his mind.

Phuong had returned to him later that same night saying the man she was living with, who had asked her to marry him, had left immediately afterwards, because Kien had returned.

How blind they had been, back then. Though now he often drowned himself in alcohol, though hundreds of times he pleaded with his inner self to calm down, he was constantly torn with pain recalling the post-war times with Phuong. His life, after ten destructive years of war, had then been punctured by the sharp thorns of love.

Kien's new life with Phuong had broken both their hearts. In hindsight, it was a love doomed from the start, doomed from the time he had heard those soft footfalls in her room.

It had ended recently, abruptly, after a fight outside a tavern where Kien had beaten up Phuong's former lover, mauling him badly. The police had been called and Kien had been described by witnesses as 'a madman'. He had returned home from the police station and met Phuong. He was speechless and distraught.

As Phuong was preparing to leave him she spoke: 'We're prisoners to our shared memories of wonderful times together. Those memories won't release us. But we've made a big mistake; I thought we would face just a few small hurdles. But they aren't small, they're as big as mountains.'

She reflected: 'I should have died that day ten years ago when our train was attacked. At least you'd have remembered me as pure and beautiful. As it is, even though I'm alive, I am a dark chapter in your life. I'm right, aren't I?' Kien remained silent. As she passed out of his life again he made no attempt to stop her.

He had thought then it was for the best, but preserving that attitude was more difficult than he'd imagined. A week went by, then two, then a month. He became increasingly restless, unable to concentrate, or even to turn up at the university. He sat uncomfortably, unable to relax or plan his days properly.

He lived on the razor's edge. Whenever he heard high heels tapping on the stairs his heart would stop. But it was never her.

Kien took to staring out of his window for hours on end, then walking the dark streets, now and then looking back in hope. On bad nights he would lose control altogether and break down, sobbing into his pillow. Yet he knew that if she returned to him both of them would suffer again.

His room began to get colder as the winter pressed in. He stood by the window one cold night, missing Phuong as usual, as he watched the slow drizzling rain, slanting with the north-east wind. Scenes from the northern battlefront began forming before him and he saw once again the Ngoc Bo Ray peak and the woods of the Screaming Souls. Then each man in his platoon reappeared before him in the room. By what magic was this happening to him? After the horrible slaughter which had wiped out his battalion, how could he see them all again? The air in his room felt strange, vibrating with images of the past. Then it shook, shuddering under waves of hundreds of artillery shells pouring into the Screaming Souls Jungle and the walls of the room shook noisily as the jets howled in on their bombing runs. Startled, Kien jumped back from the window.

Bewildered, confused, deeply troubled, he began to pace around the room away from the window. The memories flared up, again and again. He lurched over to his desk and picked up his pen then almost mechanically began to write.

All through the night he wrote, a lone figure in this untidy, littered room where the walls peeled, where books and newspapers and rubbish packed shelves and corners of the floor, where empty bottles were strewn and where the broken wardrobe was now cockroach-infested. Even the bed with its torn mosquito net and blanket was a mess. In this derelict room he wrote frantically, non-stop, with a sort of divine inspiration, knowing this might be the only time he would feel this urge.

He wrote, cruelly reviving the images of his comrades, of the mortal combat in the jungle that became the Screaming Souls, where his battalion had met its tragic end. He wrote with hands numbed by the cold, trembling with the fury of his endeavour, his lungs suffocating with cigarette smoke, his mouth dry and his breath foul, as all around him the men fought and fell, one by one, falling with loud painful screams, amidst loud, exploding shells, among thunderclaps from the rockets pouring down from the helicopter gunships.

One by one they fell in that battle in that room, until the greatest hero of them all, a soldier who had stayed behind enemy lines to harass the enemy's withdrawal, was blown into a small tattered pile of humanity on the edge of a trench.

The next morning rays from the first day of spring shone through to the darkest corner of his room.

Kien arose, wearily trudging away from the house and out along the pavement, a lonely-looking soul wandering in the beautiful sunshine. The tensions of the tumultuous night had left him yet still he felt unbalanced, an eerie feeling identical to that which beset him after being wounded for the first time.

Coming around after losing consciousness he had found himself in the middle of the battlefield, bleeding profusely. But this was the beautiful, calm Nguyen Du Street, and there was the familiar Thuyen Quang lake from his childhood. Familiar, but not quite the same, for after that long, mystical night, everything now seemed changed. Even his own soul; he felt a stranger unto himself. Even the clouds floating in from the north-east seemed to be dyed a different colour, and just below the skyline Hanoi's old grey roofs seemed to sparkle in the sunshine as though just sprinkled with water.

For that whole Sunday Kien wandered the streets in a trance, feeling a melancholy joy, like dawn mixed with dusk. He believed he had been born again, and the bitterness of his recent post-war years faded. Born again into the pre-war years, to resurrect the deep past within him, and this would continue until he had relived a succession of his life and times; the first new life was to be that of his distant past. His lost youth, before the sorrow of war.

He went to a park that afternoon, ambling along uneven rocky paths lined with grass and flowers, brushing past shrubs still wet with rain. Coming to an empty bench near a lovers' lane, he sat for hours just listening to the quiet wind blowing over the lake as he gazed into the distance, far beyond the horizons of thought to the harmonious fields of the dead and living, of unhappiness and happiness, of regret and hope. The immense sky, the pungent perfume from the beautiful new spring and a melodic sadness that seemed to play on the waves of the lake combined to conjure up within his spiritual space images of a past, previously inexplicable life.

He saw himself in a long-ago distant landscape, and from that other images and memories revived and he sat silently reviewing his past.

Memories of a midday in the dry season in beautiful sunshine, flowers in radiant blossom in the tiny forest clearing; memories also of a difficult rainy day by the flooded Sa Thay river, when he had to go into the jungle collecting bamboo-shoots and wild turnips. Memories of riverbanks, wild grass plots, deserted villages, beloved but unknown female figures who gave rise to tender nostalgia and the pain of love. An accumulation of old memories, of silent pictures as sharp as a mountain profile and as dense as deep jungle. That afternoon, not feeling the rising evening wind, he had sat and allowed his soul to take off on its flight to his eternal past.

Months passed. The novel seemed to have its own logic, its own flow. It seemed from then on to structure itself, to take its own time, to make its own detours. As for Kien, he was just the writer; the novel seemed to be in charge and he meekly accepted that, mixing his own fate with that of his heroes, passively letting the stream of his novel flow as it would, following the course of some mystical logic set by his memory or imagination.

From that winter's night when he began to write, the flames of memory led Kien deeply into a labyrinth, through circuitous paths and back out again into primitive jungles of the past. Again, seeing the Sa Thay river, Ascension Pass, the Screaming Souls Jungle, Crocodile Lake, like dim names from hell. Then the novel drifted towards the MIA team, gathering the remains, making a long trail linking the soldiers' graves scattered all over the mountains of the north and Central Highlands; this process of recalling his work in gathering remains had breathed new energy into each page of his novel.

And into the stories went also the atmosphere of the dark jungle with its noxious scents, and legends and myths about the lives of the ordinary soldiers, whose very deaths provided the rhythm for his writing.

Yet only a few of his heroes would live from the opening scenes through to the final pages, for he witnessed and then described them trapped in murderous firefights, in fighting so horrible that everyone involved prays to heaven they'll never have to experience any such terror again. Where death lay in wait, then hunted and ambushed them. Dying and surviving were separated by a thin line; they were killed one at a time, or all together; they were killed instantly, or were wounded and bled to death in agony; they could live but suffer the nightmares of white blasts which destroyed their souls and stripped their personalities bare.

Kien had perhaps watched more killings and seen more corpses than any contemporary writer. He had seen rows of youthful American soldiers, their bodies unscathed, leaning shoulder to shoulder in trenches and dugouts, sleeping an everlasting sleep because artillery barrages had blocked their exit, sucking life from them. Parachutists still in their camouflaged uniforms lying near bushes around a landing zone in the Ko Leng forest, burning in the hot noon-day sun, with only hawks above and flies below to covet their bodies. And a rain of arms and legs dropping before him onto the grass by the Sa Thay river during a night raid by B52s. Hamburger Hill, after three days of bloody fighting, looked like a dome roof built with corpses. A soldier stepping onto a mine and being blown to the top of a tree, as if he had wings. Kien's deaths had more shapes, colours and reality of atmosphere than anyone else's war stories. Kien's soldiers' stories came from beyond the grave and told of their lives beyond death.

'There is no terrible hell in death,' he had once read. 'Death is another life, a different kind to that we know here. Inside death one finds calm, tranquillity and real freedom . . .'

To Kien dead soldiers were fuzzier yet sometimes more significant than the living. They were lonely, tranquil and hopeful, like illusions. Sometimes the dead manifested themselves as sounds rather than shadows. Others in the MIA team gathering bodies in the jungles said they'd heard the dead playing musical instruments and singing. They said at the foot of Ascension Pass, deep inside the ancient forest, the ageless trees whispered along with a song that merged into harmony with an ethereal guitar, singing, '*O victorious years and months, O endless suffering and pain* . . . '.

A nameless song with a ghostly rhythm, simple and mysterious, that everyone had heard, yet each said they'd heard different versions. They said they listened to it every night and were finally able to follow the voice trail to where the singer was buried. They found a body wrapped in canvas in a shallow grave, its bones crumbled. Alongside the bones lay a hand-made guitar, intact.

True or not? Who's to know. But the story went on to say that when the bones were lifted to be placed in a grave all those present heard the song again echoing through the forest. After the burial the song ended, and was never heard again.

The yarn became folklore. For every unknown soldier, for every collection of MIA remains, there was a story.

Kien recalled the Mo Rai valley by the Sa Thay river when his group found a half-buried coffin. It had popped up like a termite hill on a riverbank, so high even the floods hadn't reached it. Inside the coffin was a thick plastic bag, similar to those the Americans used for their dead, but this one was clear plastic. The soldier seemed to be still breathing, as though in a deep sleep. He looked so alive. His handsome, youthful face had a serious air and his body appeared to be still warm, clothed in a uniform that was still in good condition.

Then before their eyes the plastic bag discoloured, whitening as though suddenly filled with smoke. The bag glowed and something seemed to escape from it, causing the bag to deflate. When the smoke cleared, only a yellowish ash remained.

Kien and his platoon were astounded and fell to their knees around it, raising their hands to heaven praying for safe flight for the departed soul. Overhead a flock of geese, flying solemnly and peacefully in formation, winged their way past.

'If you can't identify them by name we'll be burdened by their deaths for the rest of our lives,' the head of the MIA team had said. He had been an insurance clerk at one time. Now his entire life was gathering corpses. He was preoccupied with this sole duty which was to locate, identify, recover then bury the dead soldiers. He used to describe his work as though it were a sacred oath, and ask others to swear their dedication.

An oath was hardly necessary for Kien or the others in the MIA team. They'd emerged from the war full of respect and mourning for the unfortunate dead, named and nameless alike.

One of Kien's scouts was Phan, a native of Hai Hung province. He told Kien this story: 'I don't know who he was because he was from the ARVN Special Commandos, on the other side. Anyway, during one fierce battle during the rainy season this guy's company and mine became entangled in a very bloody fight. Rivers of blood; no winner, no loser, both battered. The Americans backed these ARVN units up with artillery from the top of a hill and when the artillery stopped the Phantoms came in and bombed us. I dropped into a bomb crater and escaped the big bombs. Then came the baby bombs, exploding non-stop.

'I lay there not moving and then this guy jumped in on me, heavy as a log. I was so frightened I stabbed him twice in the chest through his camouflage uniform, then once more in the belly, then again in the neck. He cried in pain and writhed around convulsing, his eyes rolling. I realised then he'd already been badly wounded before jumping in. His own artillery had blown his foot off and he was bleeding all over, even from the mouth. His hands were trying to hold in his intestines, which were spilling out of his belly and steaming. I didn't know what to do. He was so pitiful. I pushed his guts back into his belly and tore my shirt off to bandage him, but it was so hard to stop the bleeding.

'If it had been anyone else, not someone so strong and healthy, he would have died right then. But this guy just moaned louder and louder, tears running down his cheeks. I was horrified and at the same time felt deep pity for him.

'So when the raid stopped I jumped out of the crater telling him to stay there for a while. "I'm going to find some cloth and bandages," I told him. "I'll be back soon."

'He blinked at me, the rain pouring down his face, mixing water, tears and blood. Outside the crater the jungle was destroyed, with trees broken and the ground devastated. Troops from both sides had withdrawn so I searched for a while and found a bag with emergency medical equipment in it, then turned to go back to help him.

'But I'd been silly. By then it was dark and I had no idea where the crater was. The trees around me had been broken off and branches scattered all around the place. The ground was pock-marked with hundreds of craters. Where was the one I'd been sharing with the Saigonese? Darkness fell, the heavy rain continued and the water flowed in small streams down the slopes. "Hey, Saigon, Saigon, hey!" I called, running around trying to find him. I fell into a crater. The water came over my knees. That meant that someone sitting inside a crater would now have water up to his chest.

'The more I tried to find him the worse the situation became. All I did was exhaust myself. When dawn at last came and the rain eased you wouldn't believe what I saw. Horrifying. All the bomb craters were filled to the rim with water.

'I pushed off. I was going a little mad. I began to imagine his death; water slowly rising on him, a barbaric death stuck in the mud, helpless as the water came over his belly, his chest, his shoulders, his chin, his lips, then reached his nostrils . . . and he started to drown. He'd died still hoping desperately that I'd come back and save him, as I promised. In which crater had he died?

'Now, even after many years, whenever I see a flood I feel a sharp pang in my heart and think of my cruel stupidity. No human being deserved the torture I left him to suffer.'

After many years of peace Phan was still tormented by the

memory. Would the drowned man ever stop floating through his mind?

The sorrow of war inside a soldier's heart was in a strange way similar to the sorrow of love. It was a kind of nostalgia, like the immense sadness of a world at dusk. It was a sadness, a missing, a pain which could send one soaring back into the past. The sorrow of the battlefield could not normally be pinpointed to one particular event, or even one person. If you focused on any one event it would soon become a tearing pain.

It was especially important, therefore, to avoid if possible focusing on the dead.

However, Kien would remember, until the last moments of his life, his first commander, Quang. In the dry season of 1966 during the Sa Thay campaign, Kien was a novice, fighting for the first time. For three days and nights fighting against the Air Cavalry Kien followed Quang closely. He was led, helped and in reality protected. Standing, lying down, rolling away, moving forward, running, Kien was linked with Quang. Then suddenly Quang had been chopped down, hit when the company was crossing a bamboo thicket near Hill 300 to get within range of the American troops who had dropped from helicopters.

Quang had been hit by a shell exploding right at his feet, blasting him into the air then plummeting him back to earth. Kien knelt clumsily beside his commander, but didn't know how to help him. Quang's belly was torn open, his intestines pouring out, but the frightening thing was that all his bones seemed to be smashed.

His two sides had been flattened somehow, and one arm had been torn from his shoulder. Amazingly, Quang was unconscious for only a brief time. Perhaps because he was in so much pain he regained consciousness quickly. He had been a fisherman in Mong Cai, was extremely strong and healthy, well-built and tough, as well as kind-hearted. He was usually brave and silent, but now he screamed: 'Don't touch me, don't! Don't bandage me any more, aaaahhhh!'

Kien had been trying to bandage Quang's thighs.

'Stop! Stop, please!' he sobbed, and blood ran from the corners of his mouth. He lay still for a moment then moved his head and opened his eyes. 'Kien, Keeee-en, shoot me!' he said 'Shoot!'

The jungle reverberated with artillery fire. Noisy shouts echoed through the smoke. Kien trembled desperately, but kept on trying to bandage Quang. While trying his best he fervently hoped Quang would faint and be free of the horrible pain – his pain was even torturing Kien. It seemed death itself was forcing Quang to stay conscious a little longer, to prolong the cruel torture.

Then even more artillery rounds came in from the enemy, with one shell exploding near them and burying them with earth, making it even more difficult for Kien to help Quang. Miraculously, Quang had lived through the second blast.

Blood flowed from his mouth and blood bubbled through his nose as he breathed. His eyes were wide open, as though he wanted to say something. Kien bent closer to listen: 'If you pity me please don't let me go on like this. I can't stand the pain. My bones are smashed, my guts spilled . . .' His voice was barely a tiny whisper yet it was clear and he spoke firmly: 'Let me die. Just one shot. Please . . .'

Then with unexpected speed Quang summoned his remaining strength and reached with his one good arm for a grenade, then held it up.

'Got it!' he said loudly, almost cheerfully triumphant. He then began to laugh a ghastly laugh.

Kien looked on in alarm as Quang shouted to him, 'Get out quick, Kien. Go! Out of here! Get out!'

As Kien started to move he heard Quang's ghoulish laughter. He jumped up and began to back away, his eyes on the grenade's detonator. Swiftly he turned and ran as Quang's crazed laughter followed him.

Nine years later one of Kien's MIA team said he had heard crazed laughter echoing from Hill 300, on the other side of the Sa Thay river. Kien listened as the nervous man gave his version.

'I think it came from the jungle monster the Trieng people talk about,' said the soldier.

'Anyway, I'm sure it wasn't a human laugh because it was shaking and choking. It didn't last long but I froze in my tracks. Looking around a bit, I found a small grassed clearing and then a little hut. I could smell something burning, like barbecued cassava, so it meant there were human beings there. Near the hut I saw a hairy figure, someone with very long hair and a beard, sitting naked on a log staring right at the place where I was hiding.

'Then I saw a grenade in his hand, would you believe it? I crawled backwards but as I did I brushed a few leaves and the man must have heard it because he stood up, looked my way and stepped forward. I jumped up then ran away and as I ran he started that horrible laughter again, and followed me.'

'Perhaps it was the Forest Man,' said another, remembering the local folklore.

'Why would Forest Man have a grenade? And Forest Man isn't supposed to live in a hut. And would Forest Man laugh like that?' the young soldier replied.

'Maybe it was Tung. What do you think, Kien?'

'Tung who?' asked Kien.

'Crazy Tung. The guardsman, don't you remember? He went crazy and left us in the jungle when we were based near Crossroad 90 in 1971. That's quite close to that area.'

'Oh, that Tung, I remember now. Maybe you're right. He used

to laugh and laugh when he had his mad crises and he gave everyone the shivers.'

The ghost talk went on. Some said there were ghostly streams in the jungle where those who drank the water began immediately to suffer all sorts of diseases, including mental illness. But they remembered that Tung's illness had been caused by a bomb fragment penetrating his brain. At least that's what the regimental doctor had said.

Kien remembered their headquarters had been bombed and many soldiers killed and wounded. Tung appeared to escape unscratched, except for a terrible headache. The nurse gave him aspirin but that seemed to make it worse.

Then suddenly one night Tung's laughter had sounded through all the huts. Yes, that hadn't been far from here. Tung cleared out and although many tried to track him down and bring him back he skilfully avoided his trackers.

After several weeks there was still no trace of Tung. The soldiers began saying the bomb fragment had zig-zagged around in his head leading the craziness into all corners of his skull, making him crazy in several different ways.

Still, listening to the story of Tung, Kien could hardly concentrate. All he could think of was Quang's death and his laughter, and the grenade, nine years ago. It seemed to the soldiers talking about these mystical happenings that intense physical pain could mingle with the earth and grow into the trees in the jungle. Such desperate tragedies might create those ghostly sounds, sounds that would be heard forever, recreating the agonies of the past.

It was around this time that Kien began to drift over the edge from logic and started believing in ghosts. Ghosts in the winds from hell and in the mystical occurrences in the deep and gloomy jungle.

Kien and his MIA team finally decided to investigate the hut where the long-haired man had been seen. As they approached they heard a howl of laughter, coarse chuckles and roars, as though they were warning calls trying to prevent them prying.

'Who are you?' Kien called. 'We're your friends,' he added, hoping to entice them out.

There was no reply. Only the sounds of a creek running down from Hill 300.

The jungle was still. 'The war is over,' Kien shouted. 'It's peace. No war. You can come out!' he added.

The reply was a long peal of hysterical laughter which made the hair on their necks stand on end. Laughter? Or simply the howl of a lunatic? The barbaric moaning echoed on and on, the sounds clashing as though more than one voice was calling.

The MIA team waited patiently until the noises stopped, then moved towards the hut. Kien and the team felt rather than saw shadows flit from the rear of the hut into the jungle. From the top of a tree near the grass plot they heard a bird call sharply as the grass parted below the tree.

'Look!' someone shouted.

At the edge of the clearing where the bamboo jungle began, a ghostly figure was seen momentarily. Long hair flying. Then another, bent-over shadowy figure running along behind the first. Illusion and reality mixed with each other as the figures merged with the dark green jungle backdrop.

The MIA team were amazed. They left a can of rice, salt and medicines in the hut, hoping to help. But when they returned a few days later the rice and the medicine were still there, untouched. 'They might think it's a trap,' said one of the team.

'They? That means you're sure they're human?' said one who felt they'd been ghosts.

'Look,' said Kien picking up a comb. It had been fashioned from a piece of aluminium, probably from a crashed plane. Long hair was still in the comb.

'Well, they aren't ghosts. Or Forest Men,' one said.

'But who are they? Ours? Deserters? Or Saigonese?'

No one had an answer.

For weeks after that the team kept a sharp eye out for the hut-dwellers, but not once were they seen. Once some laughter was heard, and another time one of them had seen a woman bathing in the river at dusk. When he had approached she had turned and burst into ghoulish laughter and fled, into the bush or into the reeds on the edge of the stream.

'Maybe the other one's gone and ditched her,' said one soldier. 'I wouldn't be surprised if she's carrying a baby.'

In this way they mulled over the mysterious figures. The one who spoke of the baby was hoping this unfathomable story would be made less tragic by adding an air of hope, perhaps even a happy ending. By including a baby, it somehow sounded better.

He went on: 'The mental illness wouldn't affect the baby. He'd grow up, people would find him, or maybe he would find people by himself,' he suggested.

'We have to hope so,' another said, now taking the baby for granted.

'Well, let's hope so. There must be a lot of them around here like this, not to mention the more horrible stories. The dead ones left behind, for example,' another said.

'That's right! The dead ones, too,' another chimed in. 'They must also have a certain salvation.'

That's right, said Kien to himself as he listened to these ramblings. After all these we are the ones who are now confused and mired in shame. We are the ones who've become totally alienated. But we shan't be like this forever. There must be some way out for us. But when?

As the novel continued to unfold on the cluttered desk in his Hanoi room more stories came back to him. Flashes like film reels of events he had not thought about even once since they occurred.

Saigon, 30 April, V-Day. It poured with rain. Yes, on that momentous day of total victory, after that terribly hot noon, Saigon had been drenched in rain. After the downpour the sun came out from behind the clouds and the gunsmoke.

The last counter-attack by the ARVN commandos at Tan Son Nhat airport was beaten off and Kien's troops moved in from the edge of the main runway. Kien dragged himself over to the airport lounge to find his regiment.

Of the entire scout platoon sent in to the airport only he had survived.

In the city five kilometres away the anti-aircraft guns were being fired noisily in celebration. But here it remained strangely quiet. The smoke continued to billow from oil fires but the air had been cooled and soothed by the rain, creating a sleepy atmosphere. All around the airport the victorious troops were enjoying their greatest prize: sleep.

Kien lurched tiredly past a row of ARVN bodies, commandos in uniforms still wet from the rain, and stepped onto the polished granite stairs of the terminal. Everywhere soldiers were lying deeply asleep. They lay sprawled on tables, on bars, on benches, on window ledges, and in armchairs. The chorus of snores made Kien sleepy, too. He sat himself down by the door to the Customs office and lit a cigarette. After a few minutes the cigarette dropped from his fingers and he slid to the ground into a deep sleep.

He was awakened a short time later by noises, the heat of a fire and the smell of food. Next to him a group of armoured-car soldiers were burning mattresses and polished wooden railings from the bar.

They were cooking something in a huge pot. It smelled delicious.

'Smells good, don't it?' one of them said to Kien. 'Have some. Down here they call them instant noodles.'

Another soldier interrupted: 'Goddammit, be quick, so we can get looking. Fuck it, if we aren't quick the bloody infantry'll get all the good stuff. Oh, sorry mate,' he said to Kien, 'you're infantry. Well, you'd probably know where the post-office store-room is.'

'I know where it is,' Kien replied.

'Excellent. After we've had the noodles, take us there. I've got an empty armoured car out there and I've not had any souvenirs for ages.'

Then he looked disdainfully at Kien. 'Shit, don't you know you've been sleeping next to a corpse? Couldn't you smell her?'

Kien slowly turned his head to see where he'd been sleeping. A naked woman, her breasts firm and standing upright, her legs stretched out and open like scissors, her long hair covering her face, was stretched out near him, blocking the entry to the Customs office. She looked young. Her eyes were half-closed. No blood was visible.

'I was so tired I didn't notice her. I'll drag her away,' said Kien.

'Leave her. Just don't touch her. Now the war's finished it'll be bad luck for us to touch a corpse.'

'I wonder why she's naked,' said Kien.

'Beats me. We'd just shot those bastards over there and when we came in she was already lying there like that.'

'Strange. The commandos are already stinking, yet she's still fresh. Maybe women are cleaner, so their bodies don't rot as quickly,' said Kien.

'Shut up! Gabbing on about stinking corpses while we're trying to eat.'

Behind them they heard the Customs door swing open and a

crashing noise. They turned to see a huge helmeted soldier trip-ping over the girl's body and dropping a crate of Saigon 33 Beer. The bottles scattered and broke, spreading the amber fluid all over the floor. The armoured-car crew just laughed.

But the big man, embarrassed, got up and kicked at the body angrily, screaming at the dead girl. 'You fucking prostitute, lying there showing it for everyone to see. Dare trip me over, damn your ancestors! To hell with you!' he ranted.

Enraged, the big man grabbed the corpse by one leg and dragged her across the floor and down the stairs. Her skull thudded down the steps like a heavy ball. When he reached the concrete floor at the bottom of the stairs, he braced himself, lifted the dead girl and threw her out into the sunshine, next to another pile of dead southern commandos. The body bounced up, her arms spread wide and her mouth opened as if she was about to cry out. Her head dropped back with another thud on the concrete. The lout walked away jauntily, swinging his arms as if he were a hero.

The armoured-car crew had stopped eating, stiffened, and watched in silence. After the lout walked away they rose and went into the yard. The leader raised his AK and started to aim at the big man: 'Damn you!' he shrieked.

But Kien rushed over and pushed the barrel of the gun up. As he did so the soldier began firing, but the bullets went skyward and fell harmlessly to earth around them.

'Just because of that you wanted to kill him?' Kien asked the armoured-car commander.

They looked around them. The whole airport was full of officers and soldiers alike running as though they were in a market-place. They were looting, destroying, and firing rifles into the air at random. No one had paid any attention to the scene with the corpse. Even the lout hadn't realised he'd come within a whisker of being shot.

The soldier wrenched his gun back from Kien, staring at Kien with loathing and hatred.

'Maybe she was an important officer,' Kien said to the soldier, as though the treatment of her body would be justified.

'Shut up,' the soldier replied.

'What?'

'Shut up. You're talking garbage,' he said, narrowing his eyes and spoiling for a fight.

The armoured-car commander's men gathered around them. 'Drop it, the pair of you. Forget it. Today's V-Day, have you forgotten?'

The men took down curtains from the airport lounge and began to wrap the bodies up. They found some pretty clothes in a suitcase and dressed the dead girl, combing her hair into a bun and washing her face. They carried all the bodies out and laid them out in a row to wait for the body truck to take them away.

'That's it. Farewell to one regime,' Kien shouted.

The armoured-car crew took off their caps and stood to attention.

The commander, calm by now, apologised to Kien. 'Sorry for the outburst. It's just that we're fed up with corpses. We've had human flesh in the armoured-car tracks and we've had to drive through rivers to wash the bits off and wash away the stink. But I just couldn't watch that arsehole treating a body like that, and a woman, too. If you hadn't stopped me I'd have shot him and been nailed as a murderer, and that would have been senseless. We weren't any better, sleeping and eating by the corpse.'

'That's enough,' said Kien.

'No. I mean it. That slob gave us a sort of warning: Don't criticise others. Be sure of yourself first.'

Kien frowned, then walked away. 'Be sure of yourself first, what a joke!' Kien said to himself. He recalled Oanh's death a month earlier, the morning his regiment attacked the Police Headquarters at Buon Me Thuot.

That day the southern government's police force had defended themselves as staunchly as any regular soldiers in the southern armed forces. It took the NVA regulars more than an hour to fight their way into the main police building. They'd been ordered to kill all men wearing white shirts and release those wearing yellow. No one knew who'd given the order but it went down the ranks by word of mouth. The attackers fired non-stop yet the white shirts continued to pour out like bees.

In the leading force, Kien and Oanh had just taken out the machine-gunners who'd been firing on them from the third floor. They had rushed up the hallway throwing a grenade into each room they came to. The defenders were using pistols, machine-guns and grenades to fight back and refused to surrender.

Kien and Oanh got to a room at the end of the third-floor corridor. It had a plush brown door lined with leather. The door was flung open before they got to it and three figures like white blurs flashed past them and rushed upstairs to the fourth floor.

'They're women! Don't shoot,' shouted Oanh.

But Kien's AK had already sounded. Kien stopped shooting and shouted, 'Surrender and you live. Resist, you're dead!'

But he had already shot the three uniformed women and they fell back down the stairs onto the green corridor's green carpet. Dark red blood spurted from two of them onto the carpet, while the third, just a girl really, slumped at the base of the stairs against a wall.

Kien and Oanh ran over to her. The air was full of gunsmoke and the smell of blood, yet the young girl's perfume seemed stronger. She was cradling her face in her hands, her curled hair almost covering her hands. Between her hands they could see smeared lipstick and her lips twisted in pain. The whole building was in chaos and all around them were grenade explosions, gunshots, screams and footsteps.

Kien moved past the girl, heading upstairs, and Oanh said to the girl, 'Go down into the yard with your hands up. No one will shoot you.' Oanh picked up his knapsack of grenades and slung them over his shoulder as though they were avocados, and started after Kien.

Kien didn't hear the shots that killed Oanh.

With all the machine-gun fire and other noises he didn't even hear Oanh's cry as the girl shot him. He didn't realise that he had barely escaped death himself because her Walther PK 38 had run out of bullets.

She had shot Oanh in the back several times and Oanh was falling as Kien, completely unaware of her shots, turned to lean against the wall and wait for him. He was about to tell Oanh not to rush out onto the fourth floor, but to use a grenade to threaten them first.

As Oanh fell the girl lifted the pistol in both hands, bending slightly forward, and aimed at Kien. He was less than ten metres from her and knew he would be hit. She pulled the trigger, but nothing happened.

Kien shot her then, coming down the stairs past Oanh, shooting repeatedly, until he stood face to face and shot her again, in revenge. But although she had been blasted back by five rounds she still leaned on her arm on the floor, raising her head, as if she had decided to sit up. Kien fired the remainder of the magazine into her and the tiles under the girl's white uniform reddened with blood. Kien squatted down near the four bodies, shaking and retching. In ten long years of fighting, since his first day at the front, he had never felt as bad.

That day at the airport he had recalled Oanh's fate as he walked around reviling the armoured-car commander's advice to treat the dead sympathetically. Oanh had been sympathetic, and look what had happened to him.

Kien began drinking. There was plenty of free booze at the airport. He wandered around watching the soldiers looting, and joined in the drinking and destruction. The entertainment seemed riotous, but it wasn't the least bit amusing. They turned over furniture, smashed and ripped fittings and scattered them everywhere. Glasses, pots, cups, wine bottles, were all broken or shot up. They used machine-guns to shoot out the chandeliers and the ceiling lights. Everyone drank heavily and they all seemed to be drunk, half-laughing, half-crying. Some were yelling like madmen.

Peace had rushed in brutally, leaving them dazed and staggering in its wake. They were more amazed than happy with the peace.

Kien sat in the canteen of the Air France terminal, his legs up on a table, quietly drinking. One after another he downed the cups of brandy, the way a barbarian would, as if to insult life. Many of those around him had passed out, but he just kept on drinking.

A strange and horrible night.

At times the noise of machine-guns and the sight of the red, blue and violet signal flares fired into the air at random created a surreal atmosphere. It was like an apocalypse, then an earthquake. Kien shuddered, sensing the end of an era.

Some said they had been fighting for thirty years, if you included the Japanese and the French. He had been fighting for eleven years. War had been their whole world. So many lives, so many fates. The end of the fighting was like the deflation of an entire landscape, with fields, mountains and rivers collapsing in on themselves.

As dawn approached it grew noisier, then the racket died down. Kien felt the sharp contrast between the loud, chaotic night and the peaceful morning. Suddenly, he felt terribly alone; he sensed he would be lonely forever.

In later years, when he heard stories of V-Day or watched the scenes of the Fall of Saigon on film, with cheering, flags, flowers, triumphant soldiers and joyful people, his heart would ache with sadness and envy. He and his mates had not felt that soaring, brilliant happiness he saw on film. True, in the days following 30 April he had experienced unforgettable joys after the victory. But on the night itself they'd had that suffocating feeling at the airport. And why not? They'd just stepped out of their trenches.

Yes, he had drunk his way through the night sitting in the Air France lounge. It wasn't until morning that his brain started reeling. He began to have nightmares about the naked girl they'd dressed up. The floor beneath him felt as though it was heaving, a glass wall before him seemed to go up in smoke. The apparition of a naked girl appeared before him, her chest white, her hair messy, her dark eyes swarming with ants, and on her lips a terrible twisted smile. He looked steadily at her, feeling pity. This was a human being who had been killed and humiliated, someone even he had looked down on. Those who had died and those who lived on shared a common fate in this war.

He reached out unsteadily and tried to embrace the ghostly shadow of the girl. In his drunkenness he was blubbering, generating deep pity for her poor lost soul as he blethered on with words of consolation for her.

When he spoke of these events in later life others found it inconceivable he would waste his time becoming nostalgic over a girl at Tan Son Nhat airport who had not only been a corpse, but the corpse of someone Kien had never met! Yet the woman had, strangely, left a tragic and indelible imprint on his mind. She became the last of his enduring obsessions.

The manuscript pages were heaped in random order in the mute girl's attic quarters. These flimsy pages represented Kien's past; the lines told stories that were sometimes clear, but most were at best obscure and as vague and pale as twilight. They told stories from the precariously fine border dividing life from death, blurring the line itself and finally erasing it. Ages and times were mixed in confusion, as were peace and war.

The conflicts continued from the lines on pages into the real life of the author; the fighting refused to die.

The personalities, both alive and dead, breathed and spoke to the author in his special world where everyone he had known still lived and walked and smiled and ate and joked and dreamed and loved.

The mute girl might have said the author's craziest pages came when he was most unhappy; it was then he wrote part-funereally, part-insanely because of his insistent passion for life. That's what she might have said.

But she could not speak at all. That was the one last enigma bequeathed to us by the author. The mute girl had no way to express herself, for she neither read nor wrote properly, and of course could not speak.

She had opened a place in her heart and permanently reserved it for the author. When he had gone, the manuscript took his place in her heart. While she had his story she nurtured the hope of having him back.

She had moved into the apartments several years ago, during the war, when the roof was in disrepair.

Many years had elapsed since Kien's father had died, leaving the attic empty. Because of his ghastly paintings, superstitious folk said that a ghost had moved in. Perhaps it was an excuse not to fix the roof. In any case, the girl moved in quietly one day and because she could not speak and because no one else wanted to go there, she remained apart from the others in the block of apartments.

Before getting close to Kien she had passed him several times on the narrow stairways. He had stretched his lips in artificial smiles that told her he was being polite and that he was drunk and he would never remember her.

Kien himself wrote about her. That is how her story came to be among those pages that were found later. He wrote of her in the first person, then in the third. Passionately; dispassionately. This is what we pieced together:

She saw him as tall, broad in the shoulders, but thin and pale. His face was wrinkled, full of character, but he was often sad and tired.

When she first started to observe him she divined that the beautiful girl in the apartment next to his had been his lover, but was now shunning him.

She also knew that he was a writer. She would lip-read people saying it as he walked the streets. They called him 'The Sorrowful One' and nicknames like that, but there was pride in their name-calling.

By that special gift which people deprived of all normal senses develop, she also divined he was gradually becoming interested in her. She had no idea why; perhaps it was nothing but curiosity. Most people had a hidden curiosity about the handicapped. But not him, she decided. This was different.

Then, late one quiet, warm summer night, he knocked on her door. And knocked again, like the way a friend who expected to be answered would persist. From inside, she could smell alcohol. She hesitated. She was cautious, yet not afraid. In fact, she was a brave girl in many quiet ways. So she opened the door.

'Arumm . . .' he said. It wasn't a greeting, nor was it an excuse for calling near midnight. She stepped back and opened the door wider and he stepped through as though he'd been expected.

He had been expected. For many weeks, she suddenly realised, she had been waiting for him. She smiled and signalled to him to sit down.

Kien staggered a little and brushed heavily against the cane chair she offered him, tipping it over. He waved the accident aside and flopped down on her bed. She righted the cane chair and placed it near her table, signalling him to move into it. 'Doan be 'fraid,' she lip-read him saying in slurred words.

His face was distorted by the drink, but he was kind and friendly. She offered him some herbal tea, which he accepted and gulped down.

The tea sobered him slightly. He stood up and slowly walked around the room. As he spoke she realised for the first time he had been in her room hundreds of times; this had been his father's studio.

To win his confidence, and to see his lips more clearly, she sat next to him. 'People say there are ghosts here. That's not true. It's them, the ones from my father's paintings. Before his death he released them from his canvases . . . a crazy and barbarous ceremony. No paintings left now . . .'

She couldn't quite understand, but as she looked over his shoulder she saw his shadow on the wall and imagined him to be his father sitting at an easel and painting obsessively.

'And then you came,' he said clearly. 'You aren't afraid. Who are you?' But then he rambled off again. He grasped her hand tightly. 'I've got you in my novel. Understand? You've helped me remember. Right now I need to remember. Everything. To remember this attic, everything.'

She let him talk. Drunks needed to be free. She let him hold her hand tightly, twist it, until her own hand was hurting and a little swollen. He finally stopped talking and rested his head on the table. But still he held her hand. She was so tired, yet she did not try to free her hand from his.

Weeks passed without her seeing him again, though every night she could see a light at his window.

It was a light she looked for now. But was he there?

Then one day she met him at the front gate to the apartments. He had the appearance of someone returning from a long journey. He looked thinner and older, and a little absent-minded. She was deeply hurt as he brushed past her, his eyes registering no recognition. Surely he had not forgotten her? Had he shuffled her aside because she was a mute?

No. A few nights later he reappeared. He was both as friendly and as distant as he had been on the first night. And there were many more visits. He came when he was drunk; it became clear to her that he would drink himself into a certain state as he wrote, then decide he needed to see the attic, and to see her. He needed her to be there in the attic. They needed each other.

Story after story would pour out; they were horrible and they were vivid. Even she could read that on his lips and hear the sharp ends of certain words, words reserved for killing and for agony.

Then he would collapse, his head on the table. Asleep.

It took some time for her to realise that what he had been doing in all those visits was repeating stories he had just written only hours earlier. She had become his sounding-board. He was greedily demanding of her that she listen to what he had written, even though he knew she could not hear him or understand fully what he related.

It was then she wanted to scream at him in hatred for using her. Or scream in pain for the discomfort. Or punish him for his dictatorial use of her spirit; he had ignored her eyes, her lips, her smile, her cheeks, her forehead, her neck, her breasts, her soft hands, her long legs, her swaying walk, her very breath and her mute but happy smile. And worse, her natural perfume of love.

Still, he became her passion. She admitted it now to herself.

She needed those rare and wonderful evenings. She was like a vine, linked to his crises. She didn't mind his drunkenness. She needed his hand to twist hers. She needed him to talk and talk. The more confused the stories the longer he stayed, the longer he charmed her, and loved her through the rhythm of his talk.

Rumours began. Other apartment owners had seen him going to her. 'What a strange love affair,' they said. 'He's an author. She's a mute. But you must admit, she is a pretty young thing.' 'How do they do it? I mean, how do they make arrangements? One's dumb, the other's crazy!'

And so it went on. Until: 'Will they marry?'

Women whispered. Men chuckled. Both with envy.

She would have loved to know what they were saying, but of course she had no idea. She would have forgiven them. Sadly, none of it was true.

She knew she was nothing to Kien. He mistook her first for a jungle girl named Sue, then for Phuong, the girl next door. Then for the crippled Hien, on the train. Then, horridly, for a naked girl at Saigon airport, on 30 April 1975.

He also mistook her for certain ghosts. At times he wasn't aware she was even female, for he changed her name so often from masculine to feminine.

Even so, he was irresistible. She had deliberately waited for him one night, somehow knowing he would be relatively sober. He had arrived, smiling, and swung himself into the seat, just a little tipsy. He was a bit shy, but seemed at home. He seemed to be saying to her that this was the night that she should be talking. He even asked if she could speak to him. She shook her head 'No!' to him.

He continued to speak, as though it had been a polite question he had not wanted answered.

'This is the last of the novel,' he had said clearly.

'Now,' he said, equally clearly, 'I don't know what to do with the mountain of papers.' He meant his novel. Now that he had written it he had no use for it. Whatever devils he had needed to rid himself of had gone. The novel was the ash from this exorcism of devils.

Kien had written for the sake of writing, not to publish.

He had looked over the room. Then out of the window. She had watched his hands, then his eyes, then his lips as they softly formed poetry in tune with his magical glances as he described his latest story.

She leaned over. Slowly, gently, she kissed him.

Their first kiss.

He seemed unaware. He changed the subject, telling a story of his father's studio. This one, here. Now.

'I don't know what to do with all these papers,' he said.

This awakened her. She leaned over and kissed him again. This awakened him. He gently pushed her back on the bed. But his eyes were a little crazed and for a moment she expected a beating or some retribution.

He lifted from her and left. She could hear his footsteps on the stairs, as he returned to his apartment.

He did not return for some days. She waited for him with painful anxiety, but he did not come.

One night she decided she would visit him. There was another blackout, which gave her the cover of darkness to move around. She tiptoed downstairs and peered through the partly opened door. It was never locked, anyway. She could see him by the light of a kerosene lamp. The smells of alcohol and kerosene mixed in the air.

She thought she heard him groan as he wrote. He seemed obsessed and definitely didn't feel her presence. She stood by the door like that for a long time. From then on during every blackout she came down and watched him. His hair grew longer, his face grew more haggard. He looked older. Surely the writing had to end; yet she did not want it to end, fearing the end would have other consequences for her.

After some weeks, on another blackout night, she had returned later than usual and stopped to peer in on her way upstairs. Kien was kneeling by his stove shoving torn paper into it and lighting and relighting it.

She silently closed the door behind her and softly walked over and kneeled beside him. She recalled the story of the frenzied destruction of his father's paintings; she placed her hand over his, to stop him putting another page into the fire.

At first he looked startled to see her there. But he stopped the burning, letting the fire go cold. He turned and took her in his arms, away from the stove. In the total silence he then possessed her as though nothing else in the world mattered. She gasped in desperation for him and for many hours they remained locked together. His loneliness pierced her like a knife, throbbing painfully.

He had left while she was still asleep. Somehow she knew she would never see him again. This was his final departure.

She understood he had left his apartment for her. He had left the door wide open and a chilling wind had blown through, disturbing the papers and carrying many of them into the hall and down the stairs. She gathered them all together, tidied his room, and took the manuscript to her own attic.

None of the pages were numbered. There was no obvious order to them and she was able to understand only a very little of it. But she knew she had to keep them.

Months went by. Then a year. The manuscript gathered dust; it looked like an elegant old parchment.

Hanoi. Now Kien writes only at night because only then can he hope to write that which is truly his own. He drinks to stay awake, yet his recall is clear and he is more alert than ever. By night he is more creative, tapping his imagination, his poetic streak, and gathering in the plot of the story more easily.

His street neighbours are now more accustomed to his eccentricities in burning the night lights, despite their ghost-like quality in the gloom.

Professional burglars and prostitutes in the lake area soon get to know about him. The Ha Le lake was their circuit. So they nicknamed Kien's room the Ha Le lighthouse. They would greet him: 'How's the Ha Le lighthouse-keeper these days? Get plenty of writing done last night?'

He returns a smile to them when he opens his window in the morning to welcome the dawn breeze. A little further down the street a famous 'pavement girl' wolf-whistles up to greet him and make fun of him.

At nights, when all around him grows dim, Kien feels closer to life. It seems that darkness truly reflects the darkness of his soul. Now, sleepless nights have become normal for him. Unless he is very drunk he never sleeps before early morning. The nights have become more precious and urgent to him. By day, he sleeps; an unnatural, dry and uncomfortable sleep. And if he does doze off at night it is only briefly, for Time jolts him out of his sleep with a fiery reminder to his soul.

There are times when he feels that only death will give him a real rest. In his childhood he heard the saying: One's life is only a handspan; he who sleeps too much shortens it by half. Kien realises his time is running out. He is not afraid of death; there is nothing about it that frightens him. But he is sorrowful, and heavy with regret for tasks unfinished.

Once, in slumber around daybreak, he had the vivid impression he was leaving life. The images and the exalted feeling he experienced were so clear and deep that he wondered if he could ever feel the same when he really came to depart this earth. Kien felt he had died right then; however briefly, he had died. In that one-thousandth of a second something inside him that was normally so blurred, so unclear, froze and became sharp and cold and visible. He seemed to have inside him a deep slash, into which his life force was draining, pouring from him so slowly, silently, yet irrevocably. His vital force dropped from him as from a broken pot, and Kien fainted away.

It was a little death. Kien knew it as his head dropped to his desk, as his pen fell from his hand and rolled on the floor. It was not like the times he had been shot, or when he had fallen victim to a fever and been unconscious. Nor was it anything mystical. It was a new experience which had overcome him. It was the truth of all truths, the rule of all rules, the very last point of life. It was death. He recognised it.

He saw his life as a river with himself standing unsteadily at the peak of a tall hill, silently watching his life ebb from him, saying farewell to himself. The flow of his life focused and refocused and each moment of that stream was recalled, each event, each memory was a drop of water in his nameless, ageless river.

Kien saw the Buoi school as it had been back then, in April 1965, just before the outbreak of war. It was a late spring afternoon. By then its shady row of trees had been chopped down, its yard criss-crossed with deep trenches, anticipating war. The headmaster, wearing a fireman's helmet, boasted loudly that the Americans would be blown away in this war, but we wouldn't. 'The imperialist is a paper tiger,' he screamed. 'You will be the young angels of our revolution, you will rescue mankind!'

He pointed to a pupil among the tenth-form boys who were holding wooden rifles, spears, spades and hoes, showing childish bravado. 'Life is here, death is also here,' the boy said and the others sang noisily. Someone yelled, 'Kill the Invader!' and everyone cheered.

But Phuong and Kien were not at the school meeting held to preach the three golden rules of preparedness. They had escaped and had hidden behind the Octagon building on the shore of the West Lake. From where they sat, under a tree on the lake's edge, they could see the Co Ngu road, tinted red by the setting sun, and the flame trees in brilliant bloom. Cicadas sang loudly, continuously.

'Don't worry,' Phuong had said smiling, delighted she had skipped classes with Kien and also dodged trench-digging duties. She had worn her skimpy swimsuit under her school uniform, right there in the school, as if for a dare. 'Forget about the war and all the heroes, young and old heroes. Let's swim over to the Water Palace, far enough out to be dangerous . . .'

What a beautiful, warm and sweet April day it was. The delirious hugs together in the light green water. The fish brushing by them, the lilypads. Phuong's beautiful face suffused with water, the bubbles from her underwater breathing, her hair waving, heavy with water, her shoulders, her lovely long legs. All was so intimate, so perfect, that it made him ache.

The distant sound of a choir in the schoolyard reached them.

'Don't worry,' Phuong had said as they listened. She kneeled behind a shrub and removed her blouse. When she had emerged she had on a lovely black swimsuit with plunging neckline. The clarity of her pale skin contrasted beautifully with the black suit.

Kien, already nervous, was breathless. He hardly dared look at her lovely body.

As they swam the sound of the choir again reached them, the twilight deepened and they got further and further from the bank. He recalled this had been the last peaceful stretch in the river of his life; ahead of him from that moment on there was a long, new stretch of river, full of fire.

War.

*

His mind skipped from the lake to the Thanh Hoa station, which was burning fiercely after the bombing raids. Everything that could burn was burning. From the capsized train men, women and children rushed to the platform to escape. Clothes caught fire and burned on their bodies. Headless shadows stamped about. The roar of the planes continued unabated with bombs falling obliquely in the sunlight. For the first time in his life he saw people being killed, saw barbarity, saw blood flowing freely.

From then on his whole generation threw itself into the war enthusiastically, fiercely, making its own blood flow, and causing the blood of others to flow in torrents. Rushing onward, engaging in fierce hand-to-hand combat at the foot of the Ngoc Bo Ray mountain, soldiers bayoneting each other, beating each other with rifle stocks. Human forms running helter-skelter, zig-zagging from machine-gun sights only to be sent flying into the air.

Kien saw himself holding a rifle, shooting at someone's head; the sub-machine-gun bullet, as powerful as a bomb, hit him right in the mouth and his face exploded taking his left eye, his cheek-bone and his lower jaw. 'Ahaaaahhaha,' he had cried. The sound was like laughter, more likely a wail. How frenzied and aggressive this generation of his had become!

The violent and dreadful years and months. The Tet Offensive, Second Tet, the 1972 dry season, the post-Paris Agreement battles. The parched lands, dazzling under the sunlight, writhing in pain. The immense Central Highlands, cruel with a rolling red dust clouding the sky. Yamo, Dac Dam, Sa Thay, Ngoc Rinh Rua, Ngoc Bo Bieng, Chu Co Tong, all places which conjured the most terrible, fierce memories replete with suffering. There had been also the laughing, the shouting, swearing, drinking, talking, and happy times. A lot of crying, too.

Kien was again back in the jungle, at Cong Ho Rinh, an ancient, desolate village, now ruined, laid flat by fighting and now just a graveyard where human bones, broken weapons and other war materials lay around like garbage.

It must have been as beautiful as little Dien Binh village which he saw before it got caught up in the firing. It had been part of a lovely pastoral scene along the Dac Po Xi river when Kien's battalion first saw it. Now it was a heap of ash and corpses and one imagined the spirits of the dead flying away in such numbers they'd make a fog-bank along the river.

Shaking the curtain of dew and smoke from another memory he saw very clearly himself and 'Elephant' Tac both kneeling at a huge, captured M60 machine-gun and firing it non-stop at a stream of enemy stragglers from the ARVN 45th Regiment. They were running for their lives from Phuoc An, near Buon Me Thuot, being herded by tanks.

The machine-gun eagerly ate up the cartridges and spat the copper shells aside, blazing deadly fire at the stream of insane men rushing on into their sights, making themselves targets of flesh. The gun trembled violently, swivelling on its base, steam rising from its cooling tank.

Kien, in a firing frenzy, had not wanted to stop shooting but to continue would have been massacre, not fighting, for the corpses had by now piled higher than he'd ever seen before.

The T54 tanks driving the enemy into his sights now appeared. 'Stop,' shouted Tac, dropping the cartridge belt and moving over to Kien. 'Stop, cease fire,' he shouted, shaking Kien's shoulders.

Kien stopped firing. Kien and Tac watched as the T54s approached through the enemy dead. Others were kneeling, holding both hands high in surrender. The killing had been obsessive, all-devouring. But now the gun was silent the scene turned to farce. Kien looked at Tac.

Tac, the kindly 'Elephant', slowly bent down beside Kien, holding both hands to his chest as if embracing his heart. He looked at Kien with intense surprise, then his eyes turned dull and he fell forward, revealing the deadly bloom of red, flowering under his left shoulder.

Kien recalled it all. Everything. Not a single detail was missing. His fighting life was being revived in flashbacks, or in slowly unfolding scenes as heart-rending as a funeral march.

And now, in his room, Kien seemed to see the end of his stream of life. Journey's end. He seemed to hear someone calling softly to him: It is time. He closed his eyes, wanting to let himself slip away.

But life would not let him go that easily.

It paraded a variety of tempting images before him, calling to him in alluring voices from the other side of his river of life. His time would be another time. There was still too much to do. He had the burden of his generation, a debt to repay before dying. It would be tragic and unjust in the extreme if he were to pass away, to be buried deep in the wet earth, carrying with him the history of his generation. If only he could shed all other needs of everyday living and concentrate all his energies into writing, his task would be over sooner. He would then be released from the burden of life and float freely on the stream to his journey's end, where countless familiar souls awaited him.

Back to his duty. From now on his life seemed restricted to the dark hours. His table lamp came on at dusk and stayed glowing until dawn. His own form seemed no more real than the shadow he cast on the wall. As he wrote he seemed taciturn, almost immobile. But the fire within, fuelled by his powerful memory, burned fiercely.

Kien wondered about his ability to work through the nights. Not everyone could withstand this form of self-imprisonment, or self-confinement. He had probably inherited it from his father.

His father had been a sleepwalker all his life. He would silently rise from his bed, as though weightless, and slowly advance towards the bedroom door, with his eyes tightly closed, his arms by his side. He would walk all about the room, the hallways, upstairs and downstairs, out of the front door and, if the gate had been left open, out into the street. Hanoi people were kind and good-natured in those days and they would softly step aside for the old man straying from his home. No one disturbed him in his fantasies, not even the children. They intervened only if he was sleepwalking towards the lake.

His mother couldn't stand his father's gentle sleepwalking habits, considering it a humiliation and somehow proof of his failure in the world. 'A clan of muddle-headed people,' she used to say, moaning regularly about his failures. Even with his undeveloped young memory, Kien guessed then that his father's eccentricities had made her leave him.

All that remained of his mother were some photographs. Most days she left made no impression on him. He had been indifferent to her departure; it was just another sorrowful, inauspicious day in his childhood.

When he now looked at the yellow and faded photographs he saw a young woman looking back at him; but the look conveyed no meaning to him. Perhaps that was further proof of his inability to fully develop his personality. Perhaps there were innate seeds of wickedness, ruthlessness, hardness and aloofness within him, for he could never recall anything much about her, or their separation, or any comforting words from her. She had constantly told him: 'I'm a New Intellectual, dear. I'm a Party Member. I'm not an idiot, nor am I dull. You must remember that, please.'

These statements were often repeated, especially when she spoke to his father.

She had once told Kien something rather odd and awkward: 'You're a Pioneer now. One day you'll be a member of the Youth

Union, then one day you'll become a real man. So, harden your heart and be brave, my son.'

He never forgot those words. If there had been other advice, or loving caresses or any gestures of maternal love, they had long faded from his memory.

At seventeen and about to join the army he finally thought of finding his mother, to learn more about her. But he discovered she had by then been dead five years.

His father had hardly mentioned her. He had avoided talking about her for his own sake, to avoid suffering. He resigned himself to his fate of keeping his family of two in modest circumstances. Later he began drinking and retreated into deep dreams and his sleepwalking.

Only now, in his middle age, could Kien truly understand those years. His father had suddenly stopped working at the museum. He no longer carried his easel on his bicycle or wandered off to paint as he had done for years. He had started using the attic in this building as his studio and confined himself there day and night in the wet, dusty air, where bats flew. He would sit there painting quietly, occasionally telling stories to himself.

It was rumoured he had been criticised by the Party members and had been dismissed and was regarded as a suspicious malcontent, a rightist deviationist.

His health declined all of a sudden and he quickly became senile, and quite strange.

Whenever he went into his father's attic studio Kien's heart ached and he choked with compassion. The old man's paintings, seen dimly through the blue cigarette smoke, were diabolic. The smell of alcohol was permanent.

Twice a day Kien would bring frugal meals to his father, who crouched on a low chair in front of his easel. 'Who's that?' he would say gruffly.

'Here's your meal, Dad,' Kien would say.

'Alright,' he would answer, but he would rarely start eating.

The meals were on a tray placed on a small bamboo bed, one of the few pieces of furniture they had left. Piece by piece his father had sold the furniture. His mother's jewels went first in those early troubled days of marriage, and they now adorned some other woman in some other house. There was almost nothing left to sell.

No one wanted to buy the paintings. His father had long ago stopped attending exhibitions, and he had been completely forgotten by his former circle of artists.

'I'll produce a masterpiece one day. Just wait!' But he was usually dead drunk when he said this. It was a senseless boast to make, considering he no longer even exhibited his work.

His father could never have been successful in that era, no matter how many exhibitions he held or attended. He had been completely out of step with the times, which required artists to accede to certain Socialist ethics, to display material understandable to the working class.

Kien once heard him ranting: 'Scrap the aesthetics. Add a philistine touch! Define clearly the social class for mountains and rivers and all landscapes. That's what they're demanding now!' he shouted.

It was true. His paintings had been criticised because his work was seen to be alien to the working-class understanding of art. When he began closeting himself away in the attic his paintings had taken on their ferocious, diabolic nature.

Kien began to see life through his father's paintings. Human beings wore dismal expressions, their faces were long and drawn, their bodies stretched. The colours were strange, too. The paintings were utterly depressing, the subjects moronic.

Nearing the end of his life, whether painting with oils or on silk, whether painting a man or a horse or a cow, whether it was rainy or sunny, morning or evening, town or countryside, forests or mountains, rivers or springs, even skies and sea, with no exception they were all done in varying tones of yellow. Yellow. No other colours, just yellow.

In the paintings the characters wandered aimlessly across unreal landscapes, like withered puppets joined to each other like cut-out figures. The tail-ender in these processions was the aged artist himself who cast himself as a tragic figure.

It was a morbid time for young Kien, for although it was a beautiful New Year, his father saw this as his last, repeatedly saying it was spring itself which urged him to depart this world. 'At your age, when spring came, I used to look forward to all facets of life. Sunshine, happy times, plenty of wonderful activities. They were inspiring times,' he said.

But not now. Spring was finally calling him away.

And so it happened. One day an ambulance came and collected him, while Kien was at school. People came over from the hospital to tell Kien, who left his classroom. His father was barely conscious but wanted to utter his last words to Kien.

Kien held his cold hand, which felt like a piece of bronze. There was almost no pulse. He spoke softly and clearly, nor were his words confused. But his final utterances were empty, repetitions of his vain, pitiful dreams.

Then: 'Our era is over. From now on you have to be grown up, fight the battle alone. New times are coming, splendid and magnificent and trouble-free times. No more sadness,' he rambled, then fell into morbid babbling. 'Sorrow is inconsolable. There will still be great sorrow, sorrow passed down to you. I leave you nothing but that sorrow . . .'

True. Kien later discovered he had not even left his paintings. His father had destroyed them all, burning his precious, strange canvases one by one the night he imagined death had called him.

At the hospital bedside Kien, his eyes brimming with tears,

was confused. He was unable to understand his father's feelings, to comprehend what had tormented him ruthlessly. At his age it was difficult to come to terms with his father's mystical, almost insane behaviour. It took him many precious years and months to gradually understand and feel some of the bitter pain of his father's life, to understand a little of those dying words.

In later years Kien had regretted his harsh assessment of his father and his disdain for his dying words. He had been embarrassed about his eccentric father and had frequently shown dislike for his work and words when he was alive. That much was true.

It was all too late now, the love, respect, filial piety, the desire to be close and understand more of his father. All that remained was a grave, covered with earth, heaped with wreaths and josssticks and candles. That was the spring of 1965.

In later years he heard the refrain, like an air in his head:

> 'His father died in his childhood,
> His mother left him, all alone
> Like a plant, his growth is good,
> In times of war he's on his own
> So the boy creates his very own man,
> Not mourning the fate of a lonely orphan.'

The day of his father's death was the first time Hanoi sounded its air-raid sirens. Air horns on trains and sirens on top of the Municipal Theatre building howled together in a frightening cacophony.

Although people had been warned it was only a drill the city shivered with fear; hearts almost stopped beating in panic and anticipation. The sirens were the harbinger of dark days to come.

Doors slammed shut, people clattered down stairways, as exhortations rang out over the loudspeakers: 'Compatriots, pay attention please, pay attention please compatriots. Enemy aircraft are approaching . . .' Lights went out all around town. Patrol cars drove on darkened streets, their own lights masked.

Kien ran against the flow, groping his way upstairs to his father's attic studio. It was quite dark and the air was full of choking dust. The stink of wine and paint was everywhere and small bats flew by him uncertainly. 'Oh, Daddy,' he said softly.

There was a breathless silence in the attic, in the building, and across the entire city. Despite the blackout order, Kien lit a small candle. Looking around he was astounded. Where were the paintings? The unfinished one on the easel? Those in frames in the corners? All were gone, as if by magic.

The end! Kien had no doubt about it then. This was a grave-yard. Every image, every trace of his father had been wiped away, replaced by a nothingness. His father had quit the world, gone in a sleepwalker's dream, taking with him forever the deathly yellow paintings.

He had left only his son in this world.

Kien, deep in thought, slowly emerged from the building. In the east he could see, under cumulus clouds, a dim glow. The all-clear siren sounded and he realised the glow was from the moon. It was an ominous sight. Future glows in the night would not all be natural, and the sirens would not be for drills. It was the start of his seventeenth year in life, this icy spring of 1965.

Phuong knew all about the cremation of the paintings. 'It was a crazed, barbarous ceremony, a rebellion,' she recalled, when describing it to Kien later. Phuong had witnessed the scene, but no one else in the building, even Kien, had known about it.

That night his father had felt the touch of death. Quietly and systematically, he went on an orgy of self-destruction, shredding his canvases then burning them.

There had been an affinity between his father and Phuong

since she had been in her early teens. It was not a father–daughter relationship, nor an uncle–niece relationship for that matter. It was a confused, blurred relationship, based on some shared obsessions and liberal eccentricities. He became extremely fond of the girl and his affection showed in his sad, silent regard for her.

The very characteristics of his spirit, his eccentricities, his free-flying artistic expressions and disregard for normal rules that annoyed others were what attracted Phuong to him; she was a kindred soul.

The old man and the little girl would sit side by side for hours, often not uttering a word. She could sit by him calmly whereas normally she would be restless and excitable, above all merry. When she sat by him watching him paint she seemed captivated by the mood.

When she was older her visits to watch him paint were less frequent, yet she was the only one, other than Kien, who visited the secluded attic studio. Kien's father would eagerly anticipate her visits. Often she would bring alcohol and cigarettes for him, something Kien had not done. Occasionally she heard him mumbling to himself.

She was sixteen, and already very beautiful, when he said, 'You're really beautiful.' Then as a veiled warning he had added, 'You will be unhappy. Most unhappy. These are perilous times for free spirits. Your beauty one day will cost you dearly.'

He had promised her a portrait of herself in oils on her seventeenth birthday, but Phuong was horrified at the thought, imagining he would portray her with a long, drawn face as he usually painted his subjects. He had even gave his fairies long faces, with seaweed for hair and lemon-coloured skin. He died three months before she turned seventeen, rendering the fears irrelevant.

The fateful night when he had imagined Death calling him,

she had been present. He ordered her to make a fire in the back yard and to help him carry all the paintings down from the attic. She knew then he was about to die.

She seemed to understand and to agree that the burning had to take place. It had to be so. She had deliberately not called Kien, because of this. Still, she was frightened, and immersed herself in the ritual destruction to dispel her fears. It became a fantastic, flickering unreal atmosphere, giddying her as the flames leaped up. Phuong was forever haunted by that eerie night, of the lasting strange, yet pleasurable, pains that flowed over her in those passionate moments.

Only the artist himself knew precisely why he went on his orgy of self-destruction, and why he had wanted Phuong, and Phuong alone, to be his witness and helper. She didn't realise it then, but later she saw in it a prophetic message of destruction characterised by that night. The love of Kien and Phuong had been as doomed as those paintings.

She had intended to tell Kien about that frenzied night of destruction as they stood together beside his father's grave at the funeral, but she couldn't bring herself to torment him further.

It was on Kien's final night in Hanoi that she told him. He was leaving for the battlefront the next day. It was to be the last night of their pre-war lives, their last moments of youth.

These had been the final hours of their secure, pure and happy youth, those years and months counted in pleasurable days before the fateful hour arrived to leave. It came soon enough. The next day it was to be a single step onto a convoy, heading for the front.

They had been sweethearts for as long as they could remember. Phuong lived in the room next to his, they sat at the same desk in the same classroom in the same school. She rode behind him on his bicycle to and from school. His sweetheart was now the most radiant beauty in the entire Chu Van An school.

Yet neither of them had other close friends. Others seemed to be unable to penetrate their cocoon of friendship. It was a desperate, pure love, which ached within them and brought frustrations and occasional resentment for the times which imprisoned them in this unnatural state.

The Youth Union members resented them, teachers were deeply concerned, and there were so many others caught up in the patriotic campaigns which denounced any form of liberalism or romance.

There were frenzied campaigns championing the 'Three Alerts' and 'Three Responsibilities' and harshest, the 'Three Don'ts' which forbade sex, love or marriage among the young people. Love affairs for ninth- or tenth-formers were regarded as a disgrace, unpatriotic.

Phuong's burning, sensuous and conspicuous beauty had infuriated the authorities and her peers. She bore herself confidently, even rashly, paying little heed to the demands of the prudes. Kien, equally, met their objections with an uncharacteristic obstinacy.

'We've done nothing evil. We're innocent. We don't try to influence others. Our affairs are our own business,' he responded to one critical teacher.

Kien and Phuong became inseparable, like a body and its shadow. They clung to each other as if there were no tomorrows, as if there were no time to lose and every moment should be spent together. At nights, in bed, they tapped Morse Code messages to each other on their dividing wall, and dreamed of the natural progression of their love, the ultimate intimacy.

Then came that wonderful April afternoon, with the cicadas singing and the flame trees in full flower, a day made for reckless abandon. Although all students were to dig trenches across the schoolyard that day, Phuong had come to school deliberately wearing her concealed swimsuit. When the formal ceremonies for the dedication of the trenches were about to start Phuong had whispered to Kien: 'Let's go. Leave the straw heroes to their slogans. I've got a really pretty swimsuit on, so let's test it.'

They both swam out, far from the shore, not turning back until dusk. Exhausted and weary, Phuong clung to Kien. Night fell quickly and bright, scattered stars lit the sky. Kien carried Phuong in his arms, water dripping from her, and placed her gently on the fresh, cool grass. He lay down beside her, stimulated by the swim, bursting with health.

'I'm exhausted,' she said invitingly. 'I just want to lie here forever.' They lay side by side on the soft grass, hand in hand. A red streak appeared on the horizon, leaving a threadlike line down to the horizon. They whispered to each other as they watched it. 'A sunrise in the west? A flare? If it's a flare, it could be an alert. Didn't hear the siren.' Then, complete darkness and silence.

Over twenty years have passed since the evening on the lake. In that time almost everything around the lake has changed, yet the spirit of it lives on, unchanged. Immense, looming, leisurely romantic.

Kien had never returned to the school. Nor had he been back to the lakeside pavilion, or along the little path at the back of the schoolyard. He had looked from afar, unwilling to retrace old tracks.

The lake became a symbol of Phuong in her beautiful youth, symbol of the marvels and grief of youth, of love and lost opportunities. On many occasions he sat by the lake, lingering until the last trace of red had left the same sky where he and Phuong had been together twenty years ago.

They had lain together under the star-scattered sky, unwilling to move despite the cold setting in. He seemed unwilling ever to leave their special place and she sensed this, saying softly, 'The school gate's closed. Stay here.'

'Aren't you cold?' he asked, hoarsely.

'I'm . . .' Phuong moved to embrace Kien, pulling him close to her. He trembled in the embrace, first uneasily, then as he relaxed he felt a powerful, uncontrollable urge burn within him and he began tightening his grasp. He closed his eyes and buried himself in her soft fragrant embraces and she responded passionately.

As he kissed, a sudden sharp pang struck within him and he breathed in sharply, withdrawing. A sudden, darkly powerful sense of guilt had struck home; he responded prudishly, tearing himself from her arms. Astonished, Phuong reacted with fright, shame and confusion, rolling herself away and buttoning her blouse over the swimsuit.

During a long silence neither of them moved. The lake waters lapped against the shore and far away they saw an anti-aircraft gun on a pontoon in the water. From even further away a gong sounded.

'You're afraid, aren't you?' Phuong said, suddenly breaking the silence between them. 'Me, too. But just realising it makes me more keen.'

'I just think we shouldn't,' he blathered. 'I'm going off to war. I'm going away,' he said unconvincingly. 'Better not.'

'Okay,' she sighed. 'But there'll never be another time like now.'

'I'll come back,' he said urgently.

'When? A thousand years from now? You'll be changed and so will I. Hanoi will be different. So will this West Lake.'

'Our feelings won't change, that's the most important thing,' he said.

She remained silent for a moment then said, 'I can see what's going to happen. War, ruin, destruction.'

'Maybe. But we'll rebuild.'

'You're a simpleton; your father was different, he saw it coming,' she said.

'I'm different,' he said defensively.

'You didn't love him, did you?' she asked. 'Don't be angry at the question, just answer me.'

Kien simply stared at her.

'Did you ever really talk to him?'

'Of course,' he said. 'We talked about lots of things. What a question!'

'So did he tell you why he destroyed all his paintings, why he lost the will to live?' she asked.

'No, he talked about other things. Why did he destroy them? I don't understand.'

'You knew nothing about it. But I did. He confided in me. We were closer to each other than to you. When he burned the paintings I could see the future through the flames. He was burning my life as well as his own,' she said.

'What are you saying?' he shouted. 'Are you mad!'

Kien had no understanding of her emotions. Suddenly she was a stranger to him. The whole strange evening seemed to concern something in the distant future, nothing to do with his imminent departure to the battlefront, or their forced parting.

When Phuong next began speaking she spoke so softly it was almost to herself. 'Since your father's death I've often wondered why I loved you so passionately. I'm a free spirit, a rebel out of step in these warring times. You're perfectly suited to them. Despite these great differences we loved each other, regardless of everything else. You understand me, don't you?'

'Let's go home,' he said, fear in his voice. 'We're talking nonsense. What do you mean, you're a rebel?' But he knew she was right.

Phuong continued softly, 'Had your father been you I would have loved him even more than I love you.'

'I see that now,' she said, placing a finger on his lips to seal any response. 'You had little in common with your father and as you grew you resembled him less and less. You didn't love your father, nor your mother. You loved the idea of going to war; you were headstrong, you wanted to remain pure and loyal to your ideals. I don't want to sound disdainful, but there's nothing original in all that,' she said.

Kien grew uncomfortably sad. He was unable to understand everything she said, but as he listened to her, sounding like a medium telling incredible fortunes, he knew that although she sounded like someone high on magic mushrooms, he would long remember everything she had said.

'Why speak of my father now?' he asked. 'I know you often talked to him. You must know he had such wrong-headed notions. He had no comprehension of our modern values and ideals; he clung to old-fashioned values.'

'I speak now because there may be no other night like this, no time like the present. Because when you've gone your way, I'll go my own way, too,' she replied.

In his naivety he had not quite understood her. 'But where will you be going? You have university exams in three weeks. Then you'll be going to university. And as for me, well, I'll be back soon.'

'You're strange,' she said, almost giving up on him. 'War, peace, university, joining the army. What's the difference? What's good, what's bad? To volunteer for the army at seventeen is nobler than going to university isn't it? I won't bother taking the entrance exams, if that's so.'

'Where would you go?' he asked.

'To the war. See what it's like,' she replied.

'It might be horrible.'

'And it might be death. A long, permanent sleep. Still, we've only one death, haven't we. Just what makes you crave so much for that one death? It seems so attractive to you that I think I'll go along too.'

'What!' He was astonished, incredulous.

Phuong started laughing, pulling him down closer to her again, caressing his hair, pushing his face into her breasts. She said softly, 'There's no other night like this. You're offering your life for a cause so I've decided to waste mine, too. This year we're both seventeen. Let's plan to meet each other again somewhere at some future point. See if we still love each other as much as we do now.'

She gently lifted his face, softly kissing his eyelids, then his lips, then again buried his face into her breasts. 'I love you. I've loved you since we were children. I've loved your mother and your father, as I would have if I'd been your sister, or brother. From now on I'll be your wife. I'll go with you. I'll see you to the gate of the battlefront, just to see what it's like. I'll stay until we're forced to part. That moment will be with us very soon.

'But for tonight, be with me. We're here together, alone. It's here your heroic journey to the front starts. Don't be scared, of me or of anything else. From now on I'll be a lover and a wife to you; I'll never be angry at you and remember I'm not taking leave of my senses. Not yet.'

Kien trembled. The fresh cool air chilled a film of sweat on his forehead and over his back. He was both frozen with fear and brimming with love for her. He took hold of her waist, but felt weak and confused.

He couldn't. He dared not.

Phuong lay down before him gently, pulling him over to her. He placed his head inside her arm, as a little boy would. She sighed, not in anger, but in resignation. She comforted him with soft words about his father, about his paintings, about herself, and about them, words about anything and nothing, and he fell into a reverie, looking at the dark moon through a curtain of beautiful long hair which almost covered his face.

As she talked on so softly he fell into a peaceful, warm dream-like state, and he began unbuttoning her blouse, uncovering her beautiful pale breasts which rose between his eyes and the dark sky. He moved gently and began suckling her, softly at first, then with a strong passion, holding her breasts between both hands and tasting her, young and sweet.

But he dared not accept her challenge to make love to her.

The next day, they were back in class. Their last class. Then the tenth-formers, including Phuong, were allowed to go home early to prepare for their university entrance exams.

All except Kien, who got orders to report immediately to the army recruiting office. His time had come.

Kien remembers that distant night by the lake as though it were yesterday, despite the many intervening years. He needs only a little help from a dark moon and a balmy West Lake breeze and his imagination stirs. At the front, among the dead and sur-rounded by suffering, he often dreamed of and really felt her warm flesh again and tasted her virgin milk; in his dreams it was that which had given him the magical vitality to become the strongest, the luckiest, the greatest survivor of the war.

The dreams that brought her back to him were all at night. By day, strangely, Kien actually thought little of Phuong and missed her hardly at all. Certainly not as much as he missed her in later years, after she had left him for the second time. His soldier's self-defence mechanisms were working well for him in those days, especially when he was in the Central Highlands.

Perhaps that's why he developed such a fervent and disciplined attitude towards sleep. Once he was asleep, nothing could disturb him. In sleep you slept. In battle you fought. When planning you planned, thinking of what was behind as well as ahead of you, waiting at the next turn or on the other side of the pass.

By day, for some, old memories did return and persist, but only for those who were wounded, or exhausted, or in a permanently wretched condition or starving, and it usually meant one was facing further decline. In normal situations, one could keep them at bay.

Kien recalled just three occasions in ten years where he acutely missed Phuong during daylight hours, and he was haunted by those memories.

The first time was when he had been struck down by malaria in a march across Laos. Fever had gripped him for weeks and he had thought of her in his feverish state, half-imagining she was there.

The second time was when he lay wounded at Clinic 8, his regiment's code name for a divisional hospital across the border in the safety of Cambodia. His wounds stank and he had flitted between dream and reality, awaiting death yet hanging on to his flickering life. Some features of his nurse resembled Phuong's and every now and then when she passed he would fall to thinking of Phuong, the intensity of his emotions ebbing and flowing like a fever.

The third time was when he was with his scout platoon on what was officially called 'State Farm Number 3', the regiment's headquarters. The scout platoon was idle; they were on the perimeter of the Screaming Souls Jungle, playing cards and getting high by sipping tea made from *rosa canina*, when he heard news of the three jungle girls from his scouts, who had been the girls' lovers.

The three farm girls had disappeared on the other side of the mountain. He then dreamed of Phuong, every night, throughout this tragic episode. He had conveniently ignored the wild, romantic escapades of the three girls with their three lovers from his platoon because they reminded him of his romance with Phuong. Every night they had slipped out of their huts and into the jungle, secretly crossing streams and creeping along jungle paths to get to their girlfriends in their little house by the stream at the foot of the mountain. Kien lived their loves with them by proxy, using Phuong as his own jungle girl, conjuring up intense and passionately romantic dreams. Sadly, the dreams were often tinged with painful forebodings of disaster, as his romance with Phuong had been.

When they had captured the three commandos who had murdered the three girls he had decided to deal with them severely, meting out terrible deaths. Just before their executions he had forced them to dig their own graves and look at the pit where their bodies would end life on this earth. But at the last moment, as he was about to press the trigger, with the gun aimed directly at them, he gave them a reprieve.

It was not because of their pleading, nor because of prompting from his colleagues. No, it was because Phuong's words had come to him like an inner voice: 'So, you'll kill lots of men? That'll make you a hero, I suppose?'

It was unbelievable. He had let them live. It was uncanny and uncharacteristic of him, but that's how it had ended. Absurd.

When he had been at Clinic 8, the second time he had thought of her, he had been seriously wounded. He had been delirious, thinking Phuong had actually come to him, not in a dream but in reality.

It was at the start of the 1965 rainy season, after his Battalion 27 had been surrounded and almost totally wiped out by the Americans. Kien had crawled almost one day and a night, dragging himself through mud on the forest floor, his naked body badly cut up. Mates who had escaped from the massacre met up with him on the edge of the forest and carried him west, to the border. He came to at Clinic 8, safely close to the Cambodian border.

Clinic 8 consisted of a dishevelled medical team, ragged and beaten to threads after months of treating the wounded, after incessant withdrawals by men who had been continually surrounded then bombed and shelled by artillery. Doctors, nurses and wounded soldiers, carrying one another on stretchers or on their backs, withdrew from the conflict under the protection of the bamboo canopies to the safety of their camp on the Cambodian border.

Just exactly where Clinic 8 was and the general situation with the staff or even what they looked like, Kien never discovered. In the two months he had been there, before being transferred to Hospital 214, he had lain buried in a flat-roofed trench, from which water had gushed on both sides. He had a horrible wound between his legs and another on his shoulder. His rotting flesh stank so strongly that even the mosquitoes avoided it. He seemed permanently comatose and the few times he came to his senses only reconfirmed his certainty that he would surely die when he next lost consciousness.

Whenever he awakened and opened his eyes he would see Phuong in the trench with him. He called her name softly, but she never did answer him. She simply smiled and bent over close to him, placing her lips on his wet forehead.

His Phuong of the jungle hospital caressed him with her rugged, sometimes clumsy hands. Her caresses and her soft smile seemed in harmony with the rain on the trench roof and the lament of the jungle.

Despite the stink from his rotting wounds he saw her brown eyes sparkle, even in the dark. 'Phuong,' he called weakly through clenched teeth.

But the young girl just went on blithely changing his bandages, using tweezers to pull the leeches from his flesh and clean his wounds. Then she wrapped him in a torn blanket and dropped the mosquito net over him.

He tried smiling his thanks to her but he had dropped off, back into his coma.

In the following weeks Kien began to improve, coming to his senses for a little longer each time and losing consciousness for shorter periods. In the brighter, dry surroundings of Hospital 211, which was little more than a shed, Phuong did not visit him. When he recovered fully and had been given notice he would be transferred to a regrouping point he asked news of Phuong, from Clinic 8. But none of the soldiers who had been there knew anyone named Phuong.

'You're wrong,' said one soldier whose legs had both been amputated. 'I was there when you were out to the wide, so I know. You kept calling her Phuong but she couldn't correct you because she's dumb. She can't talk. She's from Da Nang, struck dumb in some bad fighting there. Yes, a lovely, delicate, good-natured young brown-eyed girl. Shit, you were in terrible shape, mate! I can hardly believe you'd be able to remember anything.

'But she's probably dead. We don't know for certain. We were transferred from there, you and me, along with other seriously wounded, to this place. Two hours later B52s bombed the place, completely wiping them out. After the bombing the enemy raided the place, too.'

'Do you know what her name was, the nurse?' asked Kien.

'Lien. Lien, or Lieu something. Never called her by name. Just "dear Sister". What a pretty girl! Struck dumb she was. Dead now, most likely.'

Kien, in later years, never told Phuong that story. They had avoided serious discussion of the ten war years. Yet when he looked at her without her being aware of it he would suddenly see a parade of war figures crossing his vision.

It was that connection with the long-gone nurse and her likeness to Phuong that brought back events and images he wished to forget. Even when he knew it was Phuong, and not the nurse, just her words, her profile, were enough to trigger the same violent memories.

Phuong had decided to break it off. She had left him, that early winter evening, brushing past him out of the door without even bothering to switch off the lights in her room next door.

Seemingly without cause Phuong had decided to end the merriment they'd shared during the autumn. The noisy, festive atmosphere was swept aside by the early cold winds of winter.

Her apartment, until recently a place of joy and laughter, was now silent and empty. The guests who so frequently bustled in had now stopped coming, as if by magic. Kien had guessed this was an annual occurrence with Phuong; she had indulged herself in all forms of partying and pleasures and then suddenly ceased, as though preparing to enter a convent.

When she was in this mood Kien too became depressed. He would rather stand by night after night listening to her lovers' noisy jokes than not have her there at all. As she wound herself down from her activities Kien noticed a decrease in the number of rather sad men knocking on her door, waiting patiently for her to unlock the door from the inside. Then they stopped coming altogether as she confined herself to her apartment.

And now Kien, himself depressed, remembered it was her birthday. He bought a bunch of roses, intending to invite her to a restaurant to celebrate. There had been another power blackout so it would be an ideal excuse not to stay at home.

Although they had separated some time ago he had wanted to see her again. He knocked gently on the door, using a secret code reserved for him alone. But it was not Phuong who answered the door. He heard the key turn and saw the door open slightly.

Through the small opening came the smell of cigarette smoke, and cognac.

'Good evening, uncle,' Kien said to the slim man standing just inside the door. He shook a smooth, soft, well-manicured hand. It belonged to a man with a wrinkled, withered face. His tiny eyes blinked rapidly as he looked at Kien, mumbling some greeting. He had a rough, uneven beard and salt-and-pepper greying hair. Kien handed some roses past him, to Phuong.

'Thank you, Kien!' Phuong said delightedly. 'I forgot my own birthday, yet you remembered Ah, let me introduce you. Kien, this is Mr Phu, an artist.' The men stood looking at each other in silence.

Phuong had dropped into a seat, near a flickering candle. Her guitar lay on a small table in front of her. 'Well,' she said, 'sorry we can't do our usual. I didn't even think of it.'

Her visitor became solicitous. 'If you've got a date, please go ahead . . .' he said.

'No. No date. Don't worry, Phu.'

Kien looked over to her, but she wouldn't return his glance. He nodded to both of them and withdrew, closing her door behind him.

Back in his room he walked over to his desk, lit a lamp, and started looking at his manuscript. He had a choking sensation in his throat and a feeling of total inadequacy, which brought on a hot rush of self-pity. He stood and looked at winter raindrops hitting the window, sliding down in gloomy patterns on the window-pane.

He poured himself a glass of wine, filled it to the brim and tossed it down hurriedly. He sat in his chair and held his head in his hands.

Suddenly his door creaked open. Phuong had come in and softly moved to his side. 'Kien,' she whispered, standing close to him and stroking his hair, 'Kien, you're in sorry shape,' she said, bending down and kissing his forehead.

Kien looked up, mumbling some foolish nonsense.

'I had to come to see you,' she said. 'I won't tell you everything, but some of the things I had to do in the past just to keep afloat, well, at times I felt like an animal. I did a number of beastly things. I'm badly soiled, rotten through and through now.'

Kien tried to say something, but she interrupted. 'Now I just can't help myself,' she said. Kien remembered hearing late-night callers squabbling amongst each other to get her favours, the losers turning away in disgust. 'I can't help myself, but I also have to live. I'll probably die some sinful, pleasurable death. But ignore me, I'm finished. This is the way I'll see my life out,' she said.

He pleaded with her to return, saying naive and foolish things, which she ignored. He said he wanted to live with her again, instead of just next door to her. But she cut in. 'Don't even think about it. It's over. We deserved to have had a happy life together, but events conspired against us. You know that. You know the circumstances as well as I do. Let's go our own separate ways from now on. Forever. It's the only way.'

Kien looked up at her, a question in his eyes.

'I met him last week, by chance,' she said. 'But I'm not leaving because of him. I've not decided anything with him yet.'

'So why?' he asked.

'Because I can't stand this tension any longer, that's why.'

'I don't see why you have to run after that old clown. It can't be that bad,' he said.

'Old? I'm no spring chicken myself. You still think I'm seventeen, that's your problem. You've never adjusted.'

'When are you leaving?'

'Tonight. Now. We won't see each other ever again,' she said.

'Just like that? Like closing a bad book?' he said.

They stood and embraced, kissing for a few moments. Phuong pushed him away. 'That's enough!' she said.

Kien followed her as she walked to the door. As she was about to leave she turned and leaned against the door. 'Forgive me, and now forget me,' she said. 'I may not know what exactly my future holds, but I do know we can't meet again.'

'Are you in love?' he said.

'I loved you, and only you, Kien. I never loved anyone else. And you?' she asked.

'I still love you,' he replied.

She departed, forever. He had had only two loves in his entire life. Phuong at seventeen in the pre-war days, and Phuong now, after the war.

He heard them going downstairs together, carrying suitcases, locking her door. She had slipped an envelope under his door as she left.

The last thing he heard was her high heels in the corridor. His own feet were dragging slightly as he went to the door. He picked up the note: 'Darling Kien, I'm leaving. Goodbye to you. It's better this way. Better for both of us. Please, please, forget me, I beg you. I wish you great success.'

Kien coaxed himself: 'I must write!'

Collar up, coat wrapped securely around him, he paced the quiet Hanoi streets night after night making promises to himself, dreaming up slogans to pull his thoughts into line.

'I must write! It's going to be like smashing granite with fists, like turning myself inside out and exposing all my secrets to the outside world.

'I must write! To rid myself of these devils, to put my tormented soul finally to rest instead of letting it float in a pool of shame and sorrow.

'I must push on! Even if some hours spent at my desk appear wasted, or some of the story-lines I begin have to be discarded, I must press on. Otherwise the pain will be unbearable.'

The writing was coming along slowly. Pacing the pavement seemed to help, and to rid him of some of the ill humour that occasionally built up. Besides, pacing the streets occasionally brought him flashbacks by association.

Passing the silk quarter one day he stood watching the girls trying on new silk fashions. He was reminded of some Khmer girls who'd been appointed jungle guides in the West Dac Ret area. They wore their bras on the outside of their garments, as adornments, or like precious jewellery. The clever young soldiers who hid bras in knapsacks won themselves any of these young girls who'd volunteered to help their troops. These country girls would give themselves to the boys and fulfil their wildest fantasies in return for a bra.

In 1973 his regiment had mistakenly been sent a batch of uniforms and assorted articles meant for a women's platoon. Side-buttoned trousers, waist-length jackets, and army-issue bras. They were rock-hard, coarsely woven, ugly things which resembled a pair of green beetles. Such was the tension that any little army supply bungle like that set the boys laughing.

Street scenes prompted him to generate stories for his book artificially. Scene: A beggar outside an expensive restaurant approaches a wealthy, well-dressed gentleman and a lady wearing gold and diamond rings. 'Show compassion for comrades in these hard times,' the beggar tells the rich man. The girl starts laughing at the beggar. The rich man says, 'If you weren't so bloody high-principled I'd give you some money. We Vietnamese are so good at fighting that we've forgotten our manners. Drop the aggression, old man, and I'll give you something.

'Just a minute, don't I know you?' he says, looking closely at the beggar.

'I'll use this scene,' Kien said to himself. 'I'll have the rich man and beggar as former schoolmates.'

Later he decided it was a foolish idea. A fictional replacement for his true stories. But it did have the soothing effect of sustaining his interest in writing. After these encounters he would return and start work again.

It was by night that the old, true stories began to flow back, bringing their own urgency to him. He needed to trap them as they emerged, to get the details down. Parts of stories he thought he'd forgotten floated through his mind, like disconnected mathematical equations, and he'd grab them and pin them down on paper forever. He found they would float into his mind more freely if he took to the pavements at night. It was a curious phenomenon, but it worked.

Occasionally he would unconsciously begin following a pedestrian, wandering behind him aimlessly until he reached his destination.

He tried imagining how this one or that one would react to living their lives as we did. The 'Holyland Boys' they called the Hanoi men as the troops lay side by side, swinging in hammocks, at some rest point. The Holylanders would test each other in trivia: Where was a certain street? Which street in Hanoi had only one house? Which had the most? Which was the oldest street? The shortest? Why was the famous Chased Market called Chased? The others would listen in fascination to these nostalgic trivia.

One of the Holylanders was 'Bullhead' Thang, who was a third-generation pedicab driver working the Hang Co station, but even Thang admitted Kien knew Hanoi better than he did.

They referred to themselves not as Hanoiese, but as Thang Long soldiers, after the original name of Hanoi. No Thang Long soldier knew Hanoi better than he did. He could name all the streets in one area starting with 'Hang', knew scores of lakes, big and small, the street where the most beautiful girls were found, on which night the Pacific Cinema would have banned films, and also how to get in to see them.

What the others didn't know was that Kien had known almost none of this inside information about Hanoi before he left. He had picked up these trivia during the war, from Hanoi units he fought with. As a teenager he had known little of Hanoi, for he was not allowed to wander the streets alone.

Military life in the jungles over those long years developed within him a deep, tender love for his home town. When he returned, some of that passion faded as the realities set in. It was not that Hanoi itself had changed – though yes, there had been changes – but he had changed. He had wanted to wind the clock back to his teenage days and relive those memories.

But the impressions of the friendliness and uniqueness of his home town that he had generated during those trivia sessions in the jungle had been based on hopes in a situation of despair.

Post-war Hanoi, in reality, was not like his jungle dreams. The streets revealed an unbroken, monotonous sorrow and suffering. There were joys, but those images blinked on and off, like cheap flashing lights in a shop window. There was a shared loneliness in poverty, and in his everyday walks he felt this mood in the stream of people he walked with. Another idea that emerged during his long walks was flashed into his mind by a written sign: 'Leave!'

'Leave this place. Leave!'

He began dreaming again of returning to Mo Hill, where someone had promised to be waiting for him. The orchard at the rear of Mother Lanh's house, the view across the stream to the forest, the peace of the rural scenes appealed to his desire for an escape.

Into his memory then flashed scenes of the B3 troop movements from Phan Rang on the coast to Ngoan Muc Pass, crossing the Da Nhim hydroelectric station, past Don Duong, Duc Trong, down to Di Linh to take Road 14. The twists and turns of that long, tiring march came to him as though it were yesterday. From Road 14 down to Loc Ninh, then turning around to regroup for an attack on western Saigon, to end the war. A mixture of marching and troop transports, across paddyfields and country paddocks.

They were in a field when most soldiers awoke, their faces weather-beaten from days of exposure to sun and dew. They spoke excitedly, knowing they were nearing the city but unsure of their exact whereabouts. The journey itself was an adventure; that's what he needed now, to go travelling. Away from Hanoi.

His visions of the war-time journey faded as he paced along by the Hoan Kien lake in central Hanoi. He turned and walked down to the Balcony Café, a nightspot hidden away at the end of a narrow alley, a place he often visited late at night. No loud music, no vain poetic ramblings by aspiring authors as in other coffee shops around the Thuyen Quang lake.

'Hello, foot-soldier,' said the fat host, smiling and pleased to see him. The host had a bright red nose.

Unasked, he brought coffee to Kien's table, adding a dish of sun-flower seeds and a half-bottle of brandy. 'Want some female company?' he asked.

'Well, well. Even you have that service now?'

The landlord smiled. 'Yes. It's the new fashion.'

People around him were playing cards, drinking coffee, smoking pot and other weeds, and talking business.

In the first days of peace the host had been as impoverished as all other demobilised soldiers. He had been so thin then that he resembled a pipe-cleaner; the effect enhanced his dark face, the result of catching malaria in Laos. When he opened the place it quickly became unofficially known as the Veteran's Club.

All the original customers were demobilised soldiers, most of them unemployed, still gathering their wits. Little by little the money they did get upon leaving the 'jungle gate' and being demobilised left their pockets and found its way into the owner's pocket, and he began to prosper.

Those early days were pleasant and hilarious. The soldiers told each other stories of their attempts to adapt to civilian life with their special brand of humour.

Helped on by a drink or two, the mood in those days was always light and for hours they would laugh almost continuously. They shared new inside knowledge of how to apply for a job, how to bribe clerks to get on the housing list, how to get a Veteran's pension, how to get admitted to the university – all sorts of helpful tips. Or they came for nostalgic conversation.

Kien on this night was sitting in a seat usually reserved for 'Vuong the Clumsy' a former armoured-car driver who now lived at the back of the railway station. When Vuong had first returned he had openly appealed to all his mates to help him find a job as a driver. 'Anything'll do,' he shouted. 'Trucks, cars, buses, even steam-rollers. Anything that's got a steering-wheel and drives on sealed roads.'

Vuong drank very little. He was a huge, tall, slightly clumsy man, but he was kind and timid.

After his unsuccessful appeal to mates to help find him a job, Vuong wasn't seen for many months. When he did return, he was whiskered, red-eyed and hung-over. 'I've given up driving, me old mates. Now alcohol drives me.'

For the next months Vuong was a fixture at the Balcony Cafe, sitting in 'his' little corner, always with a dish of food and a glass of alcohol.

When he became tipsy he sang loud military marches, or obscene ditties. 'Drink up comrades!' he would shout. 'Afraid I'm broke? Hell, don't worry. Without drivers like me you'd never be considered the world's best infantrymen. That's what the brass used to boast: "World's best infantrymen." Well, watch out, here come the infantry vehicles!' And he would go into a pantomime of his fighting days as a combat driver.

Vuong went into a steep dive, reflecting his trauma. It was sad, almost unbelievable, that such a tough and courageous fighter could fall so quickly in the post-war days. His friends said he had hit one pothole too many. But they said it with sadness, not in jest. After a while he became a ragged, beggarly drunk.

It was in those drunken times he voiced his nightmares, as though they were stories. 'Potholes are bearable,' he would say, 'but to ride on something squishy and soft, supple and pulpy, that used to make me vomit. There were nights when I couldn't sleep. I used to run over the bodies. That's what happened recently. I got a normal job driving, and had no troubles with potholes and puddles.

'It was the soft surfaces that brought back the memories. Then people around me, bicyclists, pedestrians, started looking hatefully at me. So I started to drink.

'Ever seen a tank running over bodies? You'd think we'd flatten them so much we'd never feel them. Well, I've got news for you, mates. No matter how soft they were they'd lift the tank up a bit. True! I used to feel it lift. After a while I could tell the difference between mud and bodies, logs and bodies. They were like sacks of water. They'd pop open when I ran over them. Pop! Pop!

'Now they've started running over me. I see the tanks coming and know exactly what's going to happen to me. Remember when we chased Division 18 southern soldiers all over Xuan Loc? My tank tracks were choked up with skin and hair and blood. And the bloody maggots! And the fucking flies! Had to drive through a river to get the stuff out of the tracks.'

Vuong would drink until he dropped. Every night. There were many others like that – or well on their way.

The little club got a reputation as an interesting place and soon many more veterans, including vets from the war against the French, were joining the nightly sessions. Few were easily recognised by outsiders as veterans, including the now fat owner for one, and Kien.

One night, when he was one of the few left in the club, a roughly made-up prostitute wearing an army surplus jacket dropped into a seat at his table. She reeked of cheap Chinese perfume. 'Don't stay,' he said.

'You don't like me?' she asked.

'Correct.'

'You piss off then,' she said.

'You know plenty of places. You piss off,' he said.

The whore laughed, revealing ugly broken teeth and blackened gums. Under twenty, he guessed. She looked better before she smiled, if better was the word.

'It's so cold here,' she moaned, making no move to leave. 'Fatty!' she called to the host, 'bring me a double Maxim.'

'Drinking's no good for little girls,' he replied, but went for the drink anyway.

'You're pretty small yourself,' she quipped.

She swung around and slipped her hand up between Kien's legs. 'Hah!' she shouted, then withdrew her hand. 'God, you're dull. Let's get drunk,' she said, lifting her glass to Kien.

Drunk.

In all his life he'd only been truly drunk a few times, so drunk that, like Vuong, everything around him became meaningless and he had difficulty separating reality from hallucinations.

The Air France bar at Tan Son Nhat airport in Saigon was one place, back on 30 April 1975, Victory Day.

The other time was here, at the Balcony Café, in 1975 when this tart in front of him was sucking ice-cream cones, and the owner was still a skinny returned soldier.

It had been a black day all round. He'd come for a drink and a joke with a few of his old war buddies. He'd been demobbed, one of the fortunate few to have a house to return to. He'd been admitted to the university. He'd soon be graduated and marry a very beautiful woman who'd been waiting for him to return from the war. Until then it was perfect.

He'd not been back in Hanoi very long and had just discovered the Balcony Café. The police later said the trouble had been caused by soldiers spoiling for a fight. Not true. He had simply come here to have a peaceful drink.

Four toughs had ridden up on Hondas, parking them out front. They were fashionably dressed, like singers from a band. But they were actually thugs, and dangerous, and strode about confidently, certain no one would get in their way or dare to bother them.

Vuong, sitting in the back of the café, started singing an old army song.

'Listen to that garbage,' said the leather-jacketed leader. 'Victory, shit! The victory we got was a victory for morons. Call that civilisation and progress? Garbage!'

'You sound like garbage yourself,' said Kien quietly but clearly.

Leather-jacket spun round, ready to pounce. But recognising Kien, he whistled slowly, and began to smile. 'Well, well, well,' he said, standing up and walking towards Kien's table threateningly.

The owner rushed out to stop what he thought would be a fight and Leather-jacket's mates took hold of him and sat him down. But he paid little attention to them. He moved to sit opposite Kien.

'I'm garbage? Me? What, and you're honourable, are you? I seem to remember seeing you last Sunday at the August cinema, when you waltzed in with your beautiful girlfriend. What a joke! Your girlfriend. Know why she was embarrassed? She saw me looking at you both. Shit, she's a fucking tramp,' he leered.

Kien slowly put down his cigarette, and took another sip of

coffee. But inside he was drying up and unable to respond and his heart beat loudly, anxiously.

Leather-jacket continued: 'Think I'm a liar? Meet me here tomorrow and I'll bring the last bloke who screwed her before you got her back. He'll tell you every itty-bitty detail.' Kien stared at him but didn't move or speak.

'Fuck you! You think I don't know who you are? I know old Vuong, too. Not only was I a soldier, but a Commander, that's how I know him. You're nothing special. And as for her, well, they say those with a bit of a squint like that Phuong of yours are the greatest performers. Do anything. Beautiful, sure, but real screamers. Ask the bloke I'll bring here tomorrow.'

That was as far as he got. Kien had sprayed his face with boiling coffee and sat waiting quietly for Leather-jacket's response. An awkward silence fell on the room, broken only by a snort and a snore from Vuong, who had fallen asleep at his table.

'Why tomorrow, you stinking shit? Now will do,' said Kien.

Leather-jacket started to waver. 'Right, right. Just ask Phuong. I'm Hung. She knows me. I taught her some good modern music, and how to really enjoy screwing,' he said.

Kien moved in on him, punching first, then crunching Leather-jacket's head with a chair. As Leather-jacket fell Kien grabbed him and violently shredded his clothes, pounding his head repeatedly on the floor. When Leather-jacket had had enough Kien dragged him outside, on the pavement. He was ramming Leather-jacket's bloody head into a sewer outlet when the police arrived and tried to pull him off. Kien turned on them in a blind rage and began shaping up to fight them, thinking they were Leather-jacket's mates.

The police released him the next morning. They said they had no wish to charge him. They'd seen enough of the Veterans.

Kien had just returned from the station and stepped inside his room when Phuong came in. He asked how she knew about it so quickly.

'His mates told me,' she said.

Drunk. What a night that had been. Now, many years later, he had been welcomed by the owner. That disastrous, bloody fight had been forgotten. The prosperous-looking host now embraced him, shouting for everyone to hear, 'Kien, Kien, the famous writer!'

His war buddies were proud of him now, too.

He looked over at the little tart who'd started drinking Maxim and pretended to be so worldly. She was out to the world, her head on the table. He dropped some money on the table and left her there.

His watch had stopped, but he guessed a tram was due and would rattle along soon enough. Sure enough a tram came into view in the distance, its bell clanging and its wheels throwing sparks. It was the tram old Huynh had driven before he retired. The old man had lived in the same building and by sheer coincidence, one of his three sons killed in the war had been with Kien when he had died. Kien had edged away from this memory as much as he could for he felt so deeply sorry for the old man. But, riding the same tram, it was inevitable that at times the memories would return.

Huynh sometimes left at first light, sometimes after lunch. His tram-driving shifts were irregular, but he was as regular as clockwork. He looked down when he walked, as though he was afraid of treading on his shadow. His only children, three sons, were all drafted into the army, and they had all been killed in action. The middle one, Toan, had died in front of Kien's eyes, but he'd never told father Huynh that terrible story. When news of the third son's death had arrived Huynh's wife had fallen sick and become paralysed and now the old couple lived miserably, in silence.

He had chatted with Kien sometimes, speaking as though Toan were still alive. Phuong would have been their daughter-in-law, said the old man. When you were both children, the old man confided, Toan's mother had chosen Phuong to be her son's wife because she was so lovely. Kien let this news slip by without challenge. They apparently had not known how close Kien and Phuong were in their school days. Toan had never stood a chance with Phuong.

When he was driving, Huynh had let all the children ride free on his tram. In those times the trams had been clean and kept in good condition. Not tattered and rusted, like now. The children would crowd up front, and sometimes the old man would let them ring the bell, or push a pedal.

Kien sat on the rattling tram slowly taking him home after his coffee-shop evening, remembering those days. Kien, Phuong, Toan and Sinh were all in the same class and had become close friends, often riding the tram for fun. Once they'd gone to the old terminus in the suburbs, an area not yet built over.

In a paddock near the terminus there was an old tramcar they used to play in. During one game Phuong and Kien had hidden in one of the compartments and she had embraced him, kissing him on his cheeks and his eyes, with a childish, thirteen-year-old passion.

They were interrupted by a sobbing voice: Toan had seen them and had blocked their way. 'What are you doing?' he challenged.

'Go and hide!' responded Phuong, thinking quickly. 'We're playing hide-aways,' she added.

'Liar!' he said to her. 'I saw you.'

'Don't carry on, Toan. We'll play husband and wife, just don't tell anyone if you want to play,' Phuong replied.

'Can't. Not with three people'

'Idiot. 'Course you can. I'm warning you, don't tell on us,' she repeated.

On the tram back Phuong and Kien sat together, but Toan stood near his father, blubbering. Huynh asked, 'Have you been fighting?'

'No, Daddy.'

'Why are you crying then?'

Toan didn't answer.

Phuong sighed. 'Don't worry,' she said 'he won't tell.

Half a lifetime later Toan and Kien had been together, almost by accident, on the final day of fighting, just before the attack on Saigon airport on 30 April 1975.

They were at Gate 5, Tan Son Nhat. Toan was on the machine-gun mounted on an armoured car. Kien, an infantry scout, stayed under cover by tracking behind a T54 tank. Fifteen minutes into the action they saw each other and wildly shouted to each other in greeting.

As they finished waving an anti-tank rocket fired by the defenders missed the tank Kien was using for protection and whistled past him, scoring a direct hit on Toan's armoured car, blowing it into pieces, incinerating Toan and his entire crew.

The tram turned into Kien's street, ending both his physical journey and his journey into the past with Toan, and with Phuong. As he alighted from the tram he automatically looked up to her window, hoping to see the teenage Phuong there, repeating those urgent little love cries she used to utter. But she was not there, of course. She'd long gone, from that teenage world, and from the adult world. She had now departed from both of his worlds.

Nothing would ever bring her back. He had exhausted his tears on her. He had suffered through the nights when she had openly tormented him, or brought in other lovers. Storming into her room could never have helped things. Drinking until dead drunk to remove traces of her was equally futile. It was over.

In 1965, after three months training, he had been ordered to go south with Battalion 36. There had been ten recruits from Hanoi, so when, they arrived at Hanoi station, on their way through to South Vietnam, the commander gave the ten Hanoi boys a three-hour break to go home and see their families. In those days no special leave passes were issued and progress south was usually made between bombing raids. When President Johnson halted his bombing from time to time the army would seize the opportunity and ship soldiers south.

The commander, who had brought his new troops from Yen The, ordered the ten Hanoi boys to return by 6.30p.m. to catch the troop train. That gave them two and a half hours to visit their families. Any man one minute late back to the station would be considered a deserter, he said. The boys shouted their thanks, and departed.

Kien rushed into the street with his group and hitched a ride on a flatbed truck, whose driver hardly slowed when any of the boys needed to jump off. Going into Kien's street he showed even less concern for his cargo, forcing Kien to leap clear onto the road from the moving vehicle. He landed heavily and rolled, twisting his ankle. By the time he reached his front gate he was limping, and in pain.

Taking a breath, he held on to the front gate and stared around. His street was deserted. All the houses looked empty and there was no sign of life in his own building. The population appeared to have been evacuated.

Most of the windows of his building had been boarded up. The front yard, where children were usually playing, was deserted, and there was not a soul at the community water tap, which was truly unusual. There were a few old rags hanging on clothes poles, giving the entire place an even more forlorn look.

Few families had remained in Hanoi. Most buildings had been locked. Notes were left pinned on doors, others written in chalk out front. These public messages, from wives to husbands, mothers to children, served as public notice-boards. But there were no lines, no notes from Phuong for him. Nor had he received a letter from her while he'd been in training camp. The front door was unlocked, so he quietly stepped in and began climbing the stairs to his apartment on the third floor. He stood outside the blue door, looking at the huge, brass padlock. Of course! Phuong had his key, on a string around her neck. She wore it like a necklace. He looked around for a pen and paper, or chalk, to write a line for her, but saw none, so turned and began trudging downstairs.

'Hello, fighter,' said a man's voice, startling Kien. It was Huan, Sinh's brother, a worker at the Yen Phu power station. Kien, pressed for time, apologised to Huan for not coming to his apartment, asking where everyone was. His school friend Sinh had been admitted to university, said Huan. Everyone else had been evacuated, he said, but they were all safe.

'I wonder if they'll bomb Hanoi,' Huan asked. But Kien did not respond, realising then that he had come only to see Phuong and that no one else mattered. He turned and waved goodbye in the same movement, not even telling Huan he was off to the front. Huan ran after him. 'Kien, I forgot. Did you want to find Phuong? I know you're close to her.'

'Yes. Where is she?'

'Her mother died. Word came to the university and she had to drop everything and go. I think she's at the station. I saw her heading that way with her school satchel. She's upset.'

'Are you sure it's the station?' asked Kien, grabbing him.

'All she said was, "Look after the apartment. I've got to go."
That's all I know.'

Kien made his way to the station on foot, ignoring the pain in
his ankle. The platforms were crowded, with soldiers and civilians
intermingling. People rushed helter-skelter, brushing past with
luggage, climbing on trains that were departing in quick succession. Hundreds of people could be seen in each carriage, and
on roofs, on steps, blocking all possible entrances, forcing new
arrivals to climb in through windows. It seemed hopeless.

Panic began to set in. Kien pushed angrily through the crowds,
asking himself: Which line? The train to Highway 5? North to
Lao Cai? Which damned compartment, in which carriage, on
which train?

He struggled from platform to platform for another ten minutes
before stopping, exhausted, letting himself be buffeted around as
he rested.

He had found himself standing on Platform 1, near the Thai
Nguyen train, which was about to leave. The university was
evacuating students and studies would continue in a rural area.
The long train looked like a multi-sectioned python covered with
aggressive forest ants.

From the last compartment to the final carriage there appeared
the face of a handsome young man who seemed to be looking at
Kien. No, he was looking past him and shouting: 'Come on!
What are you waiting for? No one can get seats.'

The young man continued looking in Kien's direction, adding:
'What the hell are you staring at, Phuong? Get a move on!' he
shouted angrily.

A sudden pain stabbed at Kien. He looked slowly to his right,
and there she was. 'Phuong!'

Suddenly she seemed to be the only person on the platform.
She was standing perfectly still, staring at him with her lovely
big eyes wide open in surprise. Her long hair flowed over her

forehead and cheek and twined in the shoulder strap of her satchel. Suddenly the young man reached out and pulled at her arm. 'Are you crazy? Get in!'

She shook him free and stepped out of his reach. The train began moving off, bearing him with it. He was still shouting angrily as the train took him away.

When the train had gone Phuong seemed to snap out of her reverie and broke into a big smile. 'What incredible luck!' she shouted, taking his hand and moving away from the lines. 'Let's go. We were lucky to catch each other.'

The small disquiet that arose as he saw the young man staring fiercely at him as the train pulled away stopped Kien for a moment. But the importance of the occasion was too great, and he damped down the feeling and was soon immersed into the wondrous company of his beautiful Phuong. She was speaking to him as they pushed their way through the crowd, but he could hardly hear a word. He took her school satchel and held her hand, leading her outside.

'Let's go back home,' she said, 'have dinner together, then go for a walk. You look terrific in that uniform.' She babbled on happily. 'Don't think they'll cut the power tonight. Most people are away. What's wrong with you?' she asked in the same breath, suddenly noticing his anxiety.

'I'm going to the front,' he said quickly, getting the bad news out. As he said it he realised that for the first time he was experiencing a little of what was to come in being apart from Phuong. He grew hoarse, more words would not come. It meant being hundreds of miles away down south; he would be completely powerless to return to her.

She stood still, taking it all in. 'Can't be helped,' she said quietly. 'Look, we can go home and get back here by 6.30. We'll burn a joss stick and say a prayer for your dad and my mum. Let's get a cyclo, we'll make it.'

Phuong called a cyclo and quickly bargained. 'Twenty minutes,' she told the rider. 'Do it faster and I'll pay extra.'

But when they reached their street and were about to enter the building the air-raid siren sounded. The driver, who was going to wait, panicked and ran off, without being paid, in search of a bomb shelter. It was getting dark quickly and they felt the seconds ticking by. Yet every moment was to be treasured.

'Stay overnight' Phuong whispered to him. 'The train will be gone long before the all-clear siren. Stay!'

Kien, in fear of a charge of desertion, shook his head sadly.

'No? Well we can't wait here. We'll have to take the cyclo. The coward can find it later,' she said.

Kien was reluctant.

'Pedal!' she ordered. 'We'll teach this chicken-hearted rider a lesson. The posters tell us to direct all efforts to the front line, so let's do it!'

Kien laughed. Of course, she was right. Phuong jumped into the seat and he got onto the cyclo and started pedalling. It was dangerous, as they were the only ones in the empty streets and the guards might arrest them. But as they neared the station the all-clear sounded, a signal for them to burst into ecstatic laughter. Speeding down the final, empty streets to the station, their laughter echoing from empty shopfronts, catching a train to the war. Sensational!

'And what about the look on his face when he comes out from the shelter?' they shouted, and laughed again.

But the train had gone. Battalion 36 was heading for the front. The entire force, except for one deserter.

The penalty for desertion was the firing squad.

Stunned and embarrassed, Kien stood on the now empty station, staring into the distance along the empty lines.

An unperturbed station master told them the train would stop at Dong Van or Phu Ly. 'Can't really tell. It's a troop train,' he said, looking at Kien.

Phuong tried to lighten his mood. 'The score's one-one,' she said. They'd both missed their trains.

'Look. All's not lost. Let's hitch a ride to the next station. This is wartime, there'll be plenty of ways to deal with this problem. Let's get something to eat, first.' She spoke quickly, to allay his fears.

'God, you look exhausted!' she added suddenly.

As they stood there, his war had started.

Battalion 36 had travelled to Van Trai, in the south-west. While Kien was making tracks to catch up with the other new recruits who were by then as far south as Cu Nam, B52 bombers had struck, giving them a nasty welcome to the war.

The battalion commander, who had threatened the Hanoi boys with desertion charges if they missed the train, had been one of the first to be killed. The bombers had struck first at Van Trai station, the battalion taking heavy casualties. They had then been dispersed, some continuing south by road and the others ordered to sea to continue their move south. But the B52s struck again, sinking all the sea transports, and by the time Battalion 36 had been regrouped on land there were hardly any men left and those few continued as supplementary units to others, down Road 9 to the front.

A dozen recruits went to the front. Throwing a dozen untrained men into that battle would be as effective as throwing an ice-cube into a blazing furnace.

Kien, unaware of the raids because of the wartime blackout on news, especially bad news, was still hours behind when the attack came. It was not until ten years later that he heard the details: strangely, it was on the peace train from Saigon in May 1975 that the story emerged.

One of the survivors of the attack had been his deputy com

mander, Huy. By chance, Huy was in the same compartment on the peace train. By then he had been blinded but Kien recognised him at once and called his name. Huy, however, had forgotten Kien.

'The luck of the unlucky,' he said to Kien, on hearing how he'd missed the train. 'If you hadn't missed the train you'd have probably been killed at Van Trai in the first air raid. I escaped only because I'd moved to another compartment. Pure luck.

'After the first bombing we continued with what was left of the train, thinking the B52s wouldn't be back for a while. We were wrong, of course.

'Look, if you'd deserted then no one would have noticed. What did happen, anyway?' he asked.

Kien and Phuong had hurried from the station intending to hitch-hike and get by road to the station just ahead of the troop train. They had no idea where the train would be but knew, like all trains in those times, it would be ponderously slow. Kien was urged on by an inner fear of being branded a deserter, a designation he of all people didn't deserve.

In his urgency he had ignored the perils of Phuong's presence – an attractive smartly dressed teenage student, travelling with him at night on roads ranked as strategic routes and on full war footing, with military checkpoints and road patrols at frequent intervals.

The first hints of their predicament came when drivers of passing vehicles deliberately turned their faces away from the young couple trying to hitch-hike. Deserter? The penalties for helping deserters were heavy.

'I'll stop them,' said Phuong, stepping forward. 'There's a wartime traffic priority on helping women. But I'll make a deal: I'll try cars going in either direction. If we get a ride north towards Hanoi let's go home and stay the night together. If we get a car going south, we'll catch your troop train.'

Kien was caught off balance. 'But . . .'

'Always a "but" with you! Going back to Hanoi with me makes you uneasy? You've got nothing to worry about. You can blame it on the Americans, and on me. Now, agreed?' She didn't wait for an answer, but stepped out onto the road.

From a distance they saw two cone-shaped headlights with blackout hoods covering them restricting the light to a small area ahead. It was a truck, grinding along noisily, going south.

The driver could hardly believe his eyes. A beautiful girl had stepped from the edge of the road just ahead of him. She was waving a ribboned conical hat which she'd just removed, revealing lovely long hair.

He jammed on the brakes and the truck screeched to a halt, burning rubber.

He flung the passenger door open, shouting, 'Where are you going? Don't tell me you're out for a stroll in the cool air!'

'No. I'm going to the front line. The air's not cool there at all,' she quipped back.

'The front? The war? Are you kidding?' said the driver.

'Please,' she said, 'We need to get to Phu Ly. It's important.'

The driver then saw a young soldier, in full uniform, appear beside her. It was the first time the driver had noticed him. 'I'm not going to Phu Ly. Dong Van, kid.'

Phuong turned to Kien and pulled him forward. Then she turned to the driver, offering her hand. He leaned over and lifted her in, flattered to be close to her. 'Careful, now. The step's broken,' he said warmly.

Kien reluctantly followed. He slammed the truck door, but remained silent.

'You're really kind,' said Phuong, looking at the driver for the first time. He was a rough-looking character.

'Such posh manners!' he answered.

'Indeed,' she said.

'Are you really going to the front line?' he asked warily.

'Hope so.'

'Pity.'

'Why?'

'Well, a classy little lady like you. If you're only going as far as Dong Van, even Phu Ly, you've still got a long way to go,' the driver said. He spoke only to her, ignoring Kien.

'We're chasing a troop train. Once we're on the train we'll really be moving. Think you can beat the train? It left Van Dien at seven.'

'Shit, I can beat those train-drivers any time,' he boasted. 'I'll be at your station before them.'

They rode on in silence for a few miles. He sneaked a few appreciative glances at her. His ponderous brain had problems keeping up a lively conversation.

'Any train'll stop if you stand in front of it waving your hat for a brake,' he said, flirting clumsily.

'You're an amusing chap,' she said. 'Heading into war, yet you seem light-hearted about it.'

The driver took it as a compliment. 'Sure. We're drivers, for the State. We do everything better than the bourgeois boys like your little mate here. You'll soon find out who the real men are. The front's very amusing, oh very amusing. Bloody hilarious.'

The driver had switched the cab lights off and it was now pitch dark inside. He drove at high speeds along the empty road, occasionally using the hooded lights which he operated by foot pedal. Kien was pleased he was nearing his unit, but the happiness was tinged by an undefined fear. He had ignored the crude driver; getting to the unit was more important than how he got there. With Phuong beside him it felt even better, although he had no idea of what she would do when he rejoined his unit.

He was kidding himself. He knew she was speeding headlong to the front, into certain peril.

In the background the driver, now relaxed and feeling no need to impress Phuong, swore roughly as he crashed through the gears and went about his job of getting to Dong Van on time.

Phuong was dreamily calm, rocking between the two men. When the truck hit rough patches she rested alternately on Kien's, then the driver's shoulder. Finally, the sky brightened. A full moon emerged from behind a cloudbank and moonlight filtered through into the cabin.

'There it is!' shouted the driver, pointing to a slow-moving engine and several carriages dimly visible in the moonlight across the fields.

'Your train. We'll beat it into Dong Van by five minutes,' he said confidently. He seemed to forget about flirting with Phuong and got back to his beloved driving. Beating the train into Dong Van was an important goal.

'Bloody hell! That locomotive sticks out like fire on a lake, any bloody bomber pilot could take it out without even using flares,' the driver complained.

It was true. Red sparks flew from the engine with each powerful stroke of the pistons. Kien thought it looked like thousands of big fireflies escaping into the air, tracing an obvious, fiery line for others to see.

The driver murmured, half to himself, 'I wouldn't be taking on the Americans by sending troops in a bloody slow train. That's a sure way of going straight to hell.' But Phuong's response was to giggle, and grasp Kien's hand excitedly.

Nearing the station the driver pulled the truck off the road, to keep it concealed. 'Go along the lines, that way you'll not be seen getting to the platform,' he advised. 'If it looks like not stopping just wave your hat, that'll work.'

Kien got down. Phuong went to follow him but the driver

had his strong arm around her waist, hugging her. 'Listen,' he whispered. 'I'll be coming back in two hours to make the run back to Hanoi. Wait for me here.' She began to leave but he held on. 'You're so sexy, so beautiful. I can't believe you're throwing yourself into the front line. What a waste!' He let her go. As she started down he said hopefully, 'Two hours from now, I'll come back. Be here!'

Phuong and Kien, hand in hand, ran quietly along the edge of the rail tracks. Behind them a train whistle screeched in the night and below them the ground trembled as it got closer.

Nearing the end of the platform they stopped and faced each other. Another parting. They embraced and kissed desperately, both crying their farewells as the rumbling got louder until with a deafening roar the locomotive slowly moved past them, puffing noisily and spraying out steam as it creaked to a halt.

In their embrace they had not noticed the silence that followed. No voices. No sign of human activity in the carriages. They broke from the embrace and began walking along the platform, past a luggage van, then another, then a truck piled heavy with cargo covered by a tarpaulin. It was a goods train.

The station master, carrying a lantern, approached them. Kien asked, 'The military train, brother. Where is it? The troop train from Hanoi?'

The station master lifted the lantern to get a closer look at them. 'Are you mad? Want to go to prison, or swallow a few bullets? That's military information. Piss off, or I'll call the police.'

The station master moved on, leaving them standing. 'Let me ask him,' said Phuong, and she broke away, running after the man. In a few minutes she returned, looking serious. 'Your train went through twenty minutes ago. This is a goods train, but also heading for Vinh, following the troop train. Your unit's ahead on the same line. Jump on! We'll only be twenty minutes behind them by the time it reaches Vinh.'

It was a risk. Vinh, a big port city halfway between Hanoi and the DMZ border dividing North Vietnam from South Vietnam, was an obvious destination for both men and materials going south. He'd mingle with the others there.

They clambered up, pushing the door wider. Underfoot it felt mushy, like soil. 'Shut the bloody door,' came a rough voice from the dark. 'They'll catch us with the door open. Quick, gimme yer hand.'

'Just stand aside,' said Phuong, swinging herself in easily.

'A bloody girl!' said a drunken voice.

'Get out of the way,' commanded Phuong. 'Let us through.'

When they were both in, with Kien kneeling, she whispered, 'Lie down. The train's moving.'

'You shouldn't stay,' Kien said.

'So, you want to leave me again?' she said, taking his hand. 'I'm going to go a little further with you, that's all.'

Kien started to protest again, but it was too late. The train was moving out of the station with sharp, sudden tugs as the carriages clanked against each other. Soon, it settled into a modest speed.

'Come over here,' said the voice, 'plenty of room, more comfortable. You can sleep in each other's arms. President Johnson's on holiday, he won't attack tonight.'

They moved hand-in-hand between bales of goods piled roof-high. 'Move along, move along,' the voice said, and there were grumbles from other men trying to sleep. 'Make way for a pretty young girl,' the voice continued.

Phuong entwined herself with Kien the moment they were settled. She kissed his cheeks, trying to calm him. To Kien it was part nightmare, part daydream and even in the tightest embrace a sense of the unreal stayed with him.

The crudely-made, old-fashioned goods car had a high roof

which creaked along with the joints of the car's walls. Wind howled through broken timbers.

A sensation of hopelessness swept over Kien. Phuong felt his unhappiness: 'Why don't you . . . why don't you want me?' He couldn't answer. He simply lay there listening to the puffing of the engine, smelling the damp odour of the straw and earthen floor and the mixture of coal dust and fumes in the air.

Every few minutes very small stations and sidings whizzed past his vision, some with dim lights on poles the only evidence of their existence. Then a thundering as they crossed a steel trestle bridge. They were heading into the Red River Delta where the action started and he was savouring the last moments of freedom and romance with Phuong. God knew what would happen to them when they got there.

Kien, more than a decade later, relived those last minutes in the train. Phuong had long since left him, for the second time, although for some reason a lamp still burned in her apartment. Many times, after a night of drinking, he would forget the lamp had been left on, and imagine Phuong had returned. He would stand before her apartment door knocking and calling before remembering the light had been burning ever since she had left.

From now on it was nostalgia and war recollections that drove him on. With Phuong gone this was his only hope of staying in rhythm with normal life. The sorrows of war and his nostalgia drove him down into the depths of his imagination. From there his writing could take substance.

Kien and Phuong had been just sixteen years old when they completed Ninth Form. Kien remembered the event well. It had been in August, the start of August. The Chu Van An school Youth Union had organised a vacation camp at Do Son, on the

Tonkin Gulf. Even non-Union members like Phuong and Kien were eligible to go.

The early days of the camp were wet and dismal. The sea seemed to be perpetual foam and it rained all day long. Then one afternoon the clouds parted and the sun shone brilliantly and the mood changed.

The students unpacked their gear and began pitching tents on the foreshore. As they shot up it reminded Kien of multicoloured mushrooms suddenly sprouting between rows of casuarina trees. That evening the students made a huge campfire and started a party around it. It was an extremely happy time for them all and as the flames grew higher in the night the beer, wine and music flowed and guitars and accordions started playing as the students began to sing.

It was a memorable, happy evening around the campfire amidst the trees with a background of the darkest of seas. The night wound down slowly and pleasantly, the students gradually dropping off to sleep. Kien, close to Phuong, noticed she was a little apprehensive, and asked why.

'Something abnormal about the sea,' she replied evasively. 'Frightening.'

A normal sea breeze was blowing, the waves were soft. The moonlight glittered on the waves and overhead the starry night seemed peaceful.

Kien noticed nothing unusual.

He threw some more driftwood on the campfire. Phuong gently strummed a guitar, but didn't sing. Then they heard muffled, adult voices and heavy footsteps.

From a group of men, one stepped forward. 'Why haven't you doused the fire?' he asked angrily.

'Put it out? Why?' asked Kien looking up.

A sailor with a rifle slung around his shoulder stood there

looking down at them. 'Put it out,' he said, starting to kick sand over the fire.

'Why?'

'Don't ask why. We got orders tonight. No fires on the beach. No lights. They order it, we carry it out. We aren't allowed to ask why, it's a military order.'

'Is singing banned, too?' asked Phuong, feigning innocence.

The sailor lowered his gun, softened his stance and sat down with them. 'No. Don't stop singing. That's got to go on at all costs. Sing us a song now,' he invited.

Two others from the shore patrol returned, sitting down and looking at Phuong. She said to the first sailor, 'Oh, I wasn't intending to sing. I just asked if singing was banned.'

'Sing, all the same, sister,' he said sadly. 'Sing a farewell song, to us. I'll tell you a secret; you'll know tomorrow anyway. It's war. America has entered the war. We're fighting the Americans.'

Phuong nervously started picking at the guitar, sweeping her slim fingers along the strings. After taking a deep breath, as if to calm herself, she raised her head and as her shawl fell from her shoulders, began to sing sweetly. Her audience of Kien and the patrolmen sat silently, moved to sadness as the sweet words flowed:

> 'The winds, they are a changin',
> the harsh winds blow in the world from tonight,
> no longer the peace
> we were hoping for
> Our loved ones grieve, for those who'll be lost,
> no longer in peace
> our children will live.
> From this moment on,
> the winds, they are a changin'.'

*

The first old sailor had begun to sniffle. He looked over sadly to beautiful Phuong and handsome Kien as though they were a doomed generation, already victims of a new, long war.

War! War! The sea roared out the message in the small hours of 5 August 1965. A small storm began far out across the Tonkin Gulf and the group looked on as distant forked lightning seemed to signal the start of the war. Nearby the other students in tents around the fire also began to wake up and slowly, realising something new was upon them, began to gather round the fire and talk over the news.

Kien and Phuong slipped out of the campfire circle to a quiet spot where they couldn't be heard or seen. They embraced urgently. The realisation they would certainly soon be parted and their world would soon be changed heightened the desperation. They whispered innocent, passionate vows to each other, promising never to waver in their love.

And they spoke of death.

When they returned to camp it was to an unruly scene; the wind had whipped up and the distant storm had quickly found them. Blankets rolled off along the shore, sand blew in sprays and tents broke from their pegs, and just as the howling wind died down the heavens opened and the short-lived seaside vacation was washed out.

That's how the war started, with a storm. For Kien the storm continued for nearly eleven years and even after the war his mental skies were clouded for another ten.

Now, twenty years later, he let the pictures flow back across his mental screens. He pictured himself and Phuong on the goods train, heading for Vinh. It was a crazy adventure. Kien was now a different man from then; Phuong was perhaps not so much changed.

She had in those years accumulated a mountain of sins and an avalanche of innuendo on her reputation. Yet she remained for him an enigma, someone ahead of her time in so many ways, and strangely, eternally pure.

Kien volunteered for the army in the summer of 1965, got his call-up papers in the autumn, and was soon posted to what was commonly called Long B, the military name for the battlefields of the south. Their goods train had not stopped at Phu Ly, as they expected. It turned a little east and rushed on towards Vinh, on the coast, blowing long, sorrowful whistles as it gathered speed in the night. Phu Ly, Nam Dinh, Ninh Binh, all flashed by and were left behind to the north. Everything seemed to be going so well.

'Good for us,' said Phuong, pleased the escapade was being prolonged. Her sense of adventure was heightened with every mile and she cuddled up to Kien, whispering to him, 'The further we go, the more I'm lost, the better it is. We'll see what war's like.'

Now, it seems like fiction, some imagined story on the fringe of his war memories. But it was real enough.

The train howled on through the night, never stopping at stations. Once, on a straight run through some grain fields, it stopped for a few minutes. Several men furtively climbed aboard and the train started off again.

As the newcomers moved in, everyone moved along and space became tighter and tighter. Who were they? Soldiers? Merchants doing quick deals? Highway thieves? More smoke, more stink.

One of them imitated a station master shouting after their train speeding through his small station: 'Doonnnngg Giiiaooooooo-whosh!'

Phuong laughed softly. 'How far to the killing fields?' she asked.

'So, you can't sleep either?' Kien replied.

'Sleepy, but can't sleep.'

'Tomorrow.'

'What if there's no tomorrow?'

And so their intimate nonsenses had continued for the next hour, a period of delirious romantic joy in extraordinary circumstances.

On the peace train returning home Kien had met Hien, the invalid girl. They had become friendly and on the last day they had shared a hammock. Hien, sad-eyed, sweet, the girl from Nam Dinh. She'd not been able to sleep either and kept whispering sweet nothings to him as the train clattered north, towards Hanoi.

The first day of the war, with Phuong, passing Nam Dinh. The last day of the war, with Hien, herself from Nam.

The peace train, as the soldiers called it – it was officially called the Thanh Nhat, the Unification Train – passed Thanh Hoa in the glow of dawn. Easing himself from Hien's embrace he peered out through the window. Fields, roads, mounds, villages, dewy grass, river banks, bamboo clumps, coconut plantations, ponds, hills, cemeteries, rocks, creeks, all flashed past in the dim autumn morning sky. 'Going home, going home,' the murmur of the tracks began to change gradually to 'Going south, going south.' For an eerie minute he seemed to be with Phuong, ten years earlier, in her seventeenth summer, going south, south, south.

They had clutched together in furious embrace on the floor of the rough goods car, surrounded by unseen but close, shadowy figures, snoring and smoking and murmuring.

Yet they were a world apart and Phuong stretched herself invitingly against him time and time again as if lying on a soft bed in a first-class sleeping-car. Kien's passion would rise and he would move in close, only to withdraw at the last moment, like a warrior half-drawing a sword from its sheath, then ramming it home again.

She urged him on. 'Come on, darling. Are you afraid?'

Kien was about to respond, he recalled now. What would it have been? Finally, their pure spirits joining in true love in those strange conditions?

A strange, whistling sound came to them from above, then other sounds, like the howling of engines high in the air. 'Planes! Bombers!' someone shouted and the mob in the car began scrambling in the dark.

Jet planes had found the train. High above, in the very early morning, they were circling, then diving.

Kien was slow to react. He was still dazed by the activity as he heard orders being shouted: 'Stop the train. Alert, alert!'

As the train was slowing, terror reigned. The compartment door was jerked open with a crash and men in panic began jumping from the braking but still moving car, hitting the tracks and sleepers with sickening thuds. Kien was standing up close to the door trying to get his bearings when the first direct attack came. 'Kien! Kien!' he heard a girl call. It must have been Phuong, but it came from a different corner of the car, and he couldn't see anyone in the dark. The planes dived again, strafing with increasing accuracy as flares lit the scene.

Blinded, he turned inward and saw in the blinding light the incredible sight of Phuong, lying prone on the floor, fighting a big man on top of her. She was struggling desperately, her hair flowing, her clothes being ripped from her, her mouth covered by a massive, brutal hand as he settled over her in a rhythm.

A blast hit Kien and he was flung from the car onto the rail embankment and he rolled roughly, striking metal with such force that he fainted. When he came to his chest was burning, blood had begun seeping into his mouth, bringing a salty taste, and he felt sick. He looked at the train, with cars broken but basically intact, and heard a whistle. With some urgency the engine began puffing away and the cars one by one clanged as the slack was taken up and began moving slowly on.

Kien jumped up and opened a compartment door. But Phuong was not there. Nor was she in the next, or the next. In panic, he jumped onto the steps of an escort locomotive, fearing he would otherwise be left behind. Two mechanics, wearing overalls smeared with oil, looked over at him with sympathy. Their faces were smeared with coal-dust and oil, their eyes shone chalk-white through these strange masks. One of them picked up a shovel and began stoking the furnace. The older man, the engineer, pulled on a cord and a screaming hoot was emitted. Kien sat there hardly taking any of this in. He began to fall sideways, into a faint. The young stoker supported him, wiping blood from Kien's chin with the inside of his glove. Kien looked at the blood on the glove disbelievingly.

'Cheer up, son,' the old engineer told him. 'This is kid stuff. The first whistle in the war. Nothing to it.'

As the fog lifted Kien seemed also to regain his faculties. He suddenly remembered what he thought he had seen in the compartment, and what could still be happening there. He was to remember that as his first war wound, not the blood from his injuries now staining the glove.

It was from that moment, when Phuong was violently taken from him, that the bloodshed truly began and his life entered into bloody suffering and failure. And he would understand true sacrifice; friends who would die to save others.

On the morning of 30 April, in the dying moments of fighting, when his scout units were attacking the Lang Cha Ca building in Saigon, Kien had hesitated for a moment in his run. And that second's hesitation was paid for with the life of the only other scout still alive in his unit. They were to have entered Saigon together.

Kien had hesitated when, from the vault-like window of the ground floor of the building, he heard machine-gun fire. They had shelled the building so intensely it seemed unlikely any gunner was left alive. But there it was, machine-gun fire from inside.

Kien slowed in his advance, crouching, listening. Tu, behind him, did not slow up. Kien crouched and moved cautiously but Tu raced past him and straight into the machine-gun fire. Tu's back burst open and blood showered into Kien's face.

Back came the memories of Oanh, dying on the third floor of the Banh Me Thuot police station, when the policewoman – a girl really – had feigned death then shot Oanh, sacrificing her own life in doing so.

And when Cu had laid covering fire to hold off an enemy regiment while Kien's scouts escaped after a failed raid on the ARVN Airbornes near the Phuong Hoang pass, Big Thinh, Tam and of course Cu, who had given his life in order for them to get away, were lost.

Kien and the only two others left from his scout platoon were fleeing from the southern forces who were pursuing them relentlessly in the Khanh Duong area. They were trying to reach the foot of the pass to catch up with their own units.

It was broad daylight, which made movement more dangerous.

Exhausted, they broke for a rest on the lower edge of a bamboo thicket. Tam tore a sleeve from his shirt to dress Thinh's head wound. Kien, leaning against the bank of a ditch, rested his head between his knees. He had unslung his AK and placed it beside him. Behind them to the east the southern forces were now using artillery, setting their sights with ranging shots at the northern forces to the west, who were returning the artillery fire, also using trial shells to calibrate their sights. They were at each end of the Khanh Duong valley with the three surviving scouts in no-man's-land between them. The whole area was alive with small-arms fire and the increasing thunder of artillery shells as each side bracketed their targets.

Tam was tending Thinh's head wound. Kien, sitting close by, was upset at having to leave Cu behind. They would not have escaped without him giving his life for them. 'Just the three of us left from the entire platoon,' Kien moaned.

'You can worry about that later, Kien,' said Tam, dressing the wound. 'Thank your lucky stars there's three of us still alive. It was bloody close.'

Without warning a black shadow passed over them, passing through the bamboo tops and landing with a whump! right in front of them.

A paratrooper had landed above their hideout; he stood over them on the top of a small bank looking down at the startled trio and covering them with his AR15 rifle. Their own three AKs were still on the ground near them, but they were now useless.

The paratrooper was a tall young man with flowing hair. His red beret was tucked under his epaulettes. The rest of his uniform was spotted with dark red splotches of earth indicating he had been very active in this battle. Kien stiffened as the paratrooper put his finger on the trigger, expecting bullets to burst his chest cage open, rip his face and send explosions of his blood around the jungle floor as he had so often seen it happen to others.

'Don't shoot, sir,' said Tam quickly. 'I surrender. We surrender.'

The southerner laughed. Gesturing with his free hand he gave orders. 'Get up, quick! Sons of bitches, the three of you.'

They rose, in fear of imminent death. Tam, in front of Kien, started to clamber up the small embankment as he'd been ordered. Suddenly, he lunged and grabbed one of the paratrooper's legs, pulling him sharply. He started shooting but the shots went harmlessly into the air. Tam and the paratrooper tumbled back down into the ditch and Thinh shouted to Kien, 'Run, quick, run!'

Kien was torn between going to Tam's aid and following Thinh.

More paratroopers were landing and others were now crashing through the thicket close to them. They took the only course and began running along the ditch away from Tam and the first paratrooper. The new arrivals starting shooting at them, too, and the bullets sprayed around Kien's head and behind him as he ran zig-zagging.

'Oh!' cried Thinh.

That was all he heard. Just a small cry as Thinh lifted into the air and buckled and died.

Kien continued through the bamboo cover. The paratroopers were throwing everything at him including bazooka fire, but they were wide of the mark.

Kien ran until he fell from exhaustion. As he crawled on towards his lines his emotions were storming; excruciating pain at having left and lost his mates, ecstatic elation at having survived death once more.

Strangely, that was not his most memorable escape. The most tragic, heart-rending and dangerous escape concerned Hoa. It was during the retreat after the Tet Offensives in 1968, an unfortunate time for them. For the infantry scouts even the sky was dangerous in those two weeks of withdrawal, carrying the wounded, dragging their feet through the jungles heading west towards the Cambodian border. In less than a fortnight they had been encircled twice, and twice in utter desperation had broken out of the traps, fighting fearlessly.

Kien's unit was in total disarray and badly beaten up. They fought a rearguard struggle as they headed west and together with three men from another company crossed the Poco River and wormed their way to Black Hill, which had been ground to powder by B52s. From that relative safety they ran for their lives into the sunset.

As they were crossing some low-lying jungle areas at the foot of the Ngoc Bo Ray mountain, the group came across a team of stretcher-bearers heading for Cambodian territory. Against his better judgement, Kien and his men joined the stretcher-bearers from the Sa Thay river area and went along with them. They were all short of food and their units had been torn to shreds. They were exhausted and weak and seemed lost, although they were being led by a female guide. But she was not one of the Thuong minorities who knew the borderlands territory. She was from the north.

American troops were all round them in this area and their ragged unit saw traces of them having passed earlier at various points, and other signs of their presence. They expected to run into them at any time, especially near water-holes; it was the dry season and there were precious few fresh water sources left, so they were natural ambush sites.

Overhead there were the spotter planes and bombers to contend with. After some unexpected encounters with the enemy they took more wounded, including the stretcher-bearers. They re-formed with groups of three carrying two stretchers each. They dragged and wormed their way along, heading west for the Sa Thay river. It seemed they had been wandering aimlessly around the base of Ngoc Bo Ray mountain, for they listened in vain for the welcome rippling song of the river which would spell relative safety for them.

Hoa, the guide from the north, replied confidently to Kien's comment that they were lost. Having no compass or map he was forced to rely upon her. But his intuition told him they were lost, and by the third morning their situation had become desperate. Instead of arriving on the east bank of the Sa Thay near Cambodia they arrived on the bank of an immense, unnavigable lake.

'Heavens! Crocodile Lake!' Hoa wailed in disappointment.

Kien was disgusted; he stood moodily looking over the reedy lake watching the stinking vapours rise, and seeing several lurking crocodiles slithering around in the green, wet scum along the banks.

'What's this? A sightseeing tour? You've led us to this stinking Crocodile Lake. Great!'

'My mistake,' the guide said humbly.

'It's not a mistake, it's a fucking crime,' Kien muttered cruelly. 'You ought to be shot, but bullets wouldn't be good enough.'

Hoa's eyes filled with tears and her lips trembled. 'I'll pay for my mistakes, please, let me repay. I'll find the way,' she blubbered.

'So, we'll have a wash in the mud here, shall we, while we wait for you?' he asked.

'No. It's not that bad. Crocodile Lake is close to the Sa Thay. I'll backtrack and look for the turning. It's not far. For now, let's get back under cover near the foothills we've just passed. I'll find the road and we'll march again at sunset.'

She spoke rapidly, eager to redeem herself.

Spotter planes were circling overhead. Enemy mortars pounded another target on the other side of the lake, with increasing intensity. The shock waves began arriving on their side of the lake's shoreline.

'It's my fault, comrades, I'll find the way. But first let's get the wounded under cover,' Sue repeated eagerly.

Kien by this time had no confidence in Hoa but saw her as the only hope, for none of them knew the area. The lives of scores of wounded men and their stretcher-bearers depended on her confidence in finding the way to the safety of the border. The wounded were ashen-faced, their bodies now wasted from starvation and exhaustion.

They withdrew from the lake shore to a creviced area where protective rock slabs shielded them from the harsh sun and the spotter planes. An unexpected and ominous calm fell on the area. The mortars had stopped, the roar of the jets could no longer be heard. The crackling sound of sporadic rifle-fire was heard, but apart from that only the groans of the wounded broke the silence.

The heat and humidity oppressed them all. Kien scowled at Hoa as he spoke threateningly: 'If you don't lead us to the riverbank . . . you understand the consequences . . .'

'Yes. Now, let me go now,' she said.

Kien unslung his AK and handed it to a stretcher-bearer. 'If the Americans come, use this. Not many rounds left. Take this pistol too. Still got four in it. I'll use grenades.'

Kien handed another pistol to Hoa. 'Avoid fighting. We've got to find the way out, not get into firefights, understand?'

'Let me go alone, you rest here,' she said to Kien.

'No. I'm coming with you.'

'You don't trust me. I'll find it, don't worry.'

'I don't trust you. I'll believe it when I see it. Our only duty is to these wounded; we have to find a way out at any cost,' he said.

'Understood,' she said, looking at her boots.

They backtracked for some time. When a head-shaped rock appeared before them Hoa whispered urgently: 'That's it. We turn here. This is where we missed the turning, couldn't see the rock from the other side as we came in.'

'Certain?' he replied.

She nodded. 'Remember this rock. We're near the track now,' she said quietly.

They headed off at an angle and found a lightly used track which led through a dry creekbed, and very soon they could smell and hear the fresh water of the Sa Thay. The atmosphere had changed; it was fresher, the jungle was greener there and they both regained their confidence. Hoa moved ahead through ponds and banks of shrubs blooming with red flowers.

The track they were meant to follow was by now almost

overgrown, but the sound of the river was all they needed to guide them from there. They came across an abandoned cassava field overgrown with elephant grass and found themselves looking down towards the river.

'We needn't go right down,' he said. 'The path is clear now. Let's get back and bring them all over before dark.'

'I've got to rest a bit first,' she said.

'Agreed. I'm exhausted,' he said.

They sat down out of sight looking over the fields and riverflats. Kien looked over at Hoa, his mood softening.

'Like a smoke?' she asked.

'Yes. But where'd you get them?' he said, smiling.

'I found a Salem packet. Had one left.'

She took the crushed packet from her top pocket and lit up, taking a few puffs to get it started, then handed it to Kien.

'The Americans are close, then,' he said, looking at the packet.

'Not always. We get hold of Salems, too. But we should've brought the AK,' she said.

'Yes. But I thought they'd need it if the Americans come across them. The wounded can't run so they have to fight. We're nearly out of ammunition, anyway. We have to avoid them, that's all. That's the only way we're going to get the wounded safely across.'

She nodded agreement, making a hand signal for a puff on the cigarette. Kien placed it between her lips.

'I don't usually smoke. But I want to share one with you. I don't know why I'm so nervous,' she said.

'How long have you been down here?'

'I came down south in 1966, two years ago, but I was in the Central Highlands most of the time so I don't know this area at all. This is the worst time I've had. It's really bad, isn't it? I mean, the fighting's going to go on for a long time, don't you think?'

'I'm beginning to think the real fighting's just started. It's like this everywhere now,' he replied.

A helicopter was heard. Then rifle fire.

'Don't forget the way,' she whispered urgently.

'But we both know it now,' he said.

'Yes, but you'll shoot me if I make another mistake,'

'Forget it, Hoa,' he said. 'I was angry with you then.'

'No, I mean it. The jungle is alien to me. I'm from the coast, in Hai Hau. Until we saw the head-shaped rock I was totally lost.'

Kien looked at her more closely. 'How old are you?'

'Nearly twenty. I joined when I was eighteen,' she said. 'But I'm still not used to it.'

'No one gets used to it,' he said, grinding the cigarette into the ground. 'Wait for me here. I'll go back and bring the others. You need the rest. We've still got a long way to go.'

'No, I won't. I'm the liaison guide, that's my duty,' she said. But she seemed nervous, and Kien studied her, until she looked up again.

'I'm afraid to be alone,' she admitted. 'I want to be with you, Kien.'

Kien moved to her and placed an arm around her shoulders in comfort. Gratefully, she leaned towards him, and they sat like that for some minutes, moving only when a spotter plane flew overhead, following the course of the river. Kien stood up slowly, and helped Hoa to her feet. She looked so young. He'd been about to shoot a teenage girl because she'd lost her way in unfamiliar jungle.

By the time they had reached the foot of the Ngoc Bo Ray mountain again the sun was setting behind the peaks; it was late afternoon and despite the eerie silence they were both hurrying. There was an uneasy tension in the air, broken by the rustle of dry grass, and the crunch of twigs breaking. A cobra slid across the trail in front of them, fleeing from some other movement.

They froze in their tracks, expectantly. They had just passed the turning point of the head-shaped rock and could smell the marshlands of Crocodile Lake.

There was more movement in the jungle near them. Birds, disturbed by some movement, flew out ahead of them, up and into the heat of the day before turning back into the cool to land on higher branches. As they began to move slowly forward Kien suddenly stopped, grabbing Hoa and pulling her down. An American patrol had emerged a few paces away from them, cutting a narrow path as they went. In another moment they would have stepped in front of them.

What Kien had seen first was not a man, but a tracker dog as a big as a calf, an Alsatian.

The dog was pulling at a strong leather leash which was held by a black soldier wearing a bullet-proof vest and steel helmet. Another black followed him, this one bare-chested except for a massive cartridge belt slung diagonally across his body. Following him a white American, also well muscled and naked from the waist up. Then a fourth . . . and there were others, fanned out behind the fourth. It was difficult to tell just how many, but they were quick and light-footed in the jungle and they moved relentlessly, like cunning wolves on a trail, in total silence.

The dog stopped by a shrub where Kien was hiding and began sniffing. The dog-handler had flicked something onto the sight of his gun. Kien, shivering in fear a few feet away, looked at it. It was a piece of white bandage. He moved his hand down to his grenade, expecting the worst. He realised the Americans were following their earlier trail with the wounded to Crocodile Lake. What he didn't realise was that Hoa had silently slipped away from where he was crouched.

The American patrol were still moving along, following the

eager tracker dog, following their trail of the day before. They were signalling and murmuring among themselves as they picked up the trail. We must have been obvious, thought Kien. Stretchers dragged by men, themselves probably wounded and exhausted, who were hardly likely to pay attention to bushcraft by covering their tracks.

'Our wounded are at their mercy!' He swore. A feeling of disgrace and helplessness was rising within him when suddenly, a pistol shot rang out.

It was a small, brief report, but it shook the otherwise silent jungle and reverberated in the still afternoon air. A dog yelped in pain. He saw the American soldiers react instantaneously, dropping to the jungle floor and rolling as they fell. The lead dog-handler let free the leash on the wounded dog and rolled into protective cover.

Then a second shot sounded, finding its mark on the same dog which yelped again and flew into a rage, and began charging for the source of its pain. Kien, now behind the patrol, was astonished to see little Hoa step from behind a clay ant-hill. She was a magnificent portrait of courage; she stood against the setting sun, her lovely slim body erect, arm outstretched firing at the dog, and the dog only. The final rays of the setting sun silhouetted her against the Crocodile Lakelands, tingeing her skin copper colour, giving it the appearance of a bronze statue. Her long hair swirled around her shoulders and below her shorts Kien saw that her legs were newly scratched and bleeding. The dog, which had never baulked at going for her, was finally dropped in his tracks by her last two shots.

Hoa dropped her arm, then lifted it in a throwing action, hurling the pistol towards the Americans.

The soldiers held their fire, but the point men ran towards her. Others, including one who almost trod on Kien's hand, followed. Kien looked over to Hoa again and saw her sprint away, away from the trail the patrol was following. Although she ran quickly the soldiers were athletes and they caught her after only thirty metres, and held her, cheering as they did.

Now left behind and relatively safe, Kien crawled to a safer position and tried to see what had happened to Hoa. He could have thrown his grenade and scattered them, which was what he wanted to do as it became obvious what they were doing with her.

Without losing their control, or lifting their voices, they set about stripping Hoa and, the dog-handler first, roughly fucking her. Some of them stayed back, but the way they had all come to a standstill, and with others waiting their turn, it appeared they would end their patrol with the rape.

Kien, with a single hand-grenade to fight with, was almost totally powerless. Hoa had saved fifteen sick and wounded from certain death by first shooting the dog then diverting them from the trail which would have led directly to the sick and wounded troops, almost powerless to defend themselves against such a well-armed, fit patrol force.

She gave herself to save me, too. With that thought he eased the grenade lever back to its safe position. As the almost silent but barbarous multiple rape of young Hoa continued on the small jungle clearing in the dying minutes of the harrowing day, Kien crept off, away from them, towards his wounded men.

Kien that night followed Hoa's trail to the river and made a successful crossing with the wounded.

He knew it was by then unlikely they would meet another patrol, especially at night, but he kept his hand on the grenade for hours, and the clasp felt warm. Not one of them asked about Hoa. At first he found it disagreeably strange. Then, with its acceptance he, too, began to forget about her. Was it that such sacrifices were now an everyday occurrence? Or that they were expected, even of such young people? Or worse, that they were too concerned worrying about their own safety to bother with others?

It was many years later that Kien, in the MIA team, returned to Crocodile Lake. Hoa's image came to him the moment he arrived and he set off to find the old trail to the river bank, where they had smoked the Salem together, and he had apologised for wanting to shoot her. It all seemed so long ago, and because he couldn't even find the head-shaped rock – it had been blown apart or washed away – it seemed a touch unlikely that it had ever happened. Of course it had, but not even finding the clearing where he had last seen her allowed him that escape into such possibilities.

What remained was sorrow, the immense sorrow, the sorrow of having survived. The sorrow of war.

But for Hoa and countless other loved comrades, nameless ordinary soldiers, those who sacrificed for others and for their Vietnam, raising the name of Vietnam high and proud, creating a spiritual beauty in the horrors of conflict, the war would have been another brutal, sadistic exercise.

Kien himself would have been dead long ago if it had not been for the sacrifice of others; he might even have killed himself to escape the psychological burden of killing others. He had not done that, choosing instead to live the life of an ant-like soldier, carrying the burden of every underling.

After 1975, all that had quieted. The wind of war had stopped. The branches of conflict had stopped rustling. As we had won, Kien thought, then that meant justice had won; that had been some consolation. Or had it? Think carefully; look at your own existence. Look carefully now at the peace we have, painful, bitter and sad. And look at who won the war.

To win, martyrs had sacrificed their lives in order that others might survive. Not a new phenomenon, true. But for those still living to know that the kindest, most worthy people have all fallen away, or even been tortured, humiliated before being killed, or buried and wiped away by the machinery of war, then this beautiful landscape of calm and peace is an appalling paradox. Justice may have won, but cruelty, death and inhuman violence had also won.

Just look and think: it is the truth.

Losses can be made good, damage can be repaired and wounds will heal in time. But the psychological scars of the war will remain forever.

The light which had been left on in Phuong's apartment has now finally been turned off. It now seems to Kien that he has finally lost her. His days on this earth also seem numbered, and his existence seems meaningless. But in the light of day that, too, is melodramatic. He has to finish his novel and life cannot be ended until the writing is done.

Magazines buy his articles and he makes ends meet with small editing jobs. They occupy very little of his time and require no serious concentration and his by-lines in the magazines ensure he earns at least enough to cover costs.

The manuscript, meanwhile, grows longer and longer. The drinking continues, but the work continues, too. By night he goes to an all-night café on the lake, orders coffee, lights a cigarette and buys the morning newspaper. If he goes in the afternoon heat, when it is crowded and the streets still dusty, he is often approached: How's the writing going? they ask.

'Fairly boring,' he replies.

'That's the famous author who lives on our block,' he hears them say.

One afternoon he walks past a man selling cobras on the sidewalk. The snakes look as if they're dead, exhausted by the demands of a hectic life and wishing to return to that other, safer jungle.

On the opposite side of the street, children gather around a blind man who sells colourful balloons.

Around the lake the homeless sleep on stone benches. Autumn leaves fall and make a soft carpet on the grass. The city is crowded, but sad. One day he set out to go to an office to work, but when he got to the street he turned round and went back, going upstairs and closing the door behind him.

Picture postcards from his writing life.

His friends live so far away from him now. They don't write. Why don't they write? He doesn't write to them. He doesn't speak to anyone much these days, just the mute lady who lives in the attic. His father's old studio. 'And then only when I'm pissed,' he reminds himself.

Kien is back in his apartment in Hanoi as usual, his mind tumbling over when the story he starts to write emerges as boring, heavy and senseless. He had intended to write one thing but his pen took another direction, displaying a mind of its own. He is pondering whether to leave the page or to erase it when he recalls another story. A ridiculous story of a ridiculous wound he got at Dac To. 'The South strikes again!' he mused. 'Now they're using pretty agents!' he laughed.

Wound? That's what they called it. It was VD. He was in a military clinic when another soldier was brought in. Kien himself thought nothing of it. He found it hilarious that the commander of the garrison which later occupied Saigon chose Kien to help police his troops at night. So many of them were sneaking away to find girls near the airport. But the other soldier in the clinic was outraged, and afraid. He cried, agonised and bemoaned his luck.

Kien admonished him. 'Surely this is nothing compared to your other wounds?' he asked. He turned on Kien, telling him he was a fool. 'This is worse than being blinded,' he said dramatically.

He took it so seriously! Kien imagined him drumming up a little club of soldiers who got clap in the war, then discovering how insignificant his 'wound' was.

He lay back on his bed, his hands behind his head, contemplating his present state, the condition of the heart. He looked forward to the day when his health and normal zeal would be restored, and along with it his normal sexual desires; he could be quite happy trying to relive his youth. That would help him rid himself of his burdensome past and reduce his melancholia. On the other hand, there were certain important differences in his life now.

He had discovered he was happier when looking into the past; his path in life, which he had once assumed would be towards a beautiful future, had done a U-turn and taken him backwards into the murky darkness of the hard times his homeland had experienced.

Happiness seemed to lie in the past; the older he grew the rosier the past looked to him. Life before going south as a teenage soldier now seemed to him to have been one long, beautiful day.

In one of his more peaceful moments he reviewed the new lives his colleagues had settled into after the war. Some had stayed south, for the warmer climate, or better economic opportunities, or perhaps they had just reached the end of their march in life. Others had stayed in the Central Highlands. Perhaps they wished to avoid returning north to a boring life.

Many of those who returned to the Highlands after the fighting now enjoyed healthy, outdoor, free living. They were farming pasture-lands or working in the jungles, or in new villages created along the Poco, Sa Thay, Serepoc or Ya-Mo rivers. The hells of yesteryear were now the scenes of peaceful rural tranquillity. In the dim past a political commissar had lectured him on his post-war life. He'd forgotten which commissar, but his advice went like this: 'You've been in action in the south for several years. You have suffered hardships, and stained your hands with blood. From now on, you'd do better to live close to nature and be closer to ordinary working people. That will ease your suffering and bring you happiness.'

Kien imagined his old mates working on the land, slashing and burning in the dry season, weeding in the wet. Going to the jungle in the wet season to pick mushrooms and cut bamboo shoots. Catching fish and hunting animals, delivering crops. Hardening calloused hands, broadening muscled backs.

The sacks of salt and rice, the cassavas, the sweat of hard labour, would they have generated in him the joys in life which seemed to have forever forsaken him?

There was one rural scene which frequently returned to Kien now. It was a symbol of paradise lost.

In the southern sector of the Central Highlands his units in Division 10 were making a rapid march from the Ngoan Muc pass, crossing Don Duong and Duc Trong, along Road 20 to Di Linh.

For the first time in his life he felt truly at home in the country. His heart surged with desire to quit the violence, killing and destruction and settle in the peaceful surrounds of that corner of the Highlands under a calm, peaceful sky. From that point in time he used that pastoral scene both as a measuring-stick for other rural areas, and as a symbol of what could have been.

One afternoon, Kien and his scout team were taking a jeep along Road 20 when they decided to turn off and look at a coffee plantation. There was a neatly kept gravel road running between densely planted crops leading to a nicely built house on stilts set well back from the road. They drove up carefully to the front of the pretty plantation house and parked the jeep, which had a machine-gun mounted just behind the driver and looked threatening. They politely climbed out and walked up the steps, preparing to ask for water and a place to rest.

The house was built entirely of timber and had the tall pointed roof favoured by the local hill tribes. The plantation owner greeted them courteously, taking them around the comfortable house, showing them his plough, his irrigation system and his power generator, which ran almost silently, in keeping with the peaceful scene.

Flowers were in bloom in gardens encircling the lovely house, and at the back there was a herb and vegetable patch for the kitchen.

The owner had come from the north with his wife and they now had a seven-year-old son. When Kien's team entered they came fully armed, wearing dirty, sweaty uniforms and it was clear the family were both embarrassed and nervous, although they tried not to show it.

They invited the soldiers to take a meal with them, but when they refused the couple did not press them. The owner spoke to them of plantation life while his wife went to the kitchen to brew coffee. He was surprisingly well educated, honest and very polite.

'We've not seen any guerrillas, let alone northern army regulars like yourselves. We just live a simple life, growing coffee, sugar cane and flowers,' he began. 'Thanks to Heaven, thanks to the land and the trees and Nature, and thanks to our own hands and energy and the money from our labour, we are self-sufficient. We don't need help from any government. If the President loses the fight, then let him be, even though you are Communists, on the other side. You're human too. You want peace and a calm life, families of your own, isn't that right, gentlemen?'

No one disputed what he said, although such honesty of expression was dangerous in those times. Fortunately none of them felt like handing out indoctrination lessons, so all day long the talk was of farming, labour, family happiness. The war was hardly mentioned again.

They drank excellent coffee, which added to the intimacy and warmth of the atmosphere. The wife looked on them with soft and friendly eyes, rarely speaking but feeling part of the group. The husband spoke in his frank way and treated the soldiers like friendly guests. They were soon feeling very much at home; even the occasional harsh knock of grenade or gun on the backs of their chairs as they moved positions did not break the peaceful spell. The scent of pine wood from newly hewn logs and fresh coffee brewing seemed to cast a spell over them, and they experienced a feeling of malaise, then sweet sorrow.

Inside the house they felt part of a small family circle. Outside the house was a broad circle of war.

Driving away from the plantation in the late afternoon, no one spoke for some minutes. Finally, Van, a University graduate in Economics and Planning, started to speak: 'There, you see. That's the way to live! What a peaceful, happy oasis. My lecturers with all their Marxist theories will pour in and ruin all this if we win. I'm horrified to think of what will happen to that couple, they'd soon learn what the new political order means.'

Another replied, 'Damn right they'll be unhappy. If we do win and return after the war I wonder if they'll still treat us kindly?'

'Not unless you come back as chairman of the new co-operative!' laughed Van.

But the thought had appalled them, and when Van spoke again he was sombre: 'That will be sad, really. I wonder if my own district will ever develop such lovely farms. Our landscape at Moc Chau is similar to this, yet we're always so poor.'

Kien didn't contribute anything to the conversation, but every word of it was etched in his memory and he recalled the visit several times in later years when down south. He had made half-hearted plans to go back and visit the plantation, but never seemed to have the time.

As for Van, Thanh, Tu and all the others who had been at the plantation with him on that special afternoon, they were long dead.

Of all the visitors, only he was alive to remember that visit. It had been little more than a wayside stop along the long road of conflict, yet it remained to this day a special memory, taking on increasing warmth and significance as the years went by.

He can't sleep. He thinks of Phuong, then of her apartment. No more than a room, really, identical to his. Both twenty square metres with red and white square tiles like a chess board, a stove in the corner inlaid with blue tiles, a window looking out into the street, through branches and fronds of a sheoak.

The furniture was almost identical, too. The other common characteristic was the atmosphere of loneliness, poverty, and loss. When he had first revisited Phuong's room after a ten-year absence he noticed the piano was missing. It had been her mother's precious property and had stood for many years against the window. 'I sold it,' she said simply, when he asked about it. 'It took up too much space. Anyway, I've not got the class to own something as lovely as a piano.'

It had been handed down from her father, a pianist who had died before the liberation of Hanoi from the French after the fall of Dien Bien Phu in 1954.

Phuong's mother had been a music teacher. She had retired when Phuong was sixteen, intending to concentrate on teaching her daughter classical music and the piano. She was totally different from her daughter. She was quietly spoken, thin and small. 'I'm afraid her guitar-playing and singing at all those parties and festivals are doing her no good at all, Kien. Please help me get her out of those habits,' she would say.

Phuong played the piano very well. She was a natural. But as she grew older she became lazier and lazier. 'The piano is too big, too solemn, too pretentious for these chaotic times. These days we've got to travel light,' she said.

Kien agreed. He preferred her singing, for she had such a sweet voice.

But her mother persisted, complaining to Kien, 'She's just like her father, a perfectionist. She's like a saint, or a fairy, she has their sort of perfection. But that is a delicate trait, and she must be protected. Her fine soul will be warped by the coarse style of life that's overtaking us; she will be destroyed unless she's given preferential treatment for her artistry. Yet she takes no notice of me whatsoever! She'd rather listen to your father. It frightens me that she is attracted by his frightful paintings and his disrespectful opinions. You understand, don't you?'

How could he understand, at sixteen? He hardly understood the words, let alone the sense of her mother's complaints. Yet many years later he recalled that Phuong's mother had predicted a few of the character changes in Phuong accurately. The girl's soul would become warped and twisted when she played in the mainstream of life, she had said. But then the war had come soon afterwards and there was little that could be said or done anyway.

He recalled Phuong's playing, when she was just fifteen. 'That's lovely, Phuong,' her mother had said one day. 'Now play a piece from Mozart, or the Moonlight Sonata.'

Phuong started scratchily and the music seemed lifeless. But as she bent to the task her hands flowed and she began to play passionate, inspired music. Her face flushed and her long hair fell across one side of her face but she was totally absorbed. The sonata spread its gossamer wings and embraced Kien as he drifted off into a pleasant reverie.

'It was then I knew she would be a troubled soul,' he thought to himself in later years. Towards the end of the third movement Phuong's cadence changed and a sombre, then depressing mood fell heavily over the room. Kien had openly wept for Phuong, in admiration and love. It was an ominous passion; he knew then their souls would be intertwined forever, through the last years of peace, through war, and in peace once more. He was helplessly drawn into the involvement. 'The passion will remain, and the sorrows too,' he thought.

Almost from that moment on, a harsh and cruel wind had blown across their world. In another fit of depression he sat through the morning, noon and evening recalling those few hours of so long ago.

On the table before him again, untouched, was his manuscript with the stories of so many of his dead heroes. His mind drifted from the beauty of the sonata through their wonderful final months in school until, catching the memory in a trap, he went over exactly what happened on the goods train during that air raid twenty years ago.

He had wanted to forget. It had been sheer coincidence that she had been in the carriage at all. It had been an unfortunate confluence of events leading to their presence together in a freight car at the Hang Co railway station when the bombers had struck. She had wanted to go as far as possible with him to the front, with no concern for the consequences.

There had been two raids. The first, shorter one, was when the train had been forced to stop. He had been knocked unconscious and flung onto an embankment. He was dazed. He hadn't been able to recognise which car he'd been in and when attempting to get back on the train he had missed his footing several times and got more injuries.

Now, he dimly recalled dreaming some ugly scenes, they came to him in contrasting black-and-white images, like negatives on film. Still bleeding and dizzy, he had scrambled onto the loco as the train started off again, and fallen into a deep sleep.

The authorities had then decided the raids had finished for the night and sent the train rolling south again, towards Vinh. It successfully defied the odds by crossing the Dragon Jaw Bridge in the early-morning light but then stopped at Thanh Hoa station to avoid an outgoing train. Kien was woken by a furious whistle piercing the air and the sound of a mechanic swearing angrily. He jumped down from the car without a word to anyone and looked in astonishment at what lay before him.

Thanh Hoa station was completely destroyed. Bomb craters gaped everywhere, opening their horrible mouths in the early morning sun. Their train was standing amidst the wreckage, its own freight cars heavily damaged. While Kien was taking this in some tough-looking louts jumped down in front of him. They were filthy and stank of alcohol and were swearing among themselves. They went into the ruins of the station and disappeared behind the wreckage.

He turned from them and looked back at the car they had been riding in, sensing this was where he and Phuong had been. He pushed the door open a little wider, letting more light in. There were sacks of rice piled along both sides of the car, and loose rice everywhere from burst bags. He peered into a dark corner, finding Phuong there, in a sort of twilight. She was leaning on some rice sacks, her legs folded, her arms covering her face as though asleep. Her long, tangled hair fell over her scratched shoulders.

He called her name, hoping it was not her. He stepped closer and his knees trembled at the sight. He almost collapsed as she looked up at him with a curiously unfamiliar and vacant look. Her blouse was wide open, all the buttons ripped from it, and her neck was covered in scratches. 'Phuong, Phuong, it's me, Kien,' he said gently. But she kept on staring, showing no sign of recognition. 'It's me!' he repeated. 'It's just coal-dust on my face, you can't recognise me. I had to jump on the locomotive after I got thrown out in the bombing. It's me, Kien,' he went on, not making much sense.

The black-and-white scenes from last night were confusing him; he held her shoulders between his hands. She bit her bruised lips, but no words came. She continued to stare, her eyes dull and eerie as though they wished to withdraw under Kien's questioning.

He too, was terrified. 'What's wrong with you? Don't be afraid, we'll get out. Nothing to be afraid of. But what happened to you?'

Phuong couldn't answer. Instead she shook her head, then looked down.

Kien began to close her blouse but there wasn't a single button left. Her bra had been snapped and a strap dangled loose. Her bare breasts were covered with a cold film of sweat. Kien felt himself unable to cope or to understand fully what had happened. He began to cry painful, salty tears which ran hotly down his cheeks, and he almost choked as he tried to comfort her with more words.

'Let's get out of here. Can you stand up?'

'Yes,' she said softly, her first word. Grasping his arm she stood up slowly, then staggered. He bent to prevent her falling. He saw that her slacks had been torn open, and blood ran down her inner thigh to her knees. She covered the blood with her arms, but more ran over her knees and and down her ankles.

'Why didn't you tell me you were injured? Sit down, sit down. We'll bandage it. Does it hurt?'

Phuong shook her head. No.

'Sit down. I'll make some bandages from my shirt.'

'No!' she cried, pushing him away. 'Can't you see? It's not a wound! It can't be bandaged!'

What was going on? He knew so little! Phuong lifted herself up and staggered towards the doorway. Although she was bleeding she showed no pain. Her clothes were in shreds and she was filthy.

She was preparing to jump down. Kien rushed to help her. As he did so a big, heavily muscled man wearing the top of a sailor's uniform vaulted into the doorway, blocking out the bright sunshine. Just then the train whistle shrieked, signalling departure.

'Where are you going?' the big man asked Phuong, standing in front of her and blocking Kien, whom he had ignored. 'The train's about to leave, you can't get off here!' he said roughly. It was an order.

'Here, I've got a pair of slacks for you. Got some water, food. Who's this guy?' He talked non-stop, expecting her to obey, and looking greedily at her open blouse.

'Yes,' she replied meekly. Neither she nor Kien appeared to understand what she had agreed to. She was at her wits' end and would agree to anything he said. Kien had never seen her as pale, or in fear before. 'Whaddyer want?' he then shouted at Kien. 'You know this is a military transport.' As he said it the train they'd been waiting for started to run past them. They would be leaving in a few seconds. The whole carriage shook as it passed.

'Nothin' for you to stay for,' he said. 'Her'n'me are friends.'

Kien shouted to Phuong, his voice angrily impotent, 'Let's go, go! The train's here, Phuong, let's go!'

The big man shoved Kien away from Phuong and calmly put his hands on her shoulders, grasping her firmly with his strong fingers.

'Don't tell me you're gettin' off. Is this filthy-looking bloke a friend of yours?' he asked her.

Phuong nodded, not looking at Kien.

'I see.'

The big man was about thirty years old. He had a large, square face, a moronic forehead, with a squat, fat nose and a thick chin, and he smiled with a cruel leer. He stared aggressively at them. Under the striped sailor's T-shirt his hard muscles bulged.

'I'd hoped you'd stay with me until Vinh. Otherwise I'll be bored,' he said, expecting sympathy. 'What's up? Don't you fancy a bit from me? That's not fair. I stopped those other turds lining up for you again. It's my turn now. I've not had my turn. I want some reward.'

Kien stepped up to him, imploring him. 'Let us go! We'll miss our train.'

Just then the carriage rocked and the earth all round them shook. A series of deafening explosions rent the air. There was shouting from the station. The sailor shouted, 'That's a bombing raid, and A-A guns. We'll all be killed!'

Kien grasped Phuong's wrist again and made to jump. Jets shrieked overhead and anti-aircraft artillery pounded at them. Panic broke out, with people rushing all round the train and the station.

The sailor had calmed down a little. 'Don't be scared,' he said with authority. 'They're attacking the Dragon Jaw Bridge. Stay here with me, darling. We'll sleep and eat well in here. As for you, piss off if you're scared. Go on, piss off!' he shouted at Kien.

Kien tried once more to get Phuong to leave but the big man's hand held her firmly.

'If you're scared, get out. There's a fucking war on, y'know. If we have to die, then let's die. Isn't that right, darlin'? Stay here with me. Have pity on me, darlin'. With you gone the rest of the trip's going to be ratshit,' he shouted directly to her, over the roar of the battle.

Another squadron of American jets started to descend upon them. Kien screamed, 'Let her go, leave her alone, damn you!'

Frustrated, he rushed at the big man, but the sailor had no trouble in pushing him away. Phuong stared at the two men, seemingly not taking anything of this in, even the sounds of the bombing and the A-A fire. She seemed in the sailor's spell. She would not move towards Kien, or the door.

As Kien was picking himself off the floor the sailor leaned out of the door. 'Shit! They're targeting the train now. Come on little darlin', out we go!'

Kien had fallen on something heavy, cold and flat. In his anger – and fear – he tried to get up, but fell back again, this time on top of the object. The sailor was dragging Phuong to the door to escape. A-A guns banged like huge drums, sub-machine-guns chattered and the jets screamed overhead.

He left the door and came back to Kien, putting out his hand to pull him up. 'Be quick. What the hell are you doin'? We've got to get to the shelter. Listen, I was only going to screw her until Vinh. You could have had her back after that. Hell, you're really soft. A little bourgeois softie, aren't you?'

Kien got up, still holding the object, an iron bar, behind him. As he stood, the sailor stumbled, shouting as he fell.

The shout was drowned out by the screaming of a diving jet. Kien lifted the bar then brought it down with a crack on the sailor's arm. As he was trying to get clear the sailor howled with pain. Kien went for him again, but the sailor shoved him away, and the movement caught Phuong's attention. Kien struck again. Crack! The sailor whimpered with pain.

Phuong grabbed Kien's wrist, yelling at him, but her voice was drowned out by the jets. Kien swung round, angry she should try to stop the attack; he was infuriated, surging with hatred and his face became deformed as he grabbed her and shouted, 'Get away, you whore!'

Phuong's move had given the sailor a breathing-space and he kicked out at Kien, delivering an incredible blow to the groin, which forced Kien to double up, and cry in agony. But he quickly recovered and attacked again, bashing ferociously at the man's head, drawing blood that flowed as slippery as soap across him. The sailor didn't move again. Kien, his hands bloodied, looked up as one of the jets strafed the carriage, ripping open the roof, blasting open their little hell.

Phuong, now kneeling near the door, had the look of a madwoman. 'Don't touch me!' she screamed as he came over, the sailor's blood dripping from his hands.

He wiped the blood on his trousers. 'Stand up. We're going,' he said calmly and quietly.

He flung the door open wide, looked up into the sky and, seeing no aircraft, bent down and lifted her up, then dropped her outside. 'Let me go,' she shouted angrily. But she was already down and he was beside her.

The station had been razed, like a demolition site. Kien took hold of Phuong's wrist and firmly led her over bent rail tracks and debris towards a path out.

They had not gone far when Kien dropped to the earth and pulled Phuong with him. 'Down!' he shouted, as a jet screamed in on a long dive, strafing the train. And among the tracer bullets he could detect something else; a silver napalm canister, glittering in the sunlight, its long shiny sides giving off a gleam, as it came in at horrifying speed. Then another, and another. They hit the engine and the station almost soundlessly. Kien saw a black cloud, then the air cracked like broken glass and the earth seemed to be heaving under them, then falling again. Then another raid, another bomb. Explosions punched into their faces and several times Kien was certain these were his last moments. Pressure waves shuddered through them as they lay there, helpless to defend themselves. Kien grasped Phuong's hand and their cold, quivering fingers intermingled.

Swiftly, as though coming to her senses, Phuong rolled clear then jumped up and ran for the station. A break in the bombing allowed her to get clear of the lines safely, with Kien in hot pursuit. A breeze was carrying locomotive smoke into their faces. When the smoke cleared they saw the up-line train for Hanoi was still intact, and beginning to make a run for it away from the station, a locomotive at each end, one pulling, one pushing. In the foreground their own train, completely destroyed, was just a pile of smoking ashes.

'Phuong!' he shouted, taking hold of her.

She turned to him, her eyes burning with pain and bitterness. A pent-up scream began to surface, but no sound came.

The train sped up, heading north, but as it did so four A-A batteries started firing and Kien knew instinctively the jets were back. Phuong used the chance to rip herself clear of him and she ran off once again. And once again he ran her down, trapping her and deliberately landing on top of her to keep her pinned down.

Bomb after bomb exploded, darkening the day. One series behind them, one in front of them and one right on target, hitting the rear locomotive – a direct hit. It blew up with tremendous force and for a long time it rained burning charcoal and hot water. Another jet emerged from the cloudless sky and emptied its cannon into the railcars, setting most of them on fire. The next one was for them, thought Kien, already astounded they could have lived so long, through two bombing raids.

Kien hugged Phuong closely, despite her struggles. She fought crazily, like a woman possessed, and as the raid continued he lost his temper, pressing into the back of her neck and holding her in an armlock. Then he embedded his ten fingers deeply into the flesh of her shoulder to keep her down. They were both terrified now, numb, and gasping, like animals wrestling.

Their frenzied fighting lasted only a few seconds more; then one last bomb came. It was the explosion to end all explosions that day. With the rear locomotive already blasted away the jets now attacked the centre of the train. The last bomb scored a direct hit, lifting the railcars high into the air and splitting the train in two. Half the train, pulled by the one remaining loco, kept moving north. The second half of the train, which had already lost its rear loco, now lost its entrails.

During the explosions Kien wondered which of the freight cars the sailor's body was in. Had he been incinerated by napalm? Or just ripped to pieces by the strafing?

Who cared? No one had any time for others at times like these, with an immense roaring enveloping them, and thick white smoke and fire. There was little charity or mercy in moments like these.

Unsteadily, Kien helped Phuong to stand, surprising himself with his remaining strength. He slung her onto his back and began clumping away from the heat of the burning ruins. He put her down and they leaned on each other to grope their way through more thick smoke near what remained of the station building. There were cries for help from various directions but at first they saw only corpses.

The bodies lay scattered all round. Then some people emerged, running mindlessly, falling into more debris. Kien began stepping through the bodies as though it were an everyday event for him. This was his new-found strength, to stay cool under fire. No one really knew: they could suspect, but would never really know until they faced the real test. Scores of bodies lay in all imaginable twisted positions; there was nothing to scream or take fright about. To him, in his hardened state, it seemed perfectly normal.

He was about to put Phuong down for a rest when he spotted a bicycle lying by the roadside. As he picked it up he noticed it was an old but top-quality Phoenix, in remarkably good condition. Astonishingly, it had good tyres, chain, pedals, even brakes and a bell. A black sack, nearly full, hung from the handlebars. Kien guessed the bike's owner was one of the corpses lying nearby on his back or his belly, burnt and stripped naked by napalm.

Kien got on and tried the bell. A light refined tinkling sounded, the only elegant noise in the air now crackling with frying flesh and little obscene popping noises. Then he rode it slowly for a test. Phuong, almost catatonic the whole time, uttered not a word. When he stopped beside her she offered no resistance, slipping onto the bike's rear carrier seat as skilfully as she'd done in her schooldays when they'd ridden to school together.

Kien zig-zagged through burning houses and wrecked buildings, fallen trees and power lines. There were bomb craters right down the middle of the road so every now and then he had to stop and walk the bike through. Phuong sat silently on the back all through the strange journey.

As the station receded the settled, steady pedalling action suddenly reminded him that only twelve hours earlier he'd been giving Phuong a ride in a stolen cyclo pedicab. Surely that had been one of the most dramatic entrances imaginable into the theatre of war.

There was another raid, more screams from American jets, but this time far away, down the valley.

He heard distant sirens echoing, but they were safe now, well away from the railway station and the road was clearer. Kien stopped by an A-shaped air-raid shelter along the side of the road. The earth began to rumble again and instantly the anti-aircraft guns in Ham Rong opened up.

Kien laid the bicycle down on the ground, then helped Phuong to the shelter. All round him people were stoically going about their everyday lives. Few bothered with the shelters, public or individual. The bombs were too far away. The people paid no attention to possible threats up in the bright sunny sky, or to Kien and Phuong. These were the new times. Two young people, bruised and bleeding, filthy from smoke and coal, their clothes ripped and in disarray, attracted no special attention.

An old man with a walking-stick came along. He carried a small bag made from braided bulrush leaves, and held his hand out begging for rice. Kien shook his head in disbelief that anyone would approach him looking as he did. The old man was not deterred. He prattled on, saying he had been living in a house near a station but that was now destroyed. His relatives and his friends were dead. Everything was burnt. He had no house, no food, no relatives. Why heaven had allowed him to live he would never understand. He wondered aloud if he could walk all the way to a distant relative's place. He said everyone was now certain to die. Kien just listened to him silently, as did Phuong. The old man, having spoken his piece, moved on, starting another identical speech, this time to an unseen audience.

Kien and Phuong sat in the shelter, motionless. They had no words, for they had no thoughts. They paid no attention to the distant aircraft, or to those evacuating the hamlet around them, carrying children and belongings, and their wounded. Miserable, pitiful scenes surrounded them.

They seemed determined not to speak to each other, nor even look at each other. They maintained their silent rage; not even their terrible thirst or their hunger intruded.

In later years Kien experienced several similar identical moments, long periods of withdrawal. Like the dead, one felt no fear, no enthusiasm, no joy, no sadness, no feelings for anything. No concerns and no hopes. One was totally devoid of feeling, and had no regard for the clever or the stupid, the brave or the cowardly, commanders or privates, friend or foe, life or death, happiness or sadness. It was all the same; it amounted to nothing.

A little later something else quite extraordinary occurred. A small, middle-aged man with a very thin face, carrying a fat woman on his back, stopped in front of them. The woman, whose legs were bandaged, was asleep.

Kien's bicycle had attracted the man's attention. He grew excited, asking repeatedly if they wanted to sell the bike. Phuong and Kien, both still in shock, failed to reply. All three of them were staring at the bike, as the woman on the man's back slept blissfully on.

The man's foot went out and deftly, using his toes, he lifted the bike up and carefully transferred the sleeping woman onto the back carrier seat. As the man took the wobbling bicycle to lean it against a shelter the woman moaned and held on to him.

He freed himself and returned, lifted the sack from the bicycle and placed it beside Phuong, then began searching for money in his pockets. When he found some banknotes he fished them out, counted a certain amount, then placed them on the top of the sack.

He muttered a few words in the local dialect, swung onto the seat of the bike, and rode off with the fat woman still asleep. This astonishing, simple exchange had all taken less than a minute, yet the macabre humour of it all endured for years in Kien's memories of war.

So, the man had bought the bicycle, whose real owner was a napalmed corpse near the station. Bombs were still dropping, aircraft were still roaring in the distant sky and A-A fire cracked loudly on this hot, almost suffocatingly hot day. And amid all this one of the strangest transactions had taken place. It snapped them from their silence.

Kien absently pocketed the banknotes, then picked up the sack and opened it. It contained dry rations called BA70, a torch, a water canister, a hammock and a K59 pistol. Phuong quickly looked at it from under thick lashes. Kien said, 'Let's eat something. We've got water, too.'

'Eat, maybe,' she said listlessly.

Kien opened the canister, took a sip, then passed it to her. The bag of dry food also contained green tea and sugar and some yellow-coloured cake, which had a delicious taste.

Phuong sat quietly, eating casually as though nothing had happened. Kien would like to have seen her eating with more appreciation. After all, the food had been snatched from the jaws of blood and death.

Perhaps it wasn't necessary to have such a vivid imagination, to be concerned at the source of the food and the entire circumstances they found themselves in. Kien supposed nothing was terribly wrong with eating and drinking normally to help recover after such a catastrophe. But on the other hand, watching how easily she ate and drank, he recognised that there was in Phuong, besides hunger and thirst, an unusual reserve of strength and resilience.

He ate almost nothing himself, studying her as she ate. Then he began to realise just how badly injured she was. His own clothes were dirty and torn but Phuong's clothes were almost in shreds. Through the tatters her normally white skin was bruised, scratched and bleeding. Her face was black with smoke, her lips were swollen and her eyes were flat and sullen. A small trickle of blood continued to run down the inside of one leg, though the bleeding was greatly reduced. When she uncrossed her legs to change position and stretch her legs on the grass he noticed more blood on a knee. This reminded him: this wasn't blood from a wound. It came from those tumultuous hours in the railcars.

Phuong ate only half her cake. 'Finish it, Phuong,' Kien said, 'we'll need all the energy we can muster to get back to Hanoi.'

But she sat on, shaking her head and staring. He was about to suggest she wipe the blood away, but decided not to. He said quietly: 'Let's go to that hamlet over there. You need a place to lie down. When we've recovered we'll find our way home.'

But she didn't even raise her eyes.

Kien noticed a small field on the other side of the road. Some bushes grew there, possibly a kitchen garden, for behind it were some small thatched houses. 'Come on, it's not far. Can you walk it?'

Phuong nodded sullenly.

Kien unbuttoned his shirt. 'Put this on, at least.'

She looked across at him and said sharply, 'At least! At least what? Do I look that horrible? Keep your shirt. Don't worry about me any more. Your duty is to catch up with your unit. Don't worry yourself about where I go next.'

Kien stopped unbuttoning his shirt. Embarrassed, he tried to explain himself: 'You misunderstand me. If we don't care for each other who's going to care? As far as what's happened, forget it, please. As far as I'm concerned . . .'

She interrupted sharply. 'If you want to bury a memory then just don't mention it. Secondly, you'd better ensure that no one else talks about certain memories, either.'

He had never seen her as cold and calculating as this.

'Of course,' he said, giving her his hand. 'Now, let's go.'

'Yes,' she sighed, giving him her hand to pull herself up.

They walked hand-in-hand, their shadows foreshortened by the overhead sun. The mid-afternoon heat was heavy on their backs. They looked like two very lonely souls drying themselves in the sun. The few passers-by could not avoid looking at them, especially at Phuong. Such a lovely young girl, but so dirty and tattered, and strangely casual.

'What a nice couple, look!' someone said, trying to lift their spirits.

They crossed the road and took a narrow dirt path which led

to the kitchen garden they had seen. But the garden was empty and dried-up, the earth pitted with craters from bomb shrapnel. The hot wind blew across them languidly, adding to the desolation. Perhaps no one lived there now. The thatched houses which Kien had seen from far away had led him to identify it as a small village or hamlet, but in reality the buildings were an abandoned primary school, far from any village.

Trenches had been cut across the yard and wild grass grew between them. The classrooms now looked like artillery entrenchments, covered with thick layers of earth. Phuong and Kien went into one of the former classrooms where a few desks and broken benches remained. The teacher's desk was empty, the blackboard had dropped to the floor and in the middle of the room was a heap of ashes, the remnants of a camp-fire which had been fuelled by wood from desks and chairs. The roof was ruined. Inside it was almost as light as out in the yard.

The scene of devastation tightened Kien's heart. 'Look at this,' he said to Phuong. 'How could anyone destroy a school? Don't they respect life any more?'

'Maybe it was our soldiers,' she replied. 'Soldiers do this sort of thing. War does this, war smashes and destroys.'

In her later life that tone would get her into some trouble, but Kien was so depressed he hardly noticed the cynicism.

It occurred to him that she was by now suffering from shock, some nervous disorder. He prepared a place for her to lie down. At least here they would not be disturbed by authorities wanting to question them and check their story. In addition there were enough bits and pieces here to make a bed and shelter.

'Try to get some sleep, darling,' he said.

She sat down beside him. 'You'll sleep too?' she asked.

'Yes.'

'Why don't you sling the hammock?'

'Not a good idea. Belongs to a dead person.'

'So what! Why should that bother you?'

'Enough. Don't talk like that.'

'But if you don't sling the hammock where will you sleep? You'll feel horrible lying next to me,' she said sarcastically.

Kien shook his head mechanically.

She lay down, putting her hands under her head, and faced up, making room for Kien to lie beside her. But Kien remained immobile.

'I wish there were some water somewhere near here so I could bathe,' she whispered.

'Let me check. You sleep,' he said.

'Don't go. Stay with me. I talk just to talk. I wish that I could look nicer before we say goodbye and we sleep next to each other for the last time. But then again even if I do bathe, even if I peel my entire skin away, I'll be just as unclean. That's destiny. Too bad.'

Kien looked at her. 'You're saying some rather funny things. What's all this talk about "last time" and "goodbye"?'

'Let it go. I meant we may not see each other again, but that prediction may or may not be true. I'm just making conversation,' she said.

'There are things we must ensure come true, such as my survival and return. This isn't home, it's a battlefield, it's war. We have to have confidence in ourselves,' he said.

Phuong talked on dreamily, her attitude gloomy and pessimistic. 'We were born pure and innocent. Look how innocent we are now,' she mumbled. He could hardly miss the allusion to their new status as multiple rape victim and brutal murderer. 'Don't worry about tomorrow,' she droned on. 'Don't torture yourself, what's the point? You go your way, I'll go mine. We had such a beautiful life. You and me, my love for you, your love for me. My mother and your dad, and I would have been your wife, no doubt. That was in the past. Now we have a new future, a new fate. We had no choice in the new circumstances, it was an unlucky coincidence. Now I'm like this, you go your way, I'll go mine.'

She didn't finish her semi-delirious ramblings. Her head dropped back and she fell asleep. Kien sat staring at her.

Before his eyes she had metamorphosed. Once pure and beautiful, she had spoken like a callous, uncaring pessimist, ready to bury anything tender in their past. Finally, he stroked her, lifting her head and removing her shredded blouse, replacing it with his shirt. He wiped her neck and face and her bruised body. Then he gently removed her silk slacks and wiped the streaks of blood from her thighs, trembling as he looked at the bruises.

He placed his own trousers over her legs, then slung his hammock close to her, climbed in and fell into a deep sleep.

When he awoke in the late afternoon she was gone.

Under his head, like a pillow, he found his own trousers and shirt. The smell of cigarette smoke hung in the air and there were fresh cigarette-ends on the floor, near her torn clothes.

Kien dressed, put the pistol from the sack in his belt, and began searching for her, without calling her name. In some of the other classrooms he noticed for the first time other soldiers, also sitting in hammocks. Others were sitting, playing cards.

He followed a dirt track to the garden plot they'd seen earlier, but she wasn't there. He went into the overgrown garden but after pushing through shrubs and past some trees it was obvious to him she was not there either. Two trucks, well camouflaged, were parked nearby, under a stand of trees. He approached them with apprehension, calling her name, but got no reply. A little further on he came to a marsh, with very clear water. On the far bank of the marsh was an asphalt road. It looked like Highway One, to Hanoi. He stared at the road for a while then started slowly back to the schoolroom. He'd even forgotten her need to bathe in the fresh, clear water.

As he approached he felt renewed hope that she had returned while he searched, but once inside the classroom he found no sign of her. Just swarms of mosquitoes.

He threw himself dejectedly back into the hammock, but almost in the same movement sprang out again, heading towards the soldiers' room.

Hammocks. Knapsacks. Pistols. They were all military officers. Some were lying down, others were playing cards. He hesitated a little before asking them about Phuong. A pock-marked card-player sitting on a tarpaulin looked up at Kien thoughtfully. 'Your girlfriend? Yeah. Very nice little thing. Nicely spoken, very beautiful. Slim neck, pale skin, nice face, and what a charming walk. A feast for the eyes. That her?'

'Yes, commander, that's her.'

'She was bathing over in the marsh when I saw her. Nice!' he said.

Kien was shocked.

'Why so shocked? Of course in the marsh, where else is there any water round here? But she finished long ago. Haven't you seen her since then?' he asked.

A loud voice from the other side of the room chimed in. 'Now, how could he meet her? She's over screwing the driver at Company 8, right?' The voice belonged to a large bare-chested officer, built like a wrestler.

'Yes, but . . .' Kien stammered.

'But what? I can see you're a spoiled little bourgeois, but remember you're a soldier too. Don't get sentimental, forget that emotional garbage,' he said gruffly.

Kien was embarrassed and began to stammer.

'But what?' the wrestler said, standing up, showing he was quite tall. 'What kind of bloody soldier are you? Are you love-sick? Are you from the anti-aircraft unit over at Dragon Jaw Bridge? Or are you a deserter?' he said accusingly.

The commander interrupted. 'Don't bully him, Phuc. As for you, soldier, there's nothing to worry about. If she's with the drivers it doesn't really matter. They're hidden in their trucks by the marsh over there. Those two GAZ 57s belonging to Company 8, by the old tree.'

'That's odd, I just passed there and didn't see her,' said Kien recovering a bit.

The wrestler laughed. 'If they were doing her over in the back of the truck you wouldn't have seen her. She's pretty game. Is she a city slicker?'

Kien hardly heard him. 'But I called her. No answer.'

'She didn't reply? Well, fuck me, fancy that!' he said with heavy irony. 'If I were you I'd slap her wrist for not replying. Shit, she looked good, mate. But that sort of whore, they're always running off. I wouldn't fuck her if it was free.'

Kien, now at breaking point, moved in and punched the wrestler Phuc heavily on the jaw. In the same action he stepped back sharply and drew his pistol, cocked it and fingered the trigger, aiming it directly into Phuc's big chest.

The card-players stopped playing, looking up in silence.

'You're an arsehole as well as an idiot,' Kien said to him. But he didn't fire. He simply turned and walked away, leaving them in silence. No one ran after him. No one called him. The gamblers continued their game as if nothing had happened.

Kien walked dizzily out of the schoolyard, his head bent, not caring where he was heading. Suddenly, in front of him, were the two black GA trucks. He hadn't wanted to see her in there, but his feet took him forward. Stealthily he crept up and looked into the cabin of the first one, then into the back. There was no one at all in the first truck.

He crept up on the second, lifting himself cautiously up to the cabin, but that was also empty. He looked at the covered tray behind the cabin, drawing his pistol as he approached it. He pushed the canvas aside and was hit by a stink of alcohol, food and sweat, and the sound of snoring. Four men in shorts and T-shirts were asleep, snoring and mumbling, their legs intermingled. They had left their transistor radio on, playing softly. No Phuong.

Kien jumped down, wanting to vomit and wanting to put as much distance between himself and the trucks as possible. Did he believe that shithead wrestler? Had she really jumped in with those four? His head was buzzing, driving him to distraction. The droning grew louder and he realised something else was wrong. Across the sky went another squadron of jet fighters, their presence drawing A-A fire, which was now going non-stop. Birds flew away noisily as the big iron birds above started swooping in for another round of bombing, flying in a hand-shaped formation over the A-A batteries, dropping their bombs. Though far from the area he was still able to imagine the terrible destruction and he dropped to the ground in protective cover. As he did so two things happened: a ring of fire lifted on the horizon in front of him and the shock waves lit the night, turning dusk into day for a few seconds, revealing Phuong, bathing.

She was to his left and only ten paces from him, kneeling on a smooth rock at the water's edge. Phuong was totally naked, her pale body very clear. Behind her was a grassy plot and some bushes. She faced the clear water of the lake.

Slowly, she looked up at the rain of bombs, the fire from the explosions and the thick smoke billowing up. Then she delicately stepped in a little deeper and continued bathing.

Phuong showed no interest, and no fear. Kneeling again, she scooped water into a helmet then poured it over her shoulders. She tipped her head back, raised both arms, and doused herself again.

Finally, she stood upright again to rinse and rearrange her long hair, while looking calmly at the retreating American aircraft.

She turned gracefully and walked to the bank, not troubling to see if anyone watched her. She picked up a dark green towel from the grass and began to dry herself. Her breasts shook a little as she dried her arms and shoulders. Her small waist and her pale flat stomach made the dark hair between her thighs look like a piece of velvet. She had beautiful long legs with unblemished milky skin.

Kien watched her every movement, looked over every inch of her skin, like a voyeur hypnotised by the scene.

Phuong set about dressing, wiggling into her bra and panties, then picking up her clothes. She seemed to be showing off to an unseen audience, displaying herself and her new attitudes with a boldness Kien found himself unable to come to terms with. She seemed to be welcoming her new lifestyle, embracing it with a calm, carefree approach. From being a pure, sweet and simple girl she was now a hardened experienced woman, indifferent to vulnerable emotions. To Kien she seemed to be walking away from his life, from herself, from her past and her country, without the slightest regret.

Perhaps it was all his fault. Perhaps one day she would forgive him for dragging her into this fiasco in which she had been gang-raped by thugs during an air raid, then held by force. And finally had to watch him beating a man's head in before her eyes. Perhaps she would forgive him. That was in her character.

But since the train? With the driver? Was all that true? Could he ever forgive her, that was the question. Probably not.

Kien lay there motionless. Far away he could see smoke rising from the bombing raid. The air was heavy and still and the smoke rose gently, signalling the end of the worst day of his life. He raised his pistol slowly, first looking down the barrel, then raising it slowly to his head, his finger on the trigger. Why did people claim that life was always better than death? It wasn't so. He pondered then why he was trembling now, about to take his own life, when he had not hesitated to take the life of another. He moved the pistol around to the point of his nose, his finger still on the trigger. He closed his eyes, but hesitated. He seemed to hear a distant voice calling his name, a voice from far, far away, a sad voice, as though it were calling across water. 'Kiiieeennn?' it called.

Then he heard it again. Startled, he opened his eyes and lowered the pistol, letting it drop on the grass.

She was running towards him, calling for him. He kicked the pistol into the water as she approached and it splashed like a fish jumping for an insect.

But she had not seen him. She was still searching, making her own path running through the bushes around the lake. In the dark she missed him, running within a few steps of him, calling.

He waited until she was well past, then left, walking away from the school, towards Highway One. It was getting dark by the time he reached the other side of the marsh; by then a deep mist had settled over it, reducing visibility. He groped his way over the last short distance to the road and headed for the hamlet to the north.

Even nearing town he could hear Phuong's faint voice calling his name. He imagined it was the same call he'd heard earlier, echoing somehow through the darkness.

That same evening Kien presented himself to the provincial military headquarters, telling them he'd survived the bombing raids on the station. On the following day he was placed in a newly formed platoon and marched into Nong Cong, to a liaison point. From then on he had no news at all of Phuong until the war ended nearly eleven years later.

Well, that was not quite true. He had received one letter when he was stationed by the Dac Bo La river. He was with his scout platoon enjoying the relative quiet of the post-Paris Agreement.

The letter didn't come from the North, but from Division 2 which was in the battle zone area Interzone 5. It read:

My name is Ky, but they call me 'The Beehive', the one with a pock-marked face. I am now an assistant investigator to Mr Chon. When Division 2 attacked Kontum the scouts from your regiment came to help us. Perhaps you recall that well, but if you don't it doesn't matter. But I recognised you immediately, and if I had reminded you then, you would have recognised me immediately. But the few times I did come face to face with you during that campaign I kept silent because the fighting was so fierce that it commanded our whole attention. I also hesitated because I would have reminded you of something that happened so long ago. It was in the past and it would have made you unhappy and affected your fighting spirit. But the more I observed you the more I realised you are an experienced senior scout, and would easily have been able to cope.

Now it is quiet, we can take a moment to look back. So, when I got back to the Delta, I decided to immediately write to you. Kien, do you remember the ruined and abandoned school near Thanh Hoa?

Kien put the letter down in amazement. It was not from the bare-chested officer who'd called Phuong a whore, but the officer with a pock-marked face, who'd been in the school.

After the quarrel with you we were rather uneasy. Even though we were already officers, we were still young and innocent, and didn't know how to behave properly. We felt terribly bad about what we'd said to you and wanted to run after you to console you, but you had a drawn pistol and we thought better of it.

Some time later, but not long after you had left, the young girl came to us looking for you and calling out your name, asking if we'd seen you. What we told her made her more anxious.

She kept on looking until she was exhausted. It was hard for me to persuade her to return to the classroom because you'd already gone. We had made a very big mistake in kidding you about what she did and we saw that hurt you. Contrary to what we'd told you, your girlfriend was not like that at all. She was charming and kind, and beautiful in appearance, she was very much in love with you.

We stayed in the school for another day. She was still there, waiting for you, when we left. We offered to take her as far as the Pine Forest where trustworthy drivers could give her a lift back to Hanoi, but she refused. She said she would continue south, perhaps to join the volunteer Youth Brigade. She was so young, so brave, so beautiful, even when she was sad.

We couldn't delay. Our unit left the next evening, with her still in the empty school. So, after seven years of fierce fighting I still recall the incident, and easily recognised you. And that's why I am writing to you now. If you've seen her already, before receiving this letter, that is excellent. Otherwise, I hope my letter will have some good effect. When the war is over and hopes of meeting former friends are realised, find her, Kien, if you are still alive.

The letter warmed Kien's heart, consoling and cheering him. He began to hope for something like a miracle, for some strand from his past to follow into his new post-war life. He might have something wonderful to return to, after all.

There would be a miracle, he had written. A miracle that would allow people to emerge unchanged from the war. So, despite the horrors of war, despite the cruelties, the humiliations, despite all the ridiculous prejudices and dogma which pervaded everyone's life, his Phuong would remain young forever. She would be untainted by war. She would be forever beautiful. No one would ever come close to her beauty. She was as a green meadow after spring rains, as fragrant as the flowers in bloom waving against the horizon and waves of fresh grass rustling. She was passionate, untamed, magnetic, with that same miraculous and unfathomable beauty, a beauty that made the heart ache; a vulnerable, innocent beauty forever on the brink of the abyss of destruction. That would be his miracle; Phuong would be untouched, unchanged.

Several years later, on a night when he was deep in desperation, Kien dreamed that his life had been transformed into a river stretching before him. He saw himself floating towards his death. Then at the very last moment, when he was about to go over the edge, he heard Phuong's call echoing from that bitter dusk of the marsh near the school. It was the final call of his first love. Though they hadn't had a happy life together, or moved towards a glowing future, their first love had not been in vain. They were back there in the past together, and nothing could change or rob them of that.

Fate waited to take them from the terrible present back to the happy days of the past.

Spreading before him are the past forty years. Memories, numerous memories wave to him and urge him to march forever along the road of the past. The past without end, a never-ending story of loyalty, friendship, brotherhood, comradeship and humanity.

Forever he would ache with longing to follow that shining light from the horizons of his past, to return to those moments of the first sparks of war, the glimmerings of his first adventures and the light of love shining from deep in his childhood.

When the writer left his apartment, he told no one. Frankly, no one paid any attention because he often disappeared for a week, sometimes a month. This time maybe he would disappear for a year, or for ever. It wouldn't be unusual, or cause problems either.

Those who know how to be totally free and make their own opportunities would realise that. They can change direction at will, like a gust of wind.

The day he departed, he left his door wide open. At dawn, the wind blew through his curtained window, letting drizzle into the room, wetting his furniture. Ashes blew from the stove, papers from his table, from the bookcase and from a heap of pages in the corner.

The mute woman had obviously stayed the night, and found herself alone in his bed. Silently, she tidied the messy room. She gathered all the sheets of paper and piled them on top of the manuscripts, then carted the whole stack of them up into her attic quarters.

She had no idea why or how he had left, or where he had gone. But as she couldn't speak she couldn't ask anyone. She could only ponder his departure, and her loneliness in not knowing weighed even more heavily than her handicap.

She had forgotten that he'd once decided to throw the lot into the fire. She had kept the pages, not burned them. People said of her that she was like a lost-property guardian, keeping all those messy papers.

As for me, I thought that her silent waiting for our neighbourhood writer to reappear was something akin to the loyalty of a reader towards a beloved masterpiece. If this was so, then at least the writer's unpublished work had the whole-hearted admiration of its only reader.

Later, by chance, I got the entire manuscript from her. I don't know why I should have believed her silent demand that I should patiently and carefully read everything, paragraph after paragraph. Certainly, I started. Just out of curiosity you understand.

Who was that character everybody in the street had considered so strange and hard to figure out? A haunted soul, they said. A legacy of the past. An alcoholic drinking to repent, to bury his secrets and his sins. A man who had been loved and liked by women, but really a spiritual hermaphrodite. The last true bourgeois of the district, rebellious, extremist but also timid and hesitant. So people said. But they were still not certain.

It was during this period that I was attracted by this eccentric character. That's why I tried reading his long stories, although it was difficult.

At first I tried to rearrange the manuscript pages into chronological order, to make the manuscript read like the sort of book I was familiar with. But it was useless. There was no chronological order at all. Any page seemed like the first, any page could have been the last. Even if the manuscript had been numbered, even if no pages had been burned, or moth-eaten, or withheld by the author, if by chance they were all there, this novel would still be a work created by turbulent, even manic inspirations.

One became immersed in each sequence, each page. Sometimes the descriptions were compelling. The long-forgotten name of a once-familiar battlefield moved me. The close-up fighting, the small details of the soldiers' lives. The images of former colleagues appearing for just a moment, yet so clearly. The flow of the story continually changed. From beginning to end the novel consisted of blocks of images. A certain cluster of events, then disruptions, some event wiped off the page as if it had fallen into a hole in time. Many would say this was a disruption of the plot, a disconnection, a loss of perspective. They'd say this style proved the writer's inherent weakness: his spirit was willing but his flesh wasn't.

The very same scout platoon who on page one killed with

frightening efficiency and were so skilled in battle were, on the next page, the dullest, clumsiest deadbeats imaginable. The author even turned some of them into ghosts, sorrowfully making them appear here and there, in the jungles, in dark corners, in dreams and nightmares. All of the scouts, one way or another, were killed. But then you read of them dragging themselves along the streets, living hand-to-mouth lives as city-dwellers in the post-war years.

And at the end of the day, just like the author, those ragged men became confident and happy, recalling their paradise years of long ago, remembering the smart, pretty girlfriends they'd had, recalling their naive and innocent confidence before the war. It was sad; although they had been excellent lovers, they were destined to be forever lonely. They had lost not only the capacity to live happily with others but also the capacity to be in love. The ghosts of the war haunted them and permeated their deteriorating lives.

As for the author, although he wrote 'I', who *was* he in that scout platoon? Was he any of those ghosts, or of those remains dug up in the jungle?

Was he among those kids from decent families who in fighting a war lost touch with the sources of culture? Those free spirits who were now full of prejudice?

All I knew was that the author had written because he had to write, not because he had to publish. He had to think on paper. Then of all things, he delivered everything to a lonely, mute woman, who could easily have destroyed his turbulent revelations.

Gradually, I permitted myself to read the story taking a more casual approach. I worked through the mountain of pages, one after the other, regardless of whether it seemed to be in sequence, or whether it was just a letter from his diary, or a draft of an article. Mixed among the pages I found musical scores, curriculum vitae, award certificates, a pack of cards, torn and worn and dirty, and certificates confirming that he had been wounded several times.

That relaxed reading greatly helped my understanding of him. Now, before my eyes the abandoned novel by our writer took on another form, in harmony with th : reality it described.

I've copied almost everything, all the pages I acquired by chance from the woman. I've removed only a few which were completely illegible and some other mischievous notes and letters which were incomprehensible to a third person. I simply played the role of the Rubik cube player, arranging the order.

But while copying the pages and re-reading them I was astounded to recognise that inside his story were ideas and feelings and even situations of mine. It seemed that by some coincidence of words and plot my own life and the author's had unexpectedly become entwined, enmeshed in each other. Slowly I began to realise that my earlier suspicions were true; I had known him during the war.

Yes, he was terribly changed, but I still recognised him. He was tall and slim, but not good-looking. He was stern, with wild eyes. His skin was grey, covered with small scars, brown from the sun and the gunpowder burns. His lips were tight. On his left cheek there was a deep crease. We had met each other one day along the road to war. We'd dragged ourselves through the red dust, through the mud, carrying sub-machine-guns on our shoulders, or packs on our backs. Bare-footed, on occasions. And both he and I, like the other ordinary soldiers of the war, shared one fate. We had shared all the vicissitudes, the defeats and victories, the happiness and suffering, the losses and gains. But each of us had been crushed by the war in a different way.

Each of us carried in his heart a separate war which in many ways was totally different, despite our common cause. We had different memories of people we'd known and of the war itself, and we had different destinies in the post-war years.

Our only post-war similarities stemmed from the fact that everyone had experienced difficult, painful and different fates.

But we also shared a common sorrow, the immense sorrow of war. It was a sublime sorrow, more sublime than happiness, and beyond suffering. It was thanks to our sorrow that we were able to escape the war, escape the continual killing and fighting, the terrible conditions of battle and the unhappiness of men in fierce and violent theatres of war.

It was also thanks to our mutual sorrow that we've been able to walk our respective roads again. Our lives may not be very happy, and they might well be sinful. But now we are living the most beautiful lives we could ever have hoped for, because it is a life in peace. Surely this was what the real author of this novel intended to say?

However, the sorrows of war had been much heavier for this author than they had been for me. His sorrows prevented him from relaxing by continually enticing him back into his past.

Perhaps that was not completely true. It may have been just an impasse of pessimism. Then again, his life may have been devoid of spiritual hope. Even so, I believe he derived some happiness from looking back down the road of his past.

His spirit had not been eroded by a cloudy memory. He could feel happy that his soul would find solace in the fountain of sentiments from his youth. He returned time and time again to his love, his friendship, his comradeship, those human bonds which had all helped us overcome the thousand sufferings of the war.

I envied his inspiration, his optimism in focusing back to the painful but glorious days. They were caring days, when we knew what we were living and fighting for and why we needed to suffer and sacrifice.

Those were the days when all of us were young, very pure and very sincere.